COURAGE

What Reviewers Say About Jesse J. Thoma's Work

Serenity

"*Serenity* is the perfect example of opposites attract. …I'm a sucker for stories of redemption and for characters who push their limits, prove themselves to be more than others seem to think. This lesbian opposites attract romance book is all that, and well-written too."
—*Lez Review Books*

The Chase

"The primary couple's initial meeting is a uniquely amusing yet action-packed scenario. I was definitely drawn into the dynamic events of this thoroughly gratifying book via an artfully droll and continuously exciting story. Spectacularly entertaining!"—*Rainbow Book Reviews*

Seneca Falls—*Lambda Literary Award Finalist*

"Loneliness and survival are the two themes dominating Seneca King's life in Thoma's emotionally raw contemporary lesbian romance. Thoma bluntly and uncompromisingly portrays Seneca's struggles with chronic pain, emotional trauma, and uncertainty."
—*Publishers Weekly*

"This was another extraordinary book that I could not put down. Magnificent!"—*Rainbow Book Reviews*

"…a deeply moving account of a young woman trying to raise herself from the ashes of a youth-gone-wrong. Thoma has given us a redemptive tale—and Seneca isn't the only one who needs saving. Told with just enough wit and humor to break the tension that arises from living with villainous ghosts from the past, this is a tale woven into a narrative tapestry of healing and wholeness."—*Lambda Literary*

Pedal to the Metal

"Sassy and sexy meet adventurous and slightly nerdy in Thoma's much-anticipated sequel to *The Chase*. Tongue-in-cheek wit keeps the fast-moving action from going off the rails, all balanced by richly nuanced interpersonal relationships and sweet, realistic romance."
—*Publishers Weekly*

"[*Pedal to the Metal*] has a wonderful cast of characters including the two primary women from the first book in subsidiary roles and some classy good guys versus bad guys action. ...The people, the predicaments, the multi-level layers of both the storyline and the couples populating the Rhode Island landscapes once again had me glued to the pages chapter after chapter. This book works so well on so many levels and is a wonderful complement to the opening book of this series that I truly hope the author will add several additional books to the series. Mystery, action, passion, and family linked together create one amazing reading experience. Scintillating!"
—*Rainbow Book Reviews*

Visit us at www.boldstrokesbooks.com

By the Author

Tales of Lasher, Inc.

The Chase

Pedal to the Metal

Data Capture

Seneca Falls

Serenity

COURAGE

by
Jesse J. Thoma

2021

ISBN 13: 978-1-63555-802-9

This Trade Paperback Original Is Published By
Bold Strokes Books, Inc.
P.O. Box 249
Valley Falls, NY 12185

First Edition: April 2021

CREDITS
Editors: Victoria Villasenor and Cindy Cresap
Production Design: Susan Ramundo
Cover Design By Tammy Seidick

Acknowledgments

Thank you to the entire Bold Strokes family. I could not do what I do without all of you doing what you do so well. I am especially grateful to Sandy Lowe for kindly, but firmly, telling me the first proposal for this book was never going to work. She told me to go back to work. I did and I am thankful for her suggestions and guidance.

There truly aren't words to express my gratitude for my editor, Victoria Villasenor. I am a better writer because of her wisdom and her editing always elevates anything I send her.

To my wife, thank you for loving me. After 2020, I'm grateful for many things, but that perhaps most of all.

Finally, to the readers, I wrote this book during the pandemic and nationwide calls for racial justice after so many Black men and women were killed, often at the hands of police. As I'm writing these acknowledgements, COVID vaccines are being administered to healthcare workers and the most vulnerable across the world, but the normalcy of a simple hug still seems a long way off. If you, like me, turn to books as a way to escape, I quite humbly thank you for picking up mine. I hope that wherever you are, whenever you're reading this, you are safe, healthy, and finding joy in moments both big and small.

Dedication

To Alexis, Goose, and Bird, my light in any dark
and to my father whose courage was boundless.

Grant me the serenity to accept the things I cannot change
The courage to change the things I can
And the wisdom to know the difference.

CHAPTER ONE

Natasha Parsons cautiously stepped through the door into a stranger's apartment. This kind of thing used to feel intrusive, but she'd finally gotten used to invading a stranger's space in order to do her job.

"All clear, Justin?" Natasha didn't enter the apartment all the way until her police officer partner let her know it was safe. Her job was to assess those in the midst of a mental health or substance use related crisis. The police work wasn't her purview.

"Come on in." Justin waved his hand dismissively.

Natasha had been working with the police department for over a year, but had only been partnered with Justin for about a week. He was a decent cop, but he was young and arrogant and wasn't on board with her riding along with him. They had enough history now for him to know this program worked, but he was still the same arrogant, quick to temper kid she'd been dealing with for months. She knew the captain was hoping she'd rub off on him, but so far, she still just wanted to kick him.

Once Natasha came all the way into the apartment she took a quick look around. The place was a mess, junk mail was strewn about, takeout containers had missed multiple trash pickups, and a pile of laundry was dumped in the corner, but people didn't usually call the police because of poor housekeeping. The smashed lamp next to an end table and the distraught man curled into himself on the sofa were more her concern. The feel of the place unnerved her, but she couldn't put her finger on why.

She picked her way to the sofa and sat on the coffee table in front of him. Upon closer inspection, she could see he was crying. He was no more than thirty by her estimate. His overgrown blond hair fell in his face and he swiped at it. She noticed a wedding ring but hadn't seen any sign of another occupant in the house.

"I'm Natasha." She leaned down and tried to catch the man's eye. "I'd like to help. Can you start by telling me your name?"

"What can the cops possibly do for me?"

Natasha shrugged. "No idea. You'll have to ask them. I'm not a cop. I'm a social worker and I'm here for you. We got called out because your neighbors are worried about you."

"Your vest says *Police* across the chest." He pointed at her bulletproof vest.

"I can see how that's confusing. But no gun, no badge."

He considered her for a long while. Natasha let him stare although she wasn't sure how much of her he was seeing. The tears had slowed but were still sliding down his face occasionally. He didn't seem to notice.

"I'm Billy."

"Hi, Billy. Do you know why your neighbors are worried about you?"

The tears started again in earnest. Billy's body shook with sobs. "My wife died last week. I've been struggling a little. But they shouldn't have called you." Anger flashed across Billy's face and he punched the sofa cushion next to him.

Natasha flinched. Raw, fresh grief was always difficult, on a human and clinical level. It was messy, and deep, and expressed itself differently for everyone. And there was no easy or quick fix. There was nothing wrong with Billy, except that he'd just lost his wife, and yet someone had called the cops. Now it was her job to ensure his grief, or anger, or pain didn't land him in handcuffs.

"What can we do for you now, Billy? To help you get through the next few days? The next week?"

Natasha heard Justin moving around the apartment behind her. She wished he'd just stand by the door patiently, or sit down somewhere. His wandering was distracting and felt invasive. She hadn't had to deal with this when she was partnered with Tommy.

"I don't know how to get through the next minute without her. I've been trying. I've been trying to remember that everything happens for a reason, but I get so angry. There was nothing she did to deserve to die. There was no reason for her death."

Billy pounded the couch cushion again and then jabbed his finger in Natasha's face. "Nothing you say will bring her back."

Natasha subtly put more distance between herself and Billy. Where the hell was Justin?

"You're right. I can't bring her back. I'm here for you. I'm here to help *you* and make sure you have the support you need right now."

Billy flopped against the back of the couch and looked at the ceiling.

"Tell me about her." Natasha relaxed a fraction. "I'd like to get to know her since she was someone you loved."

For the first time since she'd entered Billy's apartment, he smiled. "She was the thing that none of the rest of us are. Light, and hope, and beauty. And now she's gone and I don't know how to move on."

Natasha needed to find out if Billy had support from family and friends and make sure he wasn't a danger to himself. But before she could broach any of that, he jumped up from the couch, yelling and gesturing to something behind her.

She stood too and kicked the coffee table back as far as she could so she had more room. She stepped in front of him and held her hands out wide, trying to reestablish a connection. Her heart raced. His anger felt like a physical force radiating off of him and slamming into her.

"Don't touch that. Put it down!" Billy was gesturing furiously over Natasha's shoulder.

Natasha stole a look behind her. Justin was standing like a deer in headlights next to the fireplace, holding a heart shaped necklace in his hands with a guilty look on his face.

"What the fuck, Justin? What are you doing?" She looked pointedly from the necklace to the mantel.

Justin seemed frozen in place. He didn't move, even in the face of Billy's increasing agitation. Natasha turned back to Billy.

"He's going to put that back, Billy. And he can wait outside. I'm sorry. He shouldn't have picked up that necklace. Did it belong to your wife?"

"Put it down. Put it down."

Billy was screaming now, but he hadn't tried to push through Natasha to get to Justin. She was thankful for that, because if he attacked Justin, there wasn't much she could do to help him.

"Billy, I'm going to go talk to him. Can I trust you to stay here?"

She looked over her shoulder again. Justin was still standing there like a jewelry store mannequin. When she looked back to Billy she came nose to barrel with a handgun. Fear coursed through her body so quickly and strongly she was afraid her next heartbeat might cause it to ignite.

Justin said the room was clear. What the fuck? She took a deep breath. This wasn't the time for panic. She put her hands up slowly and took a step back. The room felt too small, with nowhere to go. She knew Justin had drawn his gun too, putting her in the middle of a deadly game of chicken. How did she always end up here?

"Billy, let's work together to find a different way for this to end. I'm still here to help you. That hasn't changed. But I work a lot better without a gun in my face."

The room was still for a few beats until Justin's radio crackled to life. Natasha didn't have time to register what was said before she heard a gunshot and was knocked over the coffee table by an impact to the left of her navel. A second shot rang out before she hit the floor.

She struggled for breath and calm while she evaluated. She heard pained grunting and chaos in the apartment. She hoped Billy wasn't coming for her. She wasn't sure she could get away since she could hardly breathe. She searched her torso. No blood. She stuck her finger in the bullet sized impression in her vest and said a prayer of thanks.

Finally, she dared to look for Billy. He was back across the room, his hands on his head, gun still clutched in his right hand, muttering to himself. She didn't want to aggravate him more, but there had been a second shot. She needed to find Justin.

She crawled toward the fireplace. Her breathing was labored, and her ribs hurt like hell. Justin was slumped against the fireplace clutching his side. She could see the blood pooling under his fingers. She pulled up his shirt and took a peek. She wasn't a doctor, but it looked like the bullet had clipped his flank in probably the only place his body armor didn't cover. Even though she was pretty confident Justin wasn't going to die on her, there was a lot of blood.

Billy looked at them but either didn't care what they were doing or was lost in his own thoughts. Natasha realized why he didn't care. He had Justin's gun as well as his own. It was sitting on the couch.

"I dropped it when he shot me." Justin nodded toward the couch. "I tried to get to it, but he saw me and got there faster."

Justin looked like he was going to cry. No time to worry about that now. One gun or two, Billy could kill them just fine with either if he wanted.

Natasha encouraged Justin to put pressure on his wound and took advantage of Billy's distraction to grab Justin's radio. Hers seemed to have gone missing when she flipped over the table. She quietly called in the officer down code, then turned off the radio. She didn't want anything else to set Billy off. She pulled out her phone and quickly tapped out a text to Tommy, just in case this went fully sideways.

Justin grimaced and grabbed her hand. She replaced his hands with her own. Her hands were covered with his blood, but she kept the pressure on. It seemed to be bleeding less profusely.

"I can't believe I didn't find that gun. Tommy's going to kill me," Justin said. "You should let me die."

"Don't be so dramatic." Natasha wasn't sure he was wrong.

"Then Harry's going to take a turn with me. Senior likes you, so he might even make Cody get involved. And if Alice...I'm a dead man."

"Let's get out of here alive, then we'll worry about Tommy."

Natasha looked at Billy again. He was pacing now.

"I've got to get him to talk to me again," Natasha pulled Justin's hands back to his flank. "That's our ticket out. More pressure on this." She pointed to his injury when he didn't comply fast enough.

"You're fucking nuts."

Sirens wailed in the distance, getting closer. Billy heard them too. He crossed the room and kneeled in front of them, leaving one of the guns on the couch. Natasha tried to shield Justin, not that it would do much good if he started firing. Billy waved the gun wildly, panic clear in his eyes.

"What did you do?" He grabbed Natasha's phone, stood up, and stomped on it. "They're going to come in and kill me. I shot a cop. I didn't mean to shoot you." He pointed at Justin. "You should've put the necklace down."

Billy was crying again. He was holding the necklace tightly in one hand, the gun in the other. She wondered if Billy was fine with the fact that he'd shot her too. She hoped not because she needed him to start talking again. She took a chance and stood.

"Billy, look at me. No one has to die today. I told you when I walked in, I'm here to help you."

His hands were shaking, and his body shuddered with sobs. Natasha stretched her hands out to the sides slowly. Drops of Justin's blood dripped slowly from her hands to the floor. Her heart was racing and sweat was dripping down her back.

"Billy, don't do this. Let me help you."

Billy raised the gun and pointed it at her again, her head this time. Natasha took a deep breath.

CHAPTER TWO

Eighteen Months Earlier

"What if you get shot?"

Natasha looked at her best friend, Kayla, who was fretting at Natasha's kitchen island but trying to hide her worry. She was surprised at the concern, not because she thought Kayla didn't care, she'd just never really considered the danger of her new job.

"I'm pretty sure they'll give me a bulletproof vest, Kay." Natasha kissed the top of Kayla's head as she moved into the kitchen and pulled out a bottle of wine.

"It's called a vest for a reason, Nat. There's still a lot of you someone could hit and do damage. Like your head. And as hardheaded as you are, I don't think your skull is bulletproof. What would I do without you?"

"No one would dare shoot at this." Natasha waved her hand in front of her face dramatically.

"Not until you opened your mouth." Kayla rolled her eyes.

"Why are you worried about people shooting me now? I piss people off all the time. No one's taken a shot yet."

Kayla looked at her like she should already know the answer. "Because everyone you'll be working with will have a gun. Except you. Which I endorse, by the way. You with a gun in your hand scares me more than almost anything else in the world, which is saying a lot. There's some scary shit out there."

"You know, when I invited you over to help me prepare for my first day tomorrow, this wasn't quite what I had in mind."

It was actually exactly what she had in mind and she knew Kayla knew it too. She was a little nervous about reporting for duty in the morning, and an evening filled with Kayla knocking the wind out of her sails was soothing. It was their routine.

"Fine, tell me more about this fancy new job then. Spare no detail."

"You know I'll be working for the police department. They hired me to be a ride along mental health clinician. So I'll head out on calls where it's suspected that mental health or substance use related issues are at play, and then they'll set me loose to work my magic." Natasha dusted off her shoulders for effect.

"So you'll be like the police dog they call out when they need it? Will you get a special handle in the back so you can let yourself out, or will your cop buddy have to open the door for you?"

"Why am I friends with you?" Natasha threw her most devastating side eye Kayla's way.

Kayla's "bitch, please" look neutralized anything Natasha could throw back. Kayla could slay any challenger with a raised eyebrow. She'd developed the skill in infancy.

"What do your parents think of this new career path?"

Kayla said it casually, but as soon as it was out of her mouth the air was heavy with suitcases full of unpacked baggage. Natasha felt the weight of it as she always did when her family was mentioned.

"My parents care about money and power, just like their whole circle of wealthy friends. They haven't been interested in Natasha Parsons in years." Natasha looked down at her perfect manicure, looking for some blemish to pick at.

"You can change your name, but I'm not sure you'll ever stop being Natasha Blackstone."

"She's dead as far as I'm concerned." Natasha set her wineglass down harder than she meant to.

"This place doesn't look like it was purchased by a dead woman." Kayla waved vaguely around the room. "You've got money, who cares? You do good with it. If I were you, I'd spend it a lot differently than you do."

"As if your family doesn't run in the same circles as mine." Natasha gave Kayla a pointed look. "And if you could you'd walk down Main Street with hundred-dollar bills shoved in your bra so you could pull them out and shower the masses."

"Who says I haven't already checked that off my bucket list?"

"Please. You'd have invited me. And then…" Natasha hesitated.

"It would've ended up in the tabloids most likely."

Kayla had known her long enough to know the price that came with the Blackstone name.

"What if you tried not hiding Ms. Parsons for once? Can we put some firecrackers on your tits and get you trending on every news outlet's social media feed? Recovering socialite is now a social worker extraordinaire?"

"Seriously, why am I friends with you?" Natasha threw the wine bottle cork at Kayla who caught it effortlessly and set it on the counter.

"Because I love you. And I'm proud of you." Kayla was still all business. "If there is someone out there who needs help, they couldn't have a better advocate than you."

Natasha fiddled with a loose piece of paper on her counter. "Forget my parents. God, Kay, what if I screw this up?"

"Not possible. You've kicked ass at every job you've ever had. Even that summer when we were ten and you decided you wanted to be a newspaper delivery girl, but you sucked at riding a bike."

Natasha ran her hand through her hair and let out a deep breath. "This feels different somehow."

"Is it the guns? And the fact that you'll be working with cops, given what happened with Joseph?"

Natasha made a "little bit" gesture with her hand. "If I screw up, someone might get shot."

"You said you weren't going to get shot." Kayla picked up the wine cork and squeezed it like she was hoping to milk one more drop of wine.

"I didn't mean me." Natasha rolled her eyes. "I meant the people I'm trying to help."

Kayla relaxed her grip on the cork and looked contemplative. "Hasn't that always been true, though? You're a social worker who chooses to work with addicted and mentally ill clients who are in ultimate crisis mode. If you screwed something up, or even if you didn't, there's a non-zero chance one of your clients could've died by the police's hands if you weren't involved too, right?"

Natasha could think of one headline grabbing case that played out exactly as Kayla described. She hadn't screwed anything up, it wasn't even her client that was killed, but it easily could've been.

"It would be different, Kay, watching it happen right in front of me instead of hearing about it the next day."

Kayla reached across the kitchen island and entwined their hands. "I know that, sweetie. But don't do anything stupid like throw yourself in the line of fire thinking one lousy vest is going to protect your ass."

"When have I ever done something reckless and stupid?"

Kayla raised her eyebrow and yanked on their joined hands, forcing Natasha to look at her. "Nat, I'm serious."

"I promise to be careful."

Natasha reclaimed her hand and put their glasses in the sink. She didn't want Kayla to see her doubts. Was that a promise she could keep?

Natasha's head was spinning as she exited Captain Gillette's office. Working within a strict hierarchy like the police department was going to take some getting used to. Who was she kidding? That was pretty far down the list of worries when it came to her learning curve. Her main concern was the less than friendly looks she was getting from the officers she was counting on to watch her back when they went out on calls.

She made her way to the desk Captain Gillette had assigned her. She was followed by what felt like the gaze of the entire station. When she got to her desk, she found the one officer she could count on for a friendly smile sitting on her desk with his feet on her chair.

"Pete, get your smelly feet off my chair and your ass off my desk. I don't want that putrid odor hanging around the rest of the day." Natasha was inordinately happy to see him.

"You'd be lucky to smell my ass the rest of the day." Pete got off her desk all the same. "Excited for your first day?"

"Sure. Who wouldn't be? The question is, how excited are you all to have me on board? Not every day someone like me comes to spice up your life."

"You are pretty zesty, and I'm thrilled to have you around. Can't speak for everyone else." Pete looked uncomfortable so Natasha knew he was holding something back. She'd known him long enough to be able to read him pretty well.

She patted his shoulder as best she could. He was six foot seven so she had to reach high to make the attempt. "It's okay, buddy. I'll win them over. Everyone likes me eventually."

Pete snorted and she punched him in the stomach. "Am I not supposed to do that here?"

"Assault a police officer? No, that's frowned upon." Pete pointed back and forth between the two of them. "But you're one of us now so I'll let it slide."

"I am *not* one of you." Natasha put her hand on her hip.

Pete leaned in close and lowered his voice. "Might not want to say that too loudly if you want to make friends." He leaned against her desk again. "Who you partnered with?"

"Some guy named Tommy." Natasha hoped he wasn't a testosterone filled meathead.

Pete made a face. Natasha didn't like the look.

"Oh, I love the captain's sense of humor." Pete looked to the heavens and put his hands together as if saying a prayer of thanks. "This is going to be fun."

"What's that supposed to mean?" Natasha considered punching him again. "What's he like?"

"I don't want to ruin the surprise. Tommy should be here soon." Pete smiled like a toddler who knew about a mess she was going to have to clean up. "Let me introduce you to a few of the others."

Pete walked Natasha around and introduced her to practically everyone in the station. It seemed everyone already knew who she was and had an opinion on her utility. Mostly, they seemed to think she had none.

Pete seemed to be taking great pleasure in making a point of noting she was partnered with Tommy. Natasha got the sense Tommy was well respected and well liked, but there was something about adding her to the mix that was amusing her co-workers. She wanted to meet him so she could evaluate for herself.

No sooner had the thought crossed her mind than she heard someone call across the room, "Tommy, ready to meet your new partner?"

Natasha turned, ready to face the man who would make or break her first few weeks. She hoped he was closer to Pete than caveman. But it turned out Tommy was a woman. A hot woman with butch sex appeal oozing out of every pore, something Natasha tried and failed to ignore, as it was, of course, totally irrelevant.

Tommy's face was unreadable while she evaluated Natasha. For some reason the fact that Tommy was an incredibly attractive woman made it easier. Natasha had endured more than one butch stare down. She winked and Tommy glared back at her. Pete laughed but covered it with fake coughing when Tommy turned her glower on him.

Natasha returned to her desk. Tommy could come to her once she was ready. Natasha needed her on board, but she wasn't going to push her.

It didn't take long before she felt a looming presence over her shoulder.

She stood and extended her hand. "I'm Natasha. The captain said we're going to be working together."

Tommy shook her hand, but it was halfhearted. "You're the social worker we're saddled with?"

"You flatter me. But I think you mean, I'm the social worker joining your station for the mutual benefit of the department and the community."

Tommy grumbled something unintelligible and beelined it for Captain Gillette's office. Natasha sighed. This wasn't how she envisioned her first day. She pulled up her email and sorted through the essential and unimportant. It was amazing how many emails she already had, given she'd been employed for only a few hours.

She'd deleted all the IT helpdesk emails when Tommy reappeared.

"Looks like I'm stuck with you." Tommy folded her arms across her chest.

"That's the spirit," Natasha said. This would be easier if Tommy didn't look so damn attractive even when she was being an obstinate, rude, ass.

"I have to take you out when I get a call for someone having a mental health crisis, right?"

Natasha nodded. "I'm here to help, not get in your way. I know it's different than the way you've worked in the past, but I hope I can show you that I can pull my weight and make your job easier."

"I don't see how that's possible. You're not a cop. You don't have any way of protecting yourself, so now that's my job. From where I'm standing, you're more work for me, not less. Which means I can't do my actual job effectively. But I don't have a choice. So I'll let you know when I need your *help*."

Tommy walked away. Natasha sprang up and followed. "Where are you going?"

"Patrol." Tommy didn't turn or stop walking.

"I should come with you," Natasha said.

"You come on mental health or substance use calls. I don't have any of those right now. Stay here. I'll let you know if something comes up."

Natasha slapped her hand against the wall. "And how the hell would I get to you?" But Tommy was gone. "Great. Now what?"

The station had emptied out considerably since her arrival as officers had gone out on patrol, detectives had exited to track down leads or interview suspects, and the daily grind of police life had begun. The only one at loose ends was her.

She returned to her desk, kicked her chair, then sat down to finish reading through her emails and start working on a plan. She couldn't leave all the power in Tommy's hands or she suspected she'd be stuck on the sidelines forever. From the looks of things, she also had some work to do with the rest of the station. She rubbed her hands together. Hard work was a universal language. Time to start talking.

CHAPTER THREE

Tommy Finch took the steps to her parents' house two at a time. She always looked forward to family dinner, but after the day she'd had, she needed to talk over a few things with her mother, sister, and brother. There were advantages to having a family full of cops.

She pushed open the door and was immediately assaulted by three surface-to-knee missiles in the form of her two nieces and one nephew. She dropped to her knees and let them tackle her.

"Auntie Tommy, can we play hide and seek? Will you buy me a unicorn for my birthday? Daddy said no."

"Did you shoot anyone today?"

"Ommy, Ommy, Ommy."

She kissed each head and tried to get up off the floor, but when they had her pinned they each seemed to grow three extra arms and a clone. She was saved by her sister walking through the door. Before Tommy could get up, her sister was on the floor next to her.

"Hey, Tommy."

"Harry, what's up?"

The kids were laughing hysterically as Tommy and Harry tossed them back and forth, stopping to tickle them until everyone was out of breath.

"Are you two going to lie on the floor all night, or are you going to come in the house and say hello to your mother?"

Tommy and Harry put the kids on their feet and got up to greet their mother, Alice.

"Hi, Mama." Tommy hugged her mother.

Her mom patted her cheek. "I baked a pie for you. And there's brownies for you, Harry."

Tommy didn't know how her mother had always been able to make each of her kids feel special and cared for and hold the family together, all while rising through the ranks of the police force. It didn't seem possible, but she'd managed somehow. Tommy always hoped someday she could have it all, like her mother. The group surged into the dining room, and eventually, everyone settled at the table to eat.

"Is something troubling you, Tommy?" Her father, Thomas Henry Finch, who everyone called Senior, had been a 9-1-1 operator and could diagnose problems in the family and dispatch a solution better than anyone Tommy had ever met.

"She's got problems all right. The kind of problems that are about five foot eight, long blond hair, and doesn't fall for any of Tommy's unique charms." Harry blew Tommy a kiss across the table.

Tommy scratched her cheek with her middle finger aimed at Harry.

"Tomasina, Henrietta, behave yourselves at my dinner table." Their mom looked pointedly at both of them.

"Yeah, behave yourselves. What's wrong with you two?" Tommy's younger brother, Cody, waved his fork in Tommy's direction. "I heard Tommy's bigger problem is she mouthed off to her captain."

"Tommy?" Her mom looked horrified.

"What? No. I didn't mouth off. Where do you two get your information?"

"I have people," Harry said.

"Well, get new people." Tommy pushed her plate away and crossed her arms.

"Tell us what's going on." Senior put his fork down and folded his hands.

Tommy thought about her levels of frustration with Natasha Parsons and what she represented. Where to begin?

"I got stuck with a new partner today. She's a civilian who feels like a public relations stunt."

"Is this the woman your sister was rather crudely trying to describe?" Her mom mimicked Senior's posture and gave Tommy her full attention.

Tommy nodded. Harry had left out a few details, namely that Natasha was gorgeous. And she didn't seem immune to Tommy's charms, since Tommy wasn't trying to charm her. She replayed their first interaction when she'd been openly appraising Natasha and instead of looking away or appearing at all uncomfortable, she'd winked. It wasn't often someone was able to so thoroughly turn the tables on her. She didn't like the feeling.

"I've heard about what you guys are trying to do with this new… what is she?" Cody paused and looked at Tommy.

"Social worker," Tommy said.

"Right, social worker. It's some kind of test program, right? If someone's crazy, you send her in instead of us? Like the bomb robots."

"Come on, Cody." Tommy might not be happy about being paired with Natasha, but she didn't like Cody comparing her to the bomb disposal robots. She wasn't disposable, not really.

"What? You're not happy to be partnered with her, are you?"

"Of course not. I thought the captain was going to tell me there was a detective spot opening up or I was finally getting a special assignment or put on a task force. Something. She's been leading me to believe that was coming for months. But no. I got miss let's-save-the-world instead. And she's going to make my damn job harder. If one hair on her pretty blond head is out of place, whose ass is on the line?" Tommy threw her napkin down and ran her hands through her hair.

"What did you do with her today?" Harry had lost her teasing tone and was all business. Her sister was a pain in the ass, but she was also a good cop and Tommy's closest confidant.

"Went out on patrol and left her on her desk." It probably wasn't the smartest course of action, but Tommy couldn't take it back now.

"Tomasina Finch." Her mom only pulled out her full name when she was pissed.

"I told her I'd call her if something relevant came up." Tommy looked down at her plate, anywhere but at her mother.

"And how was she supposed to magically appear in time to be useful? Whether you agree with the decision or not, this is your special assignment now. Your father and I didn't raise you to thumb your nose at the chain of command and ignore your duty."

"Yes, ma'am." Tommy pushed food around, suddenly not hungry.

"The captain chose you for this. If she didn't think you could protect this social worker while also serving the community she'd have given the job to someone else. If you let her down now, you can kiss detective and anything else good-bye no matter how hard you've worked." Her mom didn't lecture often, but Tommy listened when she did.

Dinner conversation moved on, becoming the light-hearted banter that usually accompanied the meal, and Tommy's shoulders eased.

After dinner, Tommy grabbed a beer and joined her sister on the back deck. Cody and his wife had to get the kids to bed so they'd already left.

"Mama went after you hard." Harry said. "You okay?"

Tommy peeled the label on her beer. "I know I screwed up today, but I'm still uneasy with the situation. I've worked hard to build trust in the communities I work in. We've all done trainings for dealing with people having mental health crises or under the influence of substances. Why are the higher-ups coming in now and saying we're—*I'm*—not good enough to do my own damn job? It feels like everyone's in an uproar and this is something to point to and say we're doing better. That's shitty on every level."

"I wouldn't want to deal with that either. And you're right about having someone else to watch out for. It's hard enough watching my own ass out there. If I've got a partner, I want to know they've got my back and I've got theirs. With a civilian, they're dependent on you and that's a lot to ask. But Mama's right. It doesn't matter why she's onboard, you've got to do your damn job."

"Do you ever wonder if people see us as anything other than Alice Finch's kids?" Tommy moved her beer bottle back and forth between her hands on the deck rail.

"Like we'll never live up to her, or we get breaks because we're her kids?"

Tommy blew out a breath. "I don't know. Either. Both. She's a lot to live up to."

"Hey, you're a great cop. You've been studying for that detective exam so damn long you'll probably get a perfect score." Harry bumped her shoulder. "And you said yourself this social worker situation is shit, so clearly no one's throwing you favors because of Mama."

They were silent for a while staring out into the dark, each with her own thoughts. Harry was the one who broke the silence.

"Is she as hot as I heard?"

"Jesus, you have no idea."

"Well, that's something." Harry saluted with her beer. "Just make sure you're thinking with this," she pointed to Tommy's head, "and not this," she pointed to her crotch.

"You're one to talk."

"Exactly. Learn from the mistakes your big sister makes."

"I knew you'd be good for something eventually." Tommy ducked the swat to the back of the head she knew was coming.

They stayed outside under the protective glow of their parents' porch light for a while longer in companionable silence. Tommy thought about Natasha and how she was going to fit into her work life. How could she do her job with an untrained sidekick? What if she had to choose between protecting Natasha and detaining a suspect? Or choose to keep Natasha safe at the expense of a civilian?

She finally headed home, her mind filled with what-ifs. The world wasn't made up of what-ifs and there was no point indulging them. She'd face whatever the day threw at her in the morning. Until then, one thing was certain, serving her community had suddenly gotten significantly more complicated.

CHAPTER FOUR

Tommy arrived at work ready to apologize to Natasha and start fresh. She didn't have to be happy about the circumstances in order to do her job. If Natasha wanted to sit shotgun all day and watch her work, that was fine. She could stay in the car, safe and sound, and write reports about how to improve the police force until she developed carpal tunnel and needed to go out on disability. As long as she stayed out of Tommy's way. If it was a political stunt, it would end eventually. If it wasn't, well, she'd make detective and hand over Natasha with her patrol car as soon as possible.

Tommy barely acknowledged her fellow officers as she moved through the station on her way to Natasha's desk. She didn't make it all the way there. Natasha was nowhere in sight. She snagged Justin, an officer not long out of the academy and still finding his footing.

"Have you seen Natasha Parsons this morning? The new social worker?"

"The captain's pet project? Blondie who's going to save the world but probably get us all killed? Nah, haven't seen her. Must not be used to showing up to work on time."

"You're right. I'm used to getting to work early. The world saving doesn't stick to a nine to five."

There was no mistaking the irritation in the voice behind her and Tommy cringed. She would've laughed at the look on Justin's face, but she had damage control to do. What would be facing her when she turned around? Hurt? Fire? Her ass about to be kicked?

She wasn't prepared for amusement. "Why do you find this funny?" Tommy heard Justin backing away. *Coward.*

"Oh, there's nothing funny about all of you being completely unwilling to give me a chance to do my job. Or denigrating me behind my back. Or trying to, at least. Your shit-talk needs work."

Natasha stepped into Tommy's space. It was a power move and Tommy recognized it for what it was. She didn't back down.

"What's funny is how damned insecure you all are. I expected a little more from tough guys. Too scared that Blondie might actually be able to bring some change for the better? That she might have something to teach you? I thought you were all about serving your community?" Natasha held eye contact, seemingly daring Tommy to look away. She didn't.

"Well, guess what? So am I. That's why I'm here. So, are you going to waste more of my time today or not?" Natasha crossed her arms and waited. They were so close her arms were only inches from Tommy's nipples, which was hard to ignore.

Justin's behavior had Tommy boxed in. She'd planned on offering Natasha the ride along anyway, but now it looked like she was acquiescing because of Justin's big mouth and Natasha's dressing down. She hadn't been at work for thirty minutes and she was already on her heels. Strike that, she was already flat on her back. In other circumstances Tommy could think of ways Natasha could get her on her back that would be a lot of fun. This wasn't one of them.

Tommy gritted her teeth. "Meet me at the car in fifteen."

Natasha's smile was almost worth the ulcer her presence was sure to create. "Don't suppose there's any way you'll let me drive?"

Tommy walked away and sent a text to Harry asking for strength, then prepared for her patrol. Five minutes before their meeting time, Natasha was nowhere to be seen. Tommy wasn't waiting for her if she was late. She headed for her car.

She opened the driver's door and jerked back, cracking her head on the doorframe. Natasha was in the passenger's seat casually reading a magazine. Why hadn't she noticed her? She was supposed to be aware of her surroundings at all times.

"What are you doing in here?" Tommy gripped the doorframe so tightly she thought she might need to check for finger imprints later.

"Figured you'd use any excuse to leave me behind again. Didn't want to chance being late. Your head okay?" Natasha didn't look up from her magazine.

"I don't have a problem with my head." Tommy adjusted her duty belt as she sat behind the wheel. "I have a problem with…" *Better not finish that sentence.*

"Me. I know. Your temper tantrum yesterday made that perfectly clear." Natasha slowly lowered the magazine and looked at her. "But I heard you're a good cop. And I thought good cops used all the tools at their disposal to do their job. So are we going out or are you going to sit here signed out for your whole shift?"

"And here I thought you weren't going to tell me how to do my job."

"Is that really what you're worried about? Deep down you think I'm going to dictate exactly how you're supposed to be a police officer?"

"Why not? There are protests in our city and across the country and suddenly here you are. I work hard to be a good cop."

"Congratulations, you're fulfilling your job description." Natasha didn't look impressed. "But if you're as good at your job as you claim, why are you so against my help? People are in the streets demanding you be better than just checking boxes on your annual review."

Tommy gritted her teeth. She was going to have a headache by the time her shift was over. "And your job description seems to be growing the longer we talk. You're really going to dismantle institutional racism, implicit bias, and reform the police department from the passenger seat of my patrol car?"

Natasha looked like she'd lost her mind. "Don't be ridiculous. I'm a social worker, not the owner of the Infinity Stones. I can't snap my fingers and undue decades of this country's history. All I can do is my job. I'm asking you to do the same, which in our case, means giving me a damn chance."

Tommy was usually composed, even-keeled, and calm under pressure. It made her a good cop. What was it about Natasha that was getting to her so easily?

She felt her phone buzz and she checked the display. It was Harry telling her to take a deep breath. She took her sister's advice.

"Do I make you nervous, Officer Finch?" Natasha folded her magazine neatly and slid it into the handbag at her feet.

"Have you gotten the impression I'm nervous?" Tommy steered into traffic. She didn't look at Natasha.

"Not exactly an answer. I'm under the impression you don't like me. I know you've said you're unhappy at this situation, but I'm pretty likable once you get to know me. So I'm wondering if I make you nervous and that's why you're determined to be mad. I don't want to be your enemy."

Tommy's knuckles turned white from her grip on the wheel. "Of course you make me nervous. You have no training, no way of watching my back, but somehow you think you can do my job better than I can. So I'm stuck protecting Pretend Cop Barbie instead of serving my community."

She was good at picking up on subtle changes in body language, but no training was necessary to detect the change in Natasha's relaxed posture. Tommy stole a glance. She didn't know Natasha well, but the fury and hurt reflected in her eyes looked like damage from old wounds.

You took it too far, Finch. Tommy cast about for something to say. Something to make up for her dickish comment.

Sometimes simple was best. "I'm sorry. That was out of line."

Before she could do or say more, dispatch crackled through the radio and the day began in earnest.

Near the end of their shift, Tommy was still trying to figure out how to make things right with Natasha. She'd barely spoken to Tommy all day, although the shift had been busy and they hadn't had much time to interact. Tommy wanted to believe that was the reason, but she knew better.

"Look, I really am sorry about earlier. We can disagree professionally, but I don't have to be a dick about it."

"Looks like we're making progress." Natasha finally looked at her. She wasn't quite smiling, but she wasn't scowling anymore. "We finally agree on something. If you were really sorry though, you wouldn't have made me listen to show tunes all day."

"What's wrong with show tunes?"

Natasha glared at her. Tommy didn't say another word.

Tommy turned down a street she regularly patrolled, figuring she'd stop in at a couple of local businesses before the end of her shift. She even considered letting Natasha come with her, to extend the olive branch a little further. Before she got to the strip of shops, something caught her eye and she pulled over.

"There's someone I have to chat with. I'll be right back."

"I know, stay in the car." Natasha propped her elbow on the doorframe and looked out the window, away from Tommy.

Tommy didn't have time to explain. She jogged across the street and intercepted her target.

"Zoo, what're you doing all the way on this side of town? Where's Parrot Master?" Tommy blocked the Zookeeper's path, forcing her to stop and talk.

The Zookeeper was a local drug dealer whose partner, Parrot Master, was the head of one of the local gangs. They were an odd pairing, but they always seemed dedicated to each other. Tommy knew the Zookeeper was protective of her man. She also knew there was more to the Zookeeper than selling drugs. What she didn't know was why she was roaming these streets. Their territory was on the other side of town, near the park and the library.

"Officer Finch, to what do I owe the pleasure?" The Zookeeper regarded her impassively.

"Not used to seeing you on my patrol. Thought I'd stop and say hello."

The Zookeeper raised an eyebrow. "I wasn't aware I was confined to a geographical perimeter. What exactly are my boundaries?"

Tommy wasn't interested in playing games. "If you and Parrot Master are looking to franchise the business, I want to know. Expanding your territory is going to ruffle feathers and we're going to be the ones to clean it up. Consider this a courtesy call."

"Your warning is noted, Officer. I'm simply out for a stroll." The Zookeeper started to move on then stopped abruptly. She'd seen something over Tommy's shoulder. "Now why, Officer Finch, do you have Natasha Parsons locked in your car?"

The Zookeeper's casual demeanor was gone. She was angry. Tommy took a step back and shifted her weight so she had better access and balance should she need to retrieve her Taser or service weapon. She'd had situations devolve fast before.

"She's not locked in my car. She's riding with me today."

The Zookeeper stepped around her and approached the patrol car. Tommy moved to stop her, but Natasha was already out of the car.

"Zookeeper. What are you doing on this side of town?" Natasha looked like she was greeting an old friend.

"I had to check on two of my flock. While I was over here, I stopped by to see that friend of yours." The Zookeeper leaned on the patrol car with her back to Tommy, who clearly wasn't invited into the conversation.

That wasn't exactly just a "stroll," and Tommy wondered at Natasha's easy connection with her. It was obvious she was telling Natasha the truth.

Tommy wanted to linger so she could continue eavesdropping, but both Natasha and the Zookeeper grew silent after their initial greeting and looked at her pointedly. Natasha actually drummed her fingers on the top of the patrol car.

Tommy could take a hint and moved farther away, but not so far that she couldn't reach Natasha if needed. She surveyed the area, curious at the Zookeeper's mention of her flock and Natasha's friend. The blooming flowers and tweeting birds provided no clues. When Tommy saw the conversation wrapping up, she moved closer again.

Before she left, the Zookeeper patted Natasha's shoulder and nodded to Tommy. Natasha slid into the passenger's seat and Tommy waited a beat, unsure if she should continue with her plan of stopping in at the businesses up ahead, or sign out for the day since her shift was over. She figured Natasha was probably tired of her by now and dropped behind the wheel.

"The Zookeeper said the domestic violence suspect you guys have been chasing your tails on has been hiding out in that apartment over there." Natasha pointed subtly. "He's off work at midnight. Might want to have someone here to pick him up."

"We checked his work. He hasn't been there since his girlfriend called us."

"Midnight. That apartment."

"And what, I'm supposed to trust secondhand information from a drug dealer on this?" Tommy blew out a breath. Everyone wanted this guy.

"You're supposed to trust me." The fire was back in Natasha's eyes. "But since you clearly don't, the guy picked up some odd job work with Parrot Master's crew. The Zookeeper isn't cool with crimes against women and she's cutting him loose. Pick him up or not, your choice."

Tommy wished she'd gotten the tip herself or better yet, had gotten it from one of her trusted informants, but she didn't think Natasha would purposefully screw her. She picked up the radio and called it in.

"Is it true she's a lawyer?"

Natasha was looking out the window and didn't look at Tommy now. "She is. Or was. Admitted to the bar and everything. I checked. I don't know why she's here and not in a courtroom. I'd like to know, but she's never told me."

"How do you know her?" Tommy headed back to the station. The Zookeeper seemed like safe conversation. Tommy wanted to get back without stepping on any more land mines.

"I know a lot of people who can help you. If you'll let me in."

They were silent for the rest of the ride. Tommy thought about what Natasha said. She might be right. But how did she change the way she approached policing when the way she worked had been drilled into her from the time she was a toddler? These weren't the kind of thoughts for the end of a long shift. She looked over at Natasha. Tomorrow wasn't likely to provide any respite to her churning gut and uneasy mind. But change seemed to be coming whether she wanted it or not.

CHAPTER FIVE

Natasha was at work early, ready to go toe to toe with Tommy again. Not even this particular butch shaped mountain was so immovable that she couldn't be won over. She'd heard chatter that the Zookeeper's tip had panned out, so hopefully that would buy her a little good will. It felt like she and Tommy had inched closer to the idea of making inroads toward getting along. She'd categorize it as both of them having picked up pencils in anticipation of negotiating rules to a game they would one day, ideally, compete in as teammates. She wondered what Tommy's team uniform policy was. She looked great in a uniform. She'd probably look even better out of it.

Whoa. Nope. Natasha jumped up and walked a lap around the station. If they didn't like the job she was there to do, she'd have to win them over herself. She circled the room and turned her charm up to level fifteen. By the time she made it back to her desk, she'd earned a few smiles and learned that Officer Ramirez could solve a Rubik's Cube in less than a minute, Officer Lopes was a very good electrician, Officer Davis was sickeningly happily married with a wife and four kids, and Officer Lipinski was the best chef in the station.

"Making friends already?" Pete was leaning against her desk when she got back.

"Getting to know my co-workers." Natasha nudged him out of the way so she could sit.

"It's not you-the-person they don't like. Remember that. It's the idea of you."

"I'm not the boogey man, Pete. And there's only one me."

"You know what I mean. They'll come around once they get to know you." Pete looked too hopeful for Natasha to trust he actually believed what he was saying.

"No one can resist me. You know that, buddy." Natasha forced her biggest smile. It faltered at the end.

"I imagine that's true," Tommy said.

Natasha jumped up and whipped around. Tommy's face was impassive.

"I'll let you two get to work." Pete bounded off too quickly.

"I wanted to let you know I have traffic duty all day today. Not much for you to do, so you might as well stay here. If anything interesting comes up, I'll call you and you can get a ride over." Tommy's expression never changed. Her voice was monotone.

"Is this progress? Are you starting to like me? Just days ago you snuck out of here without me and now look at us."

"I have to answer for my sins to a higher power. I'm trying to avoid that." Tommy's mouth quirked up. She quickly clamped down on the show of emotion, but Natasha saw it. Tommy had started to smile.

"I doubt any higher power cares whether you tell me you have traffic duty or leave me wondering where you are all day." Natasha sat back against her desk and crossed her ankles. Tommy glanced down at her legs. There was a reason these were Natasha's favorite pair of pants.

"You've never met my mother."

Natasha pushed off the desk and moved closer. "Your mother has enough power to get you to do the right thing? I can't wait to meet this woman."

"You're not going to meet my mother." Tommy took a step back and crossed her arms.

"Uh-huh. We'll see." Natasha turned and sat at her desk and waved over her shoulder. "Go have fun playing in traffic. I'll see you tomorrow." It took a few beats before she heard Tommy turn to go. "Oh, and, Tommy?" She looked over her shoulder and caught Tommy's eye. "Thanks for letting me know where you'd be today."

Although being out in the community and actively helping individuals in crisis was why she took the job, in truth, it was a relief to be stuck at her desk all day. She had plenty of computer work to do and she preferred not to take it home.

Natasha's thoughts drifted back to college and her friend Joseph. She hadn't thought of the night of his arrest in a while. That night the police were unprepared when they arrived and despite the tearful protests of his friends, a delusional, paranoid, actively psychotic Joseph was incarcerated instead of taken to the hospital. The whole incident had left a lasting mark and still featured in her dreams occasionally. She shuddered. She was in a different place now. She was stronger and wiser and in a position to make positive changes so the other Josephs in the world didn't have the same outcome.

She thought about Pete and Tommy. Knowing them, and some of the other officers she'd worked with briefly, she already had a hard time imagining them treating anyone with the callous disregard the responding officers had shown Joseph. That didn't mean she couldn't help them out with more tools to make their jobs easier and to help those who needed it most. Figuring out how best to do that was the tricky part.

Natasha got up and looked for Pete. She wasn't going to find the answers she needed staring at her computer, no matter how much work she had to do. No luck. He was massive, he didn't blend in anywhere, but she looked around again, just to be sure. She evaluated the other options still in the station. Rubik's Cube Ramirez and Top Chef Lipinski seemed like the best choices. They were sitting at desks next to each other, so she could talk to both of them.

As she drew near, their conversation caught her attention.

"Ranting and raving."

"Said he'd just bought everything he needed to build a rocket ship and was going to be the first man on Mars."

"Don't think he's slept."

"Someone you know?" Natasha stopped in front of the two desks.

"Nah, just some nut job in one of the holding cells. One of the other patrol guys picked him up banging on the door of an electrical supply store at two a.m. Got squirrelly when they tried to talk to him. Drugs or something. The guy's out of his mind."

"Any reason I can't have a talk with him?" Natasha was already headed toward the holding cells.

Cube and Chef waved her on. One ranting individual in a holding cell was probably not an unusual occurrence.

Natasha found her man easily. He was the only one in his cell.

"My name's Natasha. Do you mind if we chat for a few minutes?"

"Not at all. But be prepared for all that I have to teach you." He was pacing the floor as if driven by a malfunctioning motor.

"I look forward to it. Can you tell me your name and why you're here?"

"I'm Reginald Standish III, and I'm here because the police got in the way of my work. I was in the middle of finalizing plans for my manned spacecraft capable of traveling near the speed of light. I needed a few supplies to begin small scale testing."

"And these supplies, you could only get them at two a.m.? Did you expect the store to be open?" Natasha pulled up a chair.

"Well, I was up, and ordering was going to take too long. I've been working nonstop on this project. Why should I be forced to wait until sunrise for what I need? Do you understand the possibilities? Of course not, how could you? You're constrained by the limits of your mind. It hasn't had the awakening mine has."

Natasha considered Reginald as he paced back and forth in front of her. She didn't agree with Cube and Chef's assessment of him as a "nutjob," but she did suspect he wasn't well.

"How nonstop are we talking, Reginald? When was the last time you slept?"

"Oh, Lord. Please don't live up to every dumb blond stereotype out there. Science and human discovery cannot be confined by circadian rhythms, or monetary expenditures, or the limits we place on our own minds." Reginald's withering glare was one for the record books.

"Okay, so it's safe to say it's been a while? Are we talking hours or days? Is this project you're working on self-funded?"

Reginald jolted to a stop in front of Natasha. He looked at her intently. "I *had* to pay for everything myself. I couldn't get anyone to believe in what I'm about to achieve."

"Is this how you usually work? Nonstop like this? Paying for everything yourself?" Natasha watched his presentation carefully.

"Not at all. I've been stuck in such a dark place lately, but the past week or two such inspiration hit. I don't need sleep. The ideas are flowing so fast I can't catch them all sometimes. My mind is like a motor driving me. I'm going to solve it. Or I was, until I ended up in here."

Natasha let Reginald know she'd return shortly and stepped away. She tracked down Lieutenant Smith, a cop almost as buttoned up as Tommy.

"Explain it to me again," Lieutenant Smith said. "The guy down in holding is what? And you want to send him where?"

"Manic, most likely and I'd like to get him to agree to go to the hospital." Natasha stood as straight as she could. She wasn't sure how the officers managed that ramrod posture. Maybe she'd ask Tommy about it. Or Pete. Pete was safer.

The lieutenant evaluated her for what felt like interminable hours. Natasha felt her attempt at standing at attention starting to crack. She was going to strain something if she kept this up much longer.

"The captain said you're here to do this sort of thing. Divert mental health cases from jail to services they need. You think this guy is one of those? I don't want to let him off the hook if he's faking it."

Jesus fucking Christ. Natasha wanted to drag Lieutenant Smith to holding and ask her how Reginald could possibly be faking the manic episode, but that wasn't likely to help her case.

"It is my clinical opinion the man in holding would be better served with an evaluation at the hospital than wearing a groove in the holding room floor with his pacing."

The lieutenant nodded. "Make it happen. But if you're wrong, this lands on your ass. And that isn't how we stand at attention, but you get points for trying."

Natasha slumped as soon as Lieutenant Smith walked away. She called after her. "How many points? What do I win once I get enough?" She dug her phone out of her pocket. Reginald and others like him were the reason she took the job, clenched back muscles be damned. She called a friend in the emergency department. Once she knew there was a bed open, if he needed it, she went back to holding to talk to Reginald. Technically, the police could take him to the hospital even if he didn't agree to go, but she wanted to try to get Reginald on board.

Natasha approached holding. Reginald was still pacing animatedly.

"Reginald, I told you I'd be back once I checked in with one of the officers here. I've done that and we agree that you should go to the hospital to be seen there instead of staying here with us. What do you think about that?"

"You think I'm crazy too?" Reginald stopped in front of her again. He looked sad.

"I absolutely do not." Natasha stepped closer so Reginald could see her face clearly. "I'm worried about you and I think there are people who can help. Have any of your doctors ever talked to you about the dark times you mentioned or other times you've felt energized and inspired to work without sleep?"

Reginald nodded. "I don't want to go back to the dark. Is that what's going to happen?"

"It doesn't have to be that way. Will you agree to go to the hospital to get some help?"

Reginald's consent was almost too quiet for Natasha to hear. The second time he said it was louder and had more conviction.

Natasha seized Reginald's motivation and got the ball rolling to get him transported to the emergency department. Once he was on his way Natasha flopped back at her desk. She'd done similar assessments and hospitalizations before, but this time her adrenaline had kicked in and now she was exhausted. Her phone buzzed with a text from Tommy.

Back at it tomorrow. See you bright and early.

The police station felt like a battleground and she was a one-woman army. If only everyone around her didn't seem to be on the other side. Someday soon, she'd change that, but today she had a date with Kayla. She'd been promised an obnoxiously large fruity cocktail, and Kayla was going to have to pay up. Changing hearts and minds was going to have to wait for another day.

CHAPTER SIX

Natasha looked across the room at the door. She could probably make it if she ran. But her legs felt like jelly and she was sucking air so deeply she figured her lungs looked like two oversized balloons about to pop. Running wasn't an option.

"I see you eying the door. There is no escape."

"I really hate you right now." Natasha glared at Kayla, which allowed her to pause the ridiculous maneuver being asked of her, that in her opinion defied the natural constraints of the human body. More annoying than the fact that Kayla had talked her into this hell masquerading as a workout class was that Kayla didn't look the least bit out of breath.

"Ten more minutes." Kayla pointed to Natasha's dumbbells. They were the smallest in the room.

"Fine. But you better be taking me somewhere amazing after this. You promised me cocktails, not sweat and misery."

Forty-five minutes later, she was showered and dressed, and Kayla stood at the top of a flight of stairs taunting her with the promise of food. She was still wobbly legged and considered spending the night curled up where she stood so she didn't have to attempt even one more step up, but she didn't think Kayla would deliver dinner.

She sagged against the wall when she finally summited. "Where are you taking me?"

"I thought we could try the new place over on Main that opened last week." Kayla looked like she was trying not to laugh.

"Absolutely not."

"What? Why? You always drag me to new places. What's wrong with that one?"

"Nothing's wrong with it." Natasha pushed off the wall and took one tentative step. She wasn't looking forward to work tomorrow. "Except they don't serve meat and you're buying me a cheeseburger. After what you just put me through, I need a cheeseburger. And a milkshake."

"Fries?"

Did Kayla know her at all? She looked at her incredulously.

"So that look means I shouldn't have even asked, right?" Kayla looped her arm through Natasha's and led her toward the door. "Come on. I'll be your legs tonight. How was I supposed to know you were so out of shape?"

"Should I be insulted or proud that I survived?" Natasha leaned into Kayla.

"Be proud. Some of her classes are really hard."

Natasha jabbed Kayla in the ribs. "This wasn't one of her hard ones, was it?"

"Uh, no. This was for beginners and active seniors." Kayla wasn't doing a good job of keeping a straight face.

"Well, that's a glancing blow to my large and rock-solid ego."

Natasha and Kayla dissolved into laughter as they walked arm in arm down the street. They turned the corner toward their burger joint and crashed into two very solid figures. Natasha started to stumble and was unable to use her depleted legs to catch herself. She was caught by one of those solid bodies before she landed on her ass. When she looked up, Tommy was holding her, looking as flustered as she felt.

"Officer Finch, you do have impeccable timing." Natasha wasn't in a hurry for Tommy to let her go. Tommy looked damn good out of her uniform, and Natasha was happy to take a moment to look.

"Are you okay?" Tommy looked worried.

"Of course, why?"

"You lost your balance and you look a little flushed. Do you need me to get you home?"

Natasha patted Tommy's cheek and stepped out of her arms. "I stumbled because I ran into a Finch-sized brick wall, I'm not drunk.

But thank you for worrying about me. My friend Kayla there tortured me for over an hour at a 'beginner' exercise class and now I can't walk."

Natasha looked to Kayla and noticed the other woman with Tommy. There was no mistaking the familial resemblance. This woman looked like an older, softer Tommy, although she didn't lack butch sex appeal either. She also had the ramrod posture and neatly put together presentation. Another cop, if Natasha were a betting woman.

"Henrietta Finch, officially, but everyone calls me Harry. I'm Tommy's much better looking, wiser, and more accomplished big sister." Harry extended her hand to Natasha and Kayla.

"Family comedian is more like it." Tommy elbowed Harry in the ribs.

Natasha could see the bond between them. It was apparent in the way they moved through each other's space and traded barbs.

"Nice to meet you, Harry. I'm Natasha Parsons. I'm sure Tommy's told you all about the pain in the ass social worker she's stuck with. Now you've gotten to meet me."

"That's not…*exactly* what I said." Tommy looked from Harry to Natasha.

"Don't worry, stick with Tommy. If you're out with her, you're in good hands and you're getting the best we've got to offer. And I'm sure you've had a few choice words about her too. I usually have a few after spending an hour with her, let alone a whole day."

"All right, that's enough out of you." Tommy gave her sister a gentle shove. "I'll see you tomorrow, Natasha. Enjoy your evening."

"Good night, Tommy." Natasha turned and watched Tommy and Harry walk away. She didn't feel guilty for comparing their asses. Tommy had just bowled her over and they were off the clock. As she was making her final determination, Tommy turned around and caught her staring. Natasha didn't turn away and gave her a tiny salute.

"Officer Finch?" Kayla slapped her arm, forcing Natasha away from visions of Tommy's very nice ass and back to Kayla. "As in your jerk of a partner?"

"I don't think she's a jerk. She just hasn't given me a chance to remove the stick up her ass. We haven't gotten a chance to get to know each other yet."

"Looked like you were getting acquainted to me." Kayla grabbed Natasha's hand and pulled her down the sidewalk toward the restaurant.

Kayla waited until Natasha was done inhaling her cheeseburger, fries, and milkshake before she started asking questions.

Natasha tried to explain the first few days of work. It was hard to summarize her feelings about the job and most especially about Tommy.

"I'm happy to hear all about your day to day." Kayla took another sip of her milkshake. "But I'd rather hear more about officer hottie you were snuggling with."

"Not snuggling." Natasha jabbed a French fry at her.

Kayla waved her off. "If you did happen to go down the officer and a blonde porn reel, who tops who?"

"Well, dinner took a turn."

"Don't say in an unexpected direction." Kayla raised an eyebrow. "You've known me too long to play innocent now."

Natasha took another long drag on her milkshake. "And you've known me too long to ask dumb questions like that."

"Even a big butch cop like her, huh?"

"She doesn't scare me." That wasn't entirely true.

Kayla looked like she was going to call bullshit. "Uh-huh. You going to find out if you're right?"

"I am *not*. I've been a member of the police department for less than a week and have learned one basic lesson. Don't fuck your partner. In any sense. Besides, it's hard to separate all cops from the night with Joseph, you know?"

"She looks like the type who could create a whole vault of new memories, and you've never met a rule that couldn't be bent. But fine, no fucking. What about her sister? That one might break your butch topping streak."

Natasha leaned across the table. "Is that drool I see? I thought you swore off looking for Prince Charming."

"Oh, honey, I don't think that one's a prince, and I don't think she's looking to charm. Did you get a look at her?"

Natasha hadn't spent much time looking at Harry. She'd noticed the familial resemblance and gone back to ogling Tommy. Historically, it had been better for their friendship when she and Kayla hadn't shown any interest in the same woman, but this time she shouldn't be interested in either one.

She tried to think of Tommy leaving her at the station on her first day. Or making her wait in the car repeatedly when she might be able to help. All she saw was Tommy's ass.

"Damn it."

Kayla looked smug.

"Don't give me that look. If this blows up in my face, it's all your fault. You were the one who brought up porn and made me think about her ass."

"I never mentioned her ass." Kayla's delight was over-the-top, even for her.

Later, at home, away from Kayla egging her on, Natasha found some perspective. Sure, Tommy was hot, but she'd worked with other hot women before. No reason to lose her head just because Tommy was possibly comparable to a Greek god. Besides, she had bigger things to worry about than Tommy's pretty face. Like how to get out of the patrol car and onto the street to start doing her job. Since when was the actual job the easy part?

CHAPTER SEVEN

Tommy pulled the patrol car to the curb of a very familiar house. She'd personally responded to calls there multiple times over the past year. It was always the same. She'd go in, talk to everyone involved, no one would say anything useful, and despite knowing the situation remained volatile, she'd leave, sure she'd be back. Today she was back after a call from the mother in the house.

"This probably won't take long. We get called out here a lot. I know what's waiting for me without having to go in. Doesn't seem to be much we can do to break through though." Tommy pulled the door handle and kicked her foot out of the car.

"I can't tell if you're joking or if you're seriously expecting me to wait in the car." Natasha grabbed her own door handle and got out.

Tommy pushed the rest of the way out hurriedly. She looked over the roof of the car at Natasha. "I'm not joking. You wait here. I'll be right back."

Natasha threw her hands up. "Why would you want me in the car when I can be useful in there?"

Tommy looked at the house, then back at Natasha. "It's not one of your mental health or substance abuse calls. What would you do? Teenage son loses his temper, takes it out on his mother and sister. Rinse and repeat."

"And nothing in what you just said suggests mental health or substance use concerns? How often did you raise a hand to your mother?"

"Not the point. I've got to go." Tommy rounded the car and headed toward the house. "When people call nine-one-one, they want a quick response. Wait in the car."

She could tell Natasha was angry, but she didn't have time to unruffle her feathers. Tommy wasn't trying to be an ass, she just didn't know how to let Natasha be part of her work. She didn't see the need for what she said she could provide, and this call didn't seem to fit the criteria she'd been given. Eventually, one would come along and Natasha could show her what she could do.

She made it halfway up the walk when Pete pulled up. Tommy and Pete announced themselves at the door. A young woman opened the door and they cautiously made their way in. Tommy recognized her as the oldest child who lived in the house. She'd just graduated from high school. She looked frazzled and her shirt was ripped. She'd been well put together the last time they'd met, but Tommy saw drastic changes in people all the time.

She waved them through to the kitchen. The family matriarch was sitting in the kitchen with ice on her face. When she saw Tommy she jumped to her feet, pulling the ice away in the process. Her eye was swollen shut and a cut on her cheek was still bleeding slowly.

"I know I called you, but things are fine. You don't need to be here. False alarm. I'm fine."

"With all due respect, you don't look fine." Tommy moved farther into the kitchen looking around as she did, evaluating the scene. She saw Pete moving around the living room, doing the same.

"She said she's fine. Get out of my house."

Tommy whipped around. The youngest child, a boy in his early teens, was standing in the living room, his forward progress halted by Pete.

This was where she always ended up when she came here. The mother or sister called the police, and once she arrived, one or both of them insisted everything was fine. Whether they were afraid of him or protecting him, she wasn't sure, but he was the source of the problems.

Tommy approached the surly teenager. "Jaden, right? I'm Officer Finch. You can call me Tommy. I've got a job to do here before I can leave. Why don't you tell me what happened while my buddy here talks to your mom and sister?"

"Fuck you."

"That's one way you can play this." Tommy hooked a thumb on her duty belt, careful to avoid putting her hand anywhere near her weapon. "But believe it or not, I'm here to help."

Jaden sat on the couch, turned on the TV, and picked up a videogame controller without another word. Tommy wanted to pick up the console and toss it out the window, but she didn't let any of that frustration seep into her expression. She walked over to Pete who seemed to be having about the same luck with the mom and sister.

"Might be time for Natasha." Pete nodded toward the door.

"Why? This isn't one of hers." Tommy cocked her head and looked up at Pete.

"Trust me." Pete clapped her on the shoulder and headed for the door. "We'll be right back."

Tommy let out a breath. Was Natasha going to look victorious when she walked in? Would she rub it in Tommy's face later? That didn't seem like her style. There was nothing for her to do while she waited. It was always the times you wanted to be inconspicuous when you felt the most awkward. Tommy was sure the rest of the room could hear the random hold music on a loop in her head. It felt like Pete and Natasha had stopped for coffee on the way from the car to the house by the time they finally made it through the door.

Natasha barely glanced her way once she was in the house. Tommy watched Natasha assess the scene and each of the players carefully before heading for the mother still parked in the kitchen. Jaden didn't look up from his game as Natasha walked by. Tommy couldn't help but follow her path. She hadn't exaggerated when she'd told Harry that Natasha was ungodly hot. But they were partners and Natasha was nothing but interference. Not much of a match made in heaven there, even if Tommy was inclined to dip a toe in those waters. Which she absolutely wasn't.

Less than five minutes after Natasha pulled up a kitchen chair and started talking to Jaden's mother and sister, Natasha was passing out tissues and patting his mother's hand soothingly.

"What the fuck is happening?" Tommy started for the kitchen, but Pete held her back.

"Let her work."

Soon Natasha was up and headed for Jaden. Tommy wasn't letting her talk to him alone. She was responsible for her safety. Once again, Pete pulled her back.

"Let Nat work, Tommy. We're right here if the kid gets jumpy. Trust me, she's handled worse."

Tommy felt her hackles rise, but she stood where she was. Was it jealousy? Natasha and Pete were awfully close, which shouldn't matter, right? Wounded professional pride? She laser focused on Natasha so she didn't have to figure it out.

Natasha plopped herself on the coffee table in front of Jaden, blocking his view of his game. Tommy admired her balls. Jaden looked far less impressed. Tommy was itching to move closer, but she'd had enough corralling from Pete for one day. Tommy couldn't hear what Natasha was saying to Jaden since they were speaking quietly, but after a few minutes, Jaden's posture relaxed. They chatted for a while, far longer than Tommy had ever managed with the explosive teen.

Eventually, Natasha waved the rest of Jaden's family over. They flanked him on the couch and looked attentively at Natasha. She was ticking things off on her fingers and looking at each family member, who were nodding or shaking their heads as she moved through fingers. Tommy's jaw almost hit the floor when Jaden's mother and sister leaned in and hugged him and he reached up to wipe tears away. Natasha patted him on the knee and got up.

"So, what, you fixed them?" Tommy inclined her head toward the three on the couch.

Natasha looked back over her shoulder. "Oh no. Definitely not. But I have enough of a sense of what's going on that we came up with a plan that works for everyone and can get them the help they need. I have to make a couple of phone calls. Can I trust you to stay with your babysitter while I'm away and not burn the house down?"

Tommy swallowed her response since Natasha was too far away for Tommy to whisper. What she wanted to say wasn't "whole room" material.

"Don't worry, pal, I'm one of the cool babysitters." Pete nudged her with his elbow and winked.

"Whose side are you on?" Tommy took a step away and avoided looking at Pete.

Tommy was on the sidelines watching Natasha work far longer than she found comfortable, but finally they wrapped up and pulled away from Jaden's house. Tommy only made it around the block before her questions threatened to damage something if locked away a moment longer.

"What did you do in there?"

"My job." Natasha had fire in her eyes. "Which you should let me do more often. It helped that family today a hell of a lot more than your frequent visits."

Tommy gripped the wheel tightly. She took a deep breath. It wasn't Natasha's fault they were both stuck in this situation. "You're right, we haven't had a lot of luck with that family. What did you do that was so different?"

"Tommy, I'm a social worker, not a cop. That alone made them more willing to talk to me. But I also had something to offer them that you didn't. I could offer them hope and the help they needed."

"And I couldn't offer them those things, why?"

Tommy could feel Natasha's eyes on her, but she kept her focus on the road. "I can't tell if you're purposely being a smart-ass or if you're adorably dense, but I'll give you the benefit of the doubt because despite myself, I kinda like you."

What the hell does that mean? Tommy wasn't about to look over at Natasha for clues.

"If Jaden's mom had told you he was the one who'd blackened her eye, what would you have done?"

"Arrested him." This had to be a trap.

"Of course, because you're a police officer down to your bone marrow, and you're trained to stop people who hurt other people by removing them from the situation. But what they all needed was a social worker, someone who offered alternatives and a path to make things better. Ways that don't include hauling a kid off to jail when all he needs is real help. That's why my ass is riding shotgun with you. But you've got to let me out of the car. Pete's not always going to come let me off my leash. Deal?"

Tommy looked at Natasha. "But he broke the law and has done so repeatedly. That's not the first time I've walked in on a scene like that. Sometimes it's his sister that he's beat all to hell. Don't you care about protecting the victim?" She didn't mean to raise her voice. She'd felt bad for Jaden too, she could see he was struggling, but it didn't change the fact that he was assaulting his family.

"At ease, Officer. Of course I care about the victim. But I have a more expansive definition of who the victims are than you do. Jaden needs services, not jail, which is something his mother understands too. That's why she never talks to you. And now the entire family's getting those services. Which is good for everyone, even stubborn cops." Natasha turned away from Tommy and looked out the window.

Tommy had a decision to make. Deescalate or dig in. She liked to think that her abilities to adapt, learn, and listen, plus her people skills made her good at what she did. Now was the time to be a good cop.

"This is new to me. I'm not used to being sidelined. You might have some housetraining to do in that regard. Maybe we can call a truce?"

Natasha threw a thousand-watt smile her way. "Housetraining, you say? I can work with that. But if you start humping my leg…"

"Would you like to finish that sentence?" Tommy braked at a red light and turned to face Natasha.

"Not yet. Let's see how the housetraining goes first." Natasha smiled and winked.

How Natasha was able to upend Tommy with one closed eye was a mystery.

"Would you like to know what Jaden and his family are getting?"

"Getting?" Tommy shook her head to focus.

"As in, what services we put in place for them."

"You mean you."

"I said what I mean. I think of us as a team. Think how much we'll be able to get done when you do too."

"All right." Tommy picked up the radio to answer a dispatch call and shot a look at Natasha. "This has to be weird for you too. You're busting my balls, but you don't look like you've spent any hours in a police car."

"The scenery is certainly nicer than my old job."

Tommy's skin tingled from Natasha's gaze. When she looked over, Natasha held eye contact but pointed out the window to the city park they were driving past.

"Not many opportunities for admiring the natural beauty of the city." She grinned.

"Glad I can be of service."

Natasha's eyes lit up. "Are you at my service? That is your job description, right? Lunch first, please."

"Not exactly." Tommy couldn't help but smile. "You're missing a few key bits, but it is time for lunch. I'll buy." She wasn't sure why she'd invited Natasha, but she couldn't back out now.

"Close enough." Natasha waved her off. "Do you want to hear about the good work we did for Jaden or not?"

Tommy laughed this time. Natasha was going to keep her on her toes, but she was hard to dislike. Poor Jaden hadn't stood a chance.

Natasha explained the appointment she'd lined up for the family with a home-based service provider who would work with Jaden and his mother. Each would be supported in developing skills and creating structure to lessen Jaden's dysregulation and outbursts. She'd also been able to get them in to a new psychiatrist. Jaden's old provider had gone out of network on his mother's insurance and they'd stopped going.

Help and hope were exactly what Natasha had provided for them. She was right. She was also right that Tommy wasn't equipped to offer the same. More specifically, she personally wasn't, but clearly the resource she needed had been sitting in her car.

"I see the wheels turning in there, Officer. If you start thinking on me, I'll be forced to come to the conclusion you're the full package. How inconvenient would that be?"

Tommy pulled to the curb in front of her favorite food truck, her brow furrowed. "Did you just insult me, compliment me, and then insinuate an insult? Right before I buy you lunch?"

"Point taken. I should've waited until after you fed me."

Natasha smiled and Tommy kicked herself. She knew Natasha was teasing her, and when she smiled like that, Tommy was willing to take any insult, lap up any compliment, or put up with any social worker in the passenger seat of her car. Since when was the most dangerous thing on her beat sitting in her patrol car?

CHAPTER EIGHT

Natasha let Tommy order first from the questionable looking food truck where they'd stopped for lunch. The man in the truck leaned so far out the window to greet Tommy she thought he might tumble to the ground. It seemed unlikely that someone who was willing to risk that kind of fall would poison a cop. And the food did smell amazing.

"I never would've pictured you for a four-sausage kinda lady." Tommy balled up her napkin and tossed it in the to-go box.

"Those aren't sausages, they're fancy hot dogs. I went easy on you since it was your treat."

"I hope you're not going to be hungry the rest of our shift. When my nieces get hungry they get whiny and angry. Is that what I have to look forward to the rest of the day?"

Natasha saw a hint of a smile on Tommy's face. She liked it. "I don't need to be hungry to get angry, Officer Finch, but I very rarely whine."

Tommy raised an eyebrow but didn't say anything. Natasha's thoughts raced down all different roads wondering what Tommy's eyebrow was communicating. She moved on.

"So, Tommy, tell me, why did we have lunch clear across town from the station at a food truck that looks like it had its heyday in the sixties?"

"Cause it's Lenny's truck." Tommy looked thoughtful.

Natasha waited for more information from Tommy. None came. She gave Tommy a gentle elbow.

"Am I supposed to know Lenny? Some kind of police code word or big boss?"

Tommy laughed. "No, Lenny's just an old friend of my dad's. After he retired he started up his food truck. He'd always wanted to have one. He refuses to come close to my station or Harry's. He says it would be taking advantage of our relationship so I haul out here whenever I can to grab a bite."

"And why did he call you 'J2'?"

Tommy looked at the ground. Natasha could tell whatever J2 meant, it was personal.

"You don't have to tell me. I was curious since I've never heard anyone call you that before."

"No, it's okay. It's just, you're…"

"Your mortal enemy and now you feel like you have to share something with me that makes you vulnerable? Am I close?"

"Nailed it. You know I don't think of you as a mortal enemy, right? We just view policing differently?"

"Tommy, we don't see policing differently. Bad guys do bad things, you round them up, with as little force and as much respect as possible and toss them in jail. I'm fine with that. But we're getting a bit stuck on the gray areas of who's a bad guy and who needs someone like me more than they need someone like you."

"But if we start ignoring the law for some people, where does it end?" Tommy propped her knee and ran her hand through her hair.

"Who says we have to ignore the law? I'm not suggesting you turn a blind eye to an assault or robbery just because the perpetrator has a substance use disorder or suffers from mental health issues."

"Wait, isn't that exactly what we did with Jaden about an hour ago?" Tommy laughed and crumpled up her trash.

"We didn't ignore the assault any more than you did all the other times you were at that house. This time we did something active to prevent it from happening again. And you were never going to get his mother to press charges."

Tommy shook her head, but she was still smiling. "We agree on the last point at least. And you're right that the kid needed the services you set up. But there are a lot of hypothetical scenarios I could play out for you where I'm not sure it would be so black-and-white. What happens then?"

"Would you ever beat up a suspect to get them to confess to a crime? Or trample on someone's rights, just a little, to ensure you got your big bad criminal?"

Tommy looked taken aback. "Of course not. That would make me a really bad cop."

"There are a lot of hypothetical scenarios where some people might say it was justified. TV cops do it all the time."

"Natasha, I don't play a cop on TV. I'm a real one and I don't do that kind of bullshit."

Natasha touched Tommy's hand. "So how about we start trusting each other and face those hypotheticals you're so worried about together? I showed you some of mine today, and you seemed to like what you saw. Are you ready to reciprocate?"

She sat back, waiting for an answer. Tommy's cheeks were flushed. Off-kilter looked good on her.

"Do I want to know what reciprocating looks like?"

Natasha rubbed her hands together. "For now, I want to know why Lenny called you 'J2.'"

"I expected so much more from you."

"This is the soft toss warm-up." Natasha crossed her legs casually, turned to Tommy, and waited.

"I'll try not to strike out."

"A good-looking, strong girl like you? Don't imagine you strike out often." Natasha knew as soon as they got back in the patrol car, all bets were off, but right now, it felt like she and Tommy were making progress.

"Didn't peg you for a baseball fan." Tommy winked. "My father's name is Thomas Henry Finch. When Harry was born, my parents named her Henrietta. I was next and they named me Tomasina. I'm not sure when people started calling us Junior One and Junior Two, J1 and J2. I don't think my brother's really ever gotten over being left out. I think he became a cop so he wasn't left out of that too."

"There are three Finch family cops in this city? Good Lord. Why don't they stack the deck and put you all at one station?"

Tommy shrugged. "After the academy, we were all assigned different places. I think we like making our own way."

"I respect that. Tell me more about your brother. Is he the youngest? What's his name?" Natasha remembered Tommy's description of her mother. How could she meet this family?

"He is. His name's Cody. We used to call him AJ when he was a kid for Alice Junior so he'd feel included. That's my mother's name.

He hated it. Although now I think he actually likes it. She's a badass woman."

"Your mother's Alice Finch?" Natasha didn't need to be a lifelong police department member to know about Alice Finch, but for whatever reason she hadn't connected the name to Tommy. The woman was a legend in the city. "Wasn't she all about progressive policing and getting cops into neighborhoods to be partners with their communities?"

Tommy looked suspicious. She nodded.

"Great, so she'll definitely be on my side. When can I meet her? We can draw up teams. I know Harry will be team Tommy all the way. I'm sure you two would follow each other into the mouth of a volcano. You had that look about you."

"Look? What look? How could you tell? You couldn't even stand up. And you're not drafting my mother onto a team against me. What kind of hooligan are you?"

"Where does your father stand on this? I bet I can pull AJ to team Dark Side. So, when's the next family dinner?"

Tommy got up, shaking her head. Natasha saw a smile, even if Tommy was trying to hide it.

"I'm going to win you over, Officer Finch. You can come to my side willingly, or I'll play dirty and talk to your mother."

"Get in the car." Tommy held the door for Natasha. "We have work to do."

"Now you're talking. Are you going to let me out this time?"

"I'll take it under advisement. But stop threatening me with my mother. That's a low blow and you know it."

Natasha laughed. It was, but Tommy was talking to her and looked more relaxed than she had at any point since the day they'd met. Another roadblock in their professional relationship was likely just around the bend, but Natasha felt better equipped to handle it after a food truck lunch and learning more about Tommy. If her mother was Alice Finch and her sister and brother were cops too, it was no wonder Tommy had very specific ideas about how to do her job. She could probably recite Miranda Rights before her ABCs. So how did she convince Tommy to take a leap of faith on someone she didn't really know or trust? First things first, she had to figure out how to get Tommy to let her out of the car.

CHAPTER NINE

Tommy ducked under Harry's hook, slid to the right, and counterpunched with a quick combination. She'd always loved the sound of her gloves hitting the training pads. Having them attached to her sister's hands and seeing them fly back from the impact was an added bonus. She stuck around a second too long to admire her last jab and Harry knocked her in the side of the head with the pad.

"Keep your feet moving." Harry looked like she'd be fine if Tommy never moved again.

Tommy stepped back, shook her head to focus, raised her gloves, and approached Harry again. They danced around each other, punching, ducking, and weaving for another few rounds. After the last bell, Harry threw down the pads and Tommy peeled off her gloves. They both grabbed water.

"'Bout ready to move on? I'm tired of being your punching bag." Harry doused her face.

"What makes you think it will be any different when we spar?"

"Because I've been kicking your ass since you were in diapers. Even when you won something it was only because Mama and Senior felt like you needed a self-esteem boost, but they're not here now."

"Good thing too, I would hate for them to see you cry. I *will* tell them you'll be buying beer tonight though. You're welcome." Tommy took a last sip of water and pulled on her sparring gear.

As soon as the round timer chimed, the trash talk stopped. They sparred regularly, but they took it as seriously as their time at the gun range or any other training. This was about helping each other, not one-upmanship.

Harry spun Tommy into the ropes and landed three body blows before Tommy pushed her off. Tommy swept her leg and took Harry to the mat. They wrestled, each trying to gain the upper hand before both scrambling back to their feet.

"I hear things are settling down with your social worker problem." Harry threw a hook, Tommy avoided it.

"Natasha's not a problem. She just sees the world differently than we do." Tommy jabbed, measuring her distance before striking out and catching Harry in the shoulder.

The bell sounded signaling the end of the round. They took the thirty seconds to catch their breath. Harry started up again once the bell rang in the next round.

"So you're bringing her over to our way of thinking?"

"I don't think that's how it's supposed to work." Tommy looked for an opening in her sister's defenses she could exploit. "And you don't know her. I don't think anyone tells her how to think. But at least I don't think she's a PR stunt anymore. She wouldn't be on board with that."

Harry whooshed out a breath as Tommy connected with her abdomen. Tommy moved to follow up, but Harry skittered away.

"She's been really helpful in situations where I wouldn't have thought to include her. She might not let me ever forget it."

"Who are you, and what have you done with my sister?" Harry swatted at her.

"I'm Officer Finch, trying to do my damn job." Tommy knocked Harry's hands away and put her own hands up.

"Yeesh, touchy. No need to get your shorts in a wad. Wait, is that the problem? You have a hard-on for this woman and can't do anything about it?"

Tommy didn't answer right away. She deflected a flurry of punches from Harry and avoided a low leg kick.

"I don't have a hard-on for her. That's your department." What did she really feel about Natasha? Tommy pictured her helping Jaden and his family. She thought about her scarfing down four of Lenny's famous sausages. She dropped her hands. Natasha was a lot to sort out professionally without having to decide if she liked her as a human being. But she did.

Further contemplation was interrupted by Harry's gloved fist connecting solidly with her left cheek, just below her eye. Tommy stumbled back and landed on her ass.

"Hey, I'm sorry. Are you okay?" Harry looked a little green. She knelt next to her and tilted Tommy's head. "That eye doesn't look all that good, man."

Tommy pulled off her glove and probed the area. "I thought we pulled our punches when we sparred."

"I did pull my punch. You'd know what the back of your brain looked like if I wasn't taking it easy on you."

"Seriously, you just sucker-punched me in the face and you're bragging?" Tommy held out her hand for Harry to help her up. Her eye hadn't swollen closed and she hadn't thrown up, a telltale sign of a broken bone when she was a kid, so as far as she was concerned, she was going to be fine.

"What's wrong with you? Why did you drop your hands in the middle of a round?" Harry switched to big sister scolding. "One minute we're talking about...oh. Well, that explains it. Maybe I knocked some sense into your dumb ass. Don't do anything stupid. And I mean that professionally and personally. You're going to get yourself in trouble and knock yourself off that career ladder you're trying to climb."

"Jesus, Harry, you make it sound like she's a siren. You'd probably like her if you spent time with her. I might actually like her and I promised myself under no circumstances would I do that. She's wily."

"Take off your gloves and let's get some ice for your eye. We have to be at family dinner and that needs to look better than it does now before we show up, or Mom will kick my ass." Harry yanked her gloves off and climbed out of the ring.

Tommy touched her cheek again. It felt more swollen. Cody's wife, Priya, was a doctor and wasn't afraid to ship one of them off to get checked when they were too stubborn to go themselves.

"You caused this mess, you have to keep me away from the doc tonight."

Harry shook her head. "You dropped your hands. You're on your own."

Tommy flipped her off.

"Unless…"

Tommy knew the look on Harry's face. She was about to be offered something that only sounded like a good deal, but wouldn't actually work in her favor.

"You want to tell me more about what's up with you and the social worker? Then I'll help out with the doc."

"There's nothing to tell." Tommy threw a towel at Harry. "And you'll help me no matter what. You still owe me for keeping you out of trouble with Mama a few months ago when you were dating…what was her name again?"

"We don't speak her name." Harry looked a little pale.

"It's right on the tip of my tongue. I'm sure I'll remember it soon. A full belly usually jogs the memory. Right before dessert it will probably pop into my head. I'm sure Mama will be happy to revisit those happy memories."

"You're my least favorite sibling. Fine. The doc stays away tonight. I'll say you ran into a parking meter while playing meter maid but got checked out already. I still want to finish our conversation about the social worker, though. I'm serious about not doing anything stupid, and I'm always here to talk."

"Her name's Natasha. Not 'the social worker.' She did something for a family recently on a call out that I haven't been able to do in months. It's made me think things, Harry. Is there a place for her at our station?"

"She *is* at your station, Tommy. You know I'm with you in not seeing how she fits or makes your job easier, but she's already there. What miracle did she work on your call that's twisted you in knots?"

They packed their sparring gear and headed toward their parents' house. It wasn't far from the gym so they walked. A light breeze swirled around Tommy as she walked. It felt like each gust danced a reclusive thought closer to the surface until they'd slipped past her natural filter and were on their way to Harry uncensored.

"I knew what was happening in that house, Harry, but I couldn't do anything about it. That angry, sullen, violent kid? I figured he was just a pain in the ass, you know? On his way to being a grown-up asshole. But Natasha made that damn kid cry." Tommy shook her head at the memory, which was a bad idea given the state of her right cheek that pulsed like a drumbeat in her face.

"I could punch you in the face and make you cry. What's the follow-up with that family?"

"You did punch me in the face. I didn't cry."

Harry waved her off.

"Natasha set the family up with home-based services and got the kid an appointment with a new psychiatrist. They have to follow through with it or we'll be called back, but it was the first time I've ever seen that mother smile."

"That's…" Harry looked like she was searching for the right word. "Impressive, resourceful. I don't know. I don't have those tools on my duty belt."

"Me either. But how many houses have you walked into with kids like that kid? Or families you couldn't help but knew they needed it?"

"Too many to count."

"And what if Natasha's right, that everyone's better off if she's walking into those houses with us?"

Harry shrugged. "Maybe she is. But what happens when that house contains someone who's armed? Or her life's in danger? Or yours is? She's not going to have your back. And she's not trained to handle those situations. Someone could die. I don't want it to be you."

The sisters walked quietly the rest of the way to their parents' house. Tommy couldn't stop thinking about the way Natasha had connected with Jaden and how the Zookeeper had spoken to her so freely. Would she be rejecting the help of a fellow cop if they had a similar skill set?

"Of course not."

"Your social worker is really in your head if she's got you talking to yourself," Harry said. "You haven't done that in a long time."

Tommy climbed the steps to her parents' house and looked back at Harry. "Don't bring up Natasha tonight, and help me out of the third degree with this." She pointed to her face. "You do that and I'll forget to mention who punched me in the first place."

"And you'll never bring up the other thing we talked about. Ever."

"What did that woman do to Mama?"

Harry shook her head and shuddered.

"Fine, I'll never mention her again." They shook on it and raced to the front door. Tommy won, barely. She squeezed in just in front of Harry. Her musings about Natasha and policing skittered in before the door closed as well and distracted her the rest of the evening. She and Natasha were back on patrol the next day. If only she could figure out if the unfamiliar feeling running through her was dread or anticipation.

CHAPTER TEN

You've waited long enough, you can ask." Tommy looked at Natasha through a black-and-blue, swollen eye. "I can tell you're tying yourself up wanting to."

"Why would I need to tie myself up when I have you and your handcuffs at my disposal? As for your eye, what the hell happened to you?" Natasha had wanted to ask Tommy what happened the minute she saw her, but she didn't think Tommy would appreciate her fussing. Or maybe she didn't appreciate wanting to fuss. Either way, she'd tried, and apparently failed, at ignoring Tommy's battered face.

"Harry happened to me. I'm fine."

"Why did your sister punch you in the face?" Natasha hoped she'd done a better job hiding her gut reaction to Tommy's attacker than she had to the first sight of Tommy this morning.

"We were sparring, and I was telling her about a work thing. It looks worse than it is."

"A work thing, huh? Mysterious. Are you talking about me behind my back?"

Tommy didn't answer, but she looked uncomfortable. That was all the answer Natasha needed. She deflated.

"So it was about me. You talked to your sister about me and she punched you in the face? For curiosity's sake, which one of you was on my side?"

"No. No, it wasn't like that." Tommy was driving since they were back on patrol, but she kept glancing over. "I was telling her about what you did for Jaden and his family and I got distracted. I let my guard down. It was an accident."

"As much as I enjoy the thought that I may be a source of distraction for you, we both know there are lots of cops who would love the opportunity to take a swing if it meant getting me out of the station."

"That's not entirely true. Look, you're different and you're not a cop. That's an adjustment for all of us. But look at me. I took you to lunch at Lenny's. I'm coming around." Those words felt strange coming from her mouth.

"Is that what it's going to take? I have to go out to lunch with everyone at the station?"

Tommy's sour look righted Natasha's mood.

"No need for jealousy, Officer. I'd never cheat on Lenny." Natasha put her hand on Tommy's shoulder but pulled it away quickly. Why hadn't she anticipated what Tommy's body would feel like? She'd noticed how her uniform accentuated her muscular frame often enough that she shouldn't have been caught off guard.

"I'm sure everyone would be very happy to dine with you, but I don't think that will be required. You'll win them over on your own. I hear Lieutenant Smith is letting you talk to a few guests down in holding. Don't know how you pulled that off. It's been years and I still have no idea if she likes me."

"Not only do I get to talk to our guests in holding, but she let me transfer one to the hospital."

"No shit. A triple murderer that you thought really only needed a sympathetic ear and a blanky?" It looked like Tommy was winking since her swollen eye didn't move when she smiled.

"You *are* getting to know me."

Tommy pulled to the curb and parked. They'd been called by a small business owner about a homeless man camped on his property who was refusing to leave. The camper was acting erratically and interrupting traffic into the store.

Natasha sighed when Tommy got out of the car. No matter how much she and Tommy seemed to be clicking interpersonally, nothing was changing professionally. Tommy was still heading off to do her job, leaving Natasha on the sidelines unable to do hers. Natasha jumped when Tommy knocked on the passenger's side window.

"I've told you before, when people call us, they expect same day service. You coming?"

Natasha hurried out of the car and followed Tommy.

"You're actually letting me out? What changed your mind?"

"Wait here." Tommy put her hand up.

Natasha started to protest. Being stuck on the sidewalk wasn't any better than being in the car.

"This is part of the deal. I clear the scene before you enter. That fancy vest you're wearing only protects you from so much. I'll let you know when you can come over." Tommy gently tapped Natasha's chest in the middle of the word "Police" written across the ballistic vest she'd been given.

"Yes, ma'am." Natasha wanted to salute, but she probably wouldn't be much better at that than she'd been at standing at attention.

Tommy chatted with the man they'd come to see briefly, checked him for weapons, and then called her over. The power dynamic between herself and the man she was there to help felt more unequal than anything she'd ever experienced, which was saying something given her upbringing. It was uncomfortable having Tommy standing next to her like an armed bodyguard.

Justin pulled up as Natasha struck up a conversation. She saw Tommy motion for him to stay by his patrol car. He stayed in the general vicinity but came too close to the action for Natasha's comfort.

As at Jaden's house, Tommy held back and let her work. She gave her extra points this time though, since Pete wasn't there whispering in her ear. The man, Frank, was a Vietnam vet. He was wary of her police vest and Tommy's presence, but after some chatting she built enough rapport to get an idea how to help him.

Natasha motioned to Tommy. "Do you know if the shopkeeper intends to press charges?"

Tommy turned her head so the main players in this sidewalk drama couldn't read her lips. "He said he just wants Frank gone. If you've got something else in mind, let's make it happen."

"God, I love it when people say that to me."

"Why does that not surprise me? Get back to work, please."

Frank was suffering greatly. He was homeless, he had mental health issues related to his military services, he wasn't currently receiving treatment, and he had significant substance abuse issues. Natasha suspected the mental health diagnoses and substance use were intertwined, but whether Frank connected the two didn't matter.

"Frank, we have options to get you some help." Natasha squatted a few feet from Frank, who was sitting blocking the entrance to the shopkeepers' store.

"Look, lady. You're real pretty, and nice enough, but I'm fine right here where I am. Ain't no one bothered me before you showed up."

"Frank, I've been honest with you, so you level with me. We both know that's not really true. We wouldn't be here right now if you were fine and no one bothered you. And you can't stay where you are now because the owner of this store needs people to be able to get in the door. So let's talk about where you can go instead."

Frank needed treatment for his substance use and an evaluation for the mental health comorbidities. There was a psychiatric hospital in the area that could provide both as well as help transfer him to long term care at the local Veteran's Affairs outpatient services, but he'd need to be cleared medically before being considered for admission.

"Frank, I'd like to get you over to the hospital so we can get you the help you need. From there the doctors can decide if you should go for more treatment in the hospital or see someone at the VA to help you figure out your next steps."

"I was doing pretty well a few years ago when I had a doctor at the VA. She was like you. Pretty and really smart. And she kept my mind right. Maybe she's still there?"

Natasha stood up. "How about we find out? Will you ride over to the hospital with me and Officer Finch?"

Frank glanced at Tommy and the patrol car behind her. He looked around wildly. Natasha thought he might bolt.

"Frank, look at me. You okay?"

"I'm not getting in that car. That car is a prison and I'm not going back."

Tommy, who'd been staying a few steps away, moved next to Natasha. She wanted to shoo Tommy away, but Tommy was her partner. She could come to the party if she wanted.

"Frank, I have a pretty good idea why you don't want to get in the back of my car. Is there anything we can do to help you feel safe enough to ride to the hospital?"

It was Natasha's turn to step back and let Tommy work. She was impressed, although she probably shouldn't have been. Tommy was a good officer and it wasn't like she hadn't interacted with the Franks of the world daily before Natasha showed up. As she and everyone else had said, over and over, they knew what they were doing on the street.

Frank cursed at no one in particular. He seemed lost in a memory, but he looked at Tommy, pointed, and shook his head. "Absolutely not. Your car is a prison."

Tommy stepped back to her. "He's not going to get in the patrol car willingly. He said the car was like a prison but there's nothing on his record to say he's been jailed before."

"Ambulance?" Natasha hoped Frank would get in the ambulance when it arrived.

"I'll call, you convince him."

While Tommy made the request for a ride for Frank, Justin sidled up. He didn't seem like the type who fancied himself suited for the sidelines.

"What's taking so long?"

Natasha didn't feel like explaining to Justin, but this was part of her job. She needed more officers than just Tommy to see the value of her work.

"Frank needs to be evaluated at the hospital but is reluctant to get in the patrol car. Tommy's calling for an ambulance."

"Oh, come on." Justin crossed his arms. "We're right here. He can't drive five minutes in the back of the damn car? I'll get him in. He doesn't need to waste the time of our paramedic brothers and sisters. They aren't a taxi service."

Justin headed to Frank who had wandered a few hundred feet up the block.

"Tommy, Justin's about to do something stupid." Natasha took off toward Frank.

Natasha was only a few steps behind Justin, but she was already too late to prevent the shit storm Justin probably didn't know he was creating.

"Look, man, get in the car. It's a short ride and you'll get checked out. Tommy's a decent driver, so you won't even get bounced around back there."

Frank was shaking his head. Natasha could tell he was getting agitated. Why couldn't Justin see that he was making things worse?

Justin raised his voice and ordered Frank in the car. His inexperience was showing, but Natasha had a hard time picturing Tommy ever treating someone like this. Justin reminded her of the cops who responded the night of Joseph's psychotic episode. He reminded her of her brother, using his power like a bludgeon.

"Enough, Justin. Natasha and I will get Frank to the hospital. Why don't you go about your business?" Tommy stepped between Justin and Frank.

"What's wrong with you, Tommy? Blondie get in your head? Just toss this guy in your back seat and get him to the hospital. He's not worth all this time and energy. Put him in the car."

Natasha felt like her head might explode. Frank actually did.

"I'm not worthless! You won't put me back in the cage."

Frank took a swing at Justin but connected with Tommy instead. He hit her on the side of her eye that wasn't already bruised and swollen. Frank raised his fist for another strike, but Tommy and Justin restrained him before he could swing.

Natasha watched as Frank was wrestled to the ground. She ran her hands through her hair and kicked at a rock on the ground. She was so angry tears were close to popping free to relieve some pressure. It didn't have to end up like this. It shouldn't have ended like this.

Screaming at Justin would probably get her a curbside seat next to Frank on the ground, so she kept quiet. Tommy would get an earful later.

The paramedics arrived before Natasha was done stewing. Another officer appeared as well. How many cops were needed to subdue one scared homeless man? At least Frank was restrained and unharmed. That wasn't always the outcome for the mentally ill when they interacted with police.

"Justin's lucky he's not headed to the hospital on that damn stretcher. There is no way this call should've ended like this."

Natasha jumped. "You're not allowed to sneak up on me when I'm pissed off, Tommy."

"Why not? We can be pissed together. And for the record, I stomped over here."

"Why are you bent out of shape? Didn't you get what you want? Bad guy arrested. Now we move on?" Natasha crossed her arms and turned on Tommy.

Tommy looked stunned. She took a step forward. "You really think there's a part of me that has shriveled and deformed so badly that I'd think Frank is a bad guy who needs to be arrested and thrown in jail? Or do you have that low an opinion of cops?"

Natasha's shoulders sagged. "No, neither. I can't kick Justin in the balls, which I want to do, so I'm yelling at you. That's not fair, I'm sorry. But that doesn't change what's happening to Frank right now."

The paramedics were finished securing Frank to the stretcher and were getting ready to load him into the waiting ambulance. He was still agitated and tears ran down his face. Natasha jogged over.

"Frank, listen to me. You can still get the help we talked about. Talk to the doctors when you get to the hospital. Tell them what you told me. I'll call over and tell them you're coming."

He nodded. There was fear in his eyes. Natasha turned away so he didn't see the sadness and anger in hers. The officer she didn't know climbed in the back with Frank and the ambulance took off for the hospital. As promised, she called and let them know what she could about Frank and his needs. Maybe it would help.

When she got off the phone the crowd that had flocked as soon as a police officer was on the scene had dispersed.

Tommy was standing a few inches from Justin and was jamming her finger into his chest every time she wanted to make a point. Tommy was speaking quietly, but her body language, and the tone that was drifting Natasha's way conveyed all that needed to be said about the conversation.

When Justin was released and walked away, he looked like a chastised dog with his tail between his legs.

"What's going to happen to Frank?"

"You're the one who called the hospital." Tommy headed back to the car. "He should get the same care and treatment as he would've if Justin hadn't mucked this all up. He needs psychiatric care, not jail."

"Even after he punched you?" Natasha stopped Tommy and looked at her face. She had a small cut where Frank had gotten her, but she looked okay.

"I got checked before they loaded Frank. I'm fine, but thank you for caring."

Natasha gave Tommy's chin a little shove. "Who says I care? Maybe I'm mad at you and deciding if I can bop you and blame it on Harry or Frank."

"You can always blame something on Harry. But you don't need to bop me. I'm on your side. Ask Justin."

"Does that feel strange coming out of your mouth? It's okay, you can tell me." Natasha settled into the car and turned to Tommy in time to catch a hint of a smile.

"You built a connection with Frank quickly under difficult circumstances. That was impressive. I wish we'd been able to get him to the hospital in a less traumatic way. I hope he's still able to follow the path you helped him map out."

Natasha fanned herself dramatically. "Was that a compliment? Be still my heart."

They rode in silence for a while. It felt companionable in a way it never had. They almost felt like a team.

"Tommy, thank you for being on my side back there."

"It was the right side, Natasha. Maybe we can stop thinking about things as your side or the police side. It might help if you and I are going to work together. And I'm sorry it ended up the way it did back there. That frustrates the hell out of me. I wish we'd been able to get him to the hospital without tossing him in my car. Lots can go wrong waiting for an ambulance."

Tommy was right. Sometimes catching people in exactly the right moment of motivation was crucial. By the time transport arrived it might be too late. Especially if their call was triaged further down the list on a busy day. And what if everyone on scene had as little experience as Justin? She'd just witnessed how rapidly her work could be undone. It was disheartening. But what was the solution?

Natasha stared out the window as if the answers were hidden in random letters that popped into focus from the bus stop advertisements, graffiti, and storefront signs as they passed. Her head was full of "what-ifs" and "hows." She needed answers, but those would have to come later. Right now she and Tommy had more work to do.

CHAPTER ELEVEN

Tommy flagged the bartender, Chet, and dropped onto a barstool. It had been a day that begged to be washed away with a cold one, but that wasn't why she was there. Although they were making progress, Natasha still felt like a runaway freight train bound for a destination she wasn't sure she was ready for. Tonight she wanted something so familiar it hadn't changed in her memory.

She closed her eyes. Most of the voices she could pull out of the din were familiar ones. Someone swore at the pool table, and she knew the cue ball with the chip had accidently gotten on the table. Chet hollered at his son working the other end of the bar, and Tommy knew Chet the Younger hadn't restocked, again. The floor under her feet was just as sticky as it had been for years.

"You look like you've had a shitty day." Pete leaned against the bar and raised his hand to catch Chet's attention. "Is it drink alone kind of shitty, or you need a drinking buddy kind of shitty?"

Tommy kicked out a barstool. "Have a seat. Who said my day's been crap?"

"Well, Justin came back to the station looking like someone ground up his balls and handed them back to him in a little Ziploc. Not the sandwich size either, just smashed them in the tiny little snack bags. Natasha wouldn't talk to me. She barely looked at me. And then there's you, sitting here drinking all alone, surrounded by friends."

"So no one told you anything, you're just being nosy."

Pete lost his jovial look. "I'm looking out for a friend. What the hell happened today? Natasha never clams up like that."

Tommy wasn't sure. Natasha had barely spoken to her the day she'd crossed the line and made Natasha mad, either. Maybe she'd never been pissed at Pete. Tommy couldn't imagine anyone being angry with Pete. He was the equivalent of a human Saint Bernard, big, goofy, cute, and if you got lost, he'd bring you the alcohol of your choosing in a cask around his neck.

"She's pissed at a day that didn't have to end the way it did. So am I." Tommy took a sip of her beer.

"Justin to blame for that? That why you handed him his balls in a to-go bag?"

Tommy sighed and put her beer back down, not taking the sip she was lining up. "Come on, Pete, we both know Justin's green as they come, but he's not a bad cop. We were both young and stupid when we first came out of the academy and graduated from the watchful eyes of our field training officer. Everything looks different on the street."

Pete raised his glass to that.

"Justin fucked up today and I told him that. If he's a good cop, he won't make that mistake again. Natasha's right to be pissed though. Justin's teachable moment was at the expense of another man's mental health."

Now it was Pete's turn to stop mid-sip. "Oh, that wouldn't sit well with Nat. No wonder she was mad at everyone in a uniform."

"How do you two know each other?"

Pete's smile looked nostalgic. "Before Nat joined our ranks and before I got transferred to our station, she worked at the free behavioral health clinic. They take all comers there, and it wasn't unusual for them to give my old station a call from time to time. I caught the call a few times early on."

"And she was fine with you swooping in and taking over?" Tommy studied Pete as intently as she would an eyewitness giving a statement.

"Don't imagine she would've been if that's what I'd done. You and I are talking about the same Nat, right? About yay tall?" Pete held his hand to his mid-chest. "I can't count the number of times Nat calmed the situation down and I didn't have to do much except stand there and look pretty. I arrived once to find her in the middle of a scrum breaking up a fight between an actively psychotic man and another high out of his mind on the latest designer drug."

"Holy shit. How many of us would you need to feel comfortable taking on that combo?"

"I can tell you I wouldn't want to do it alone."

"So who won?"

"She did, of course. No one was seriously injured, everyone eventually got evaluated and linked to services, and significant jail time was avoided. Mr. Designer Drugs had to do a little explaining in court since he had quite a stash on him, but he eventually found his way into treatment after paying his debt to society." He shook his head. "I got to know Nat pretty well during that time, and she's damn good at what she does."

Tommy wished she had a better grasp on what it was Natasha was so good at and how that was supposed to slot into her daily work. Natasha's role in her work life felt like mercury. She could see it and watch it move, but the moment she tried to grasp it, it slipped through her fingers. They sat in silence for the rest of her beer. Tommy stared at the liquor bottles lined up across from her. She turned and looked at the other patrons, mostly police, in the room. Just about everyone had beer in their hands.

"Have you ever seen anyone order anything here except beer?"

Pete shook his head. "Don't think so, why?"

"If this place only sells beer, why do they have twenty different kinds of vodka?"

"Invite Nat here one day after work. I guarantee she'll order one of those fancy drinks that requires one of those twenty bottles."

Tommy set her bottle back on the bar harder than she meant to. The crack startled Pete. Tommy yanked the label off, crumpled it and tossed it aside. "If you know Natasha so well, why aren't you partnered with her? You seem cool following her lead on how to police and deal with the folks she cares about, so why is she in my car and not yours?"

"Whoa, easy man. I never said anything about her yanking my jock about how to do my job. I was called to help at the clinic, and unless there was an immediate threat, I was okay not always dictating terms. But there were plenty of times everyone left pissed."

"Then why don't you know that Natasha clams up when she's angry? That she goes so silent you want to vomit out any inane thought just to break the quiet?" Why was she snapping at Pete? It wasn't his fault Natasha was her personal sore spot.

Pete shrugged and flagged Chet to order another round. "Our interaction ended when the call was done and then I didn't see her again for a bit. Sometimes days, sometimes weeks. How far under your skin has she gotten?"

Tommy glared at Pete. "You didn't answer why she's in my car and not yours."

Pete banged his hand on the bar. "I'm not the captain. I don't know. But if I had to guess it's because everyone loves you. And respects you. So if *you* can make it work with her and say she's cool, then everyone at the station will follow your lead. Not everyone has the balls to change when change is needed, but I've always respected your courage."

"Jesus. No pressure."

"Give her a chance, Tommy. She's amazing. Just give her a chance to show you what she does. Then show her what you do. I promise there's a middle ground you'll both be okay with."

"Now your beer's talking for you."

"I'm twelve feet tall. I'd need all those bottles of vodka to get a good buzz."

"Complete lie, buddy, but as long as you're not driving anywhere soon, I'll let you keep telling people that." Tommy tapped her bottle to Pete's and turned to face the rest of the bar.

"Tommy, I trust you and I trust her. Maybe I'm in the minority, but I think Nat could help the station and those we're sworn to protect. That's her goal too, so we're all on the same team. So it's on the two of you to get it figured out."

Tommy nodded. She kicked back into work mode. She'd been thinking of Natasha in terms of things she lacked: the ability to defend herself or Tommy, basic police training, a gun. Maybe it was time to start thinking about the things she brought to the table, like creative solutions to challenging situations, personal networks and contacts, and bravery.

She tried to refocus. If she was going to think about work, she might as well invite Natasha to the bar next time, like Pete suggested. Date night and business meeting rolled into one.

Date night? Tommy threw some cash on the bar, said good-bye to Pete, and rushed for the door. Natasha had pushed her back on the speeding freight train in one of the places she thought was safe. And date night had to invade her thoughts too? She should squash that thought immediately. But she didn't seem able to, whatever that meant. And now that the thought had seen the light of day, she wasn't sure she wanted to.

CHAPTER TWELVE

Natasha checked her watch when she pulled open the door to the coffee shop. She was five minutes early, but she could see the two women she was meeting already seated across the room. Closing out the day with Tommy had taken longer than she'd anticipated, and these two were never late.

She set her things down and was content to start the meeting without coffee, but they both shooed her to the counter. She reflected on her shift with Tommy while she waited to order. Although there was still too much sitting in the car for her taste, today Tommy had asked her to help out talking to witnesses at a domestic violence incident. Tommy had looked shocked when she'd gotten nowhere and Natasha was able to jog memory after memory.

It was going to take more time for Tommy to really appreciate that the lettering on her vest might identify her as an employee of the police department, but the community didn't see her in the same light as those who wore the uniform. Whether that was good or bad was an open debate, but it did make folks more comfortable talking to her as opposed to Tommy.

Once she had her triple espresso, Natasha returned to the table. She was meeting with Luanne, the director of Star Recovery, a substance abuse crisis and recovery center, and Dinah, her old boss at the free behavioral health clinic.

"Let's get a good look at you." Dinah grabbed Natasha's chin and turned it side to side. "I don't see any real difference. Luanne, you?"

Luanne shook her head, laughing. "Looks about the same to me."

Dinah patted Natasha on the cheek. "Guess the cop stink hasn't sunk in too deep yet. I'll consider taking you back."

"Cop stink is the sweat from the damn vest they make me wear. Lemme give you a hug."

"Get off me." Dinah was laughing now too.

"What can we do for you, sweetie? I assume you're not coming back to the light?" Luanne folded her hands and was all business.

"Has it always been like this, us vs them? Good or bad, light or dark?"

"I guess you'd have to ask our clients, but I don't think many of them are overly eager to interact with the police." Dinah pushed her cup aside. "And you watch the news, right?"

"That doesn't necessarily mean the police are the enemy though, right?" Natasha drummed the table.

"Don't suppose so, but the criminal justice system hasn't always been kind to our flock. Why don't you answer for us? How are they treating you?"

Luanne had always been good at drilling down to the point.

Natasha's shoulders sagged. "It's been a bit rockier than I expected, but I'm making progress, slowly."

"That's why we're here now I suspect. What can we do to help?" Dinah patted her hand.

Natasha was grateful for their support. She had a big favor to ask. She needed them to start thinking in shades of gray. She explained the recent Frank fiasco in general terms to protect his privacy.

"You want to know why it's us vs them, that rookie cop proves my point. What was he thinking?"

"Justin's not the point. Tommy pointed out where he went wrong, quite forcefully. The Justin shit show could've been avoided if I'd had more options than getting my guy in the patrol car or calling for an ambulance. I'm not sure he needed to even go to the hospital, but there isn't another way to get services as things are configured now. Can you think of another way that could've played out?" Natasha sat back in her chair and waited. Luanne and Dinah looked pensive.

"You know our clinic handles cases like your fella all the time," Dinah said.

"Substance use is rarely the only thing working against folks, so we've got a wide range of services too." Luanne sat back and matched Natasha's position. "I think you know all this though. What are you getting at?"

"How do I get them to you?" Natasha pointed between the two women. "The folks I find that need help?"

"You have a police partner. You can't just sneak people out from under her nose, Natasha. Are we going to be watching a crime show based on your life in a few years? Prison isn't as much fun as they make it look on TV." Everything on Dinah's face screamed "disapproving mom."

"No." Natasha pointed to Dinah, then Luanne. "No sneaking. Those that deserve it go to jail. Sometimes the hospital is the best option. But there's a group that would be best served by one of your operations. So how do I get them hooked up with you? Tommy's not a taxi service, and as we found out the hard way, not everyone is thrilled with the idea of riding in the back of a police car."

Natasha lifted her cup and went to take a sip of her espresso while Dinah and Luanne got back to her. It was empty. Disappointed, she put the cup back down and waited.

"I'm not going to commit to anything, no matter how much you sweet talk me," Luanne said. "But we do have a mobile crisis unit in the works. I'm sure you know nothing about it and all the anonymous funding that came in to make it a reality."

"I don't know a thing." Natasha squirmed.

"I've been around people who lie a lot for too many years, and I know that you're terrible at it. So whoever your friend is who gave all that money, please thank them." Luanne reached out and grabbed Natasha's hand.

Natasha tried not to dramatically sigh with relief. There was no way Luanne would know she was the anonymous donor, but she wouldn't have expected Luanne to figure out she was connected at all. She needed to work on her poker face. She needed to improve one of the things she hated most about her family name—lying to get what she wanted, lying to deceive, lying to maintain control and power.

"Did we lose you to thoughts of anonymous billionaires?" Dinah waved her hand in front of Natasha's face.

If only they knew. "Not at all. I'm excited the mobile crisis program is getting going. I know how important it is to Star."

Luanne looked skeptical. "Like I was saying, I'd only be willing to consider offering up our services during regular business hours for now though, when we have the most staffing."

"I'm the only one of me in the department right now, and I'm on the day shift." Natasha's heart raced. Could they actually make this work?

"I'll have to talk to Kit and Zeke. They've been heading up the mobile crisis team." Luanne pulled out her phone and sent a text. "I asked Kit to set up a meeting for the three of us to talk it through and see how we'd make it work. I'll get back to you after we have a chance to talk. I'm supportive and want to help, but there are a lot of logistical nightmares to sort out here. That's the best I can do."

Natasha didn't know the two people Luanne referenced, but she'd work with anyone Luanne wanted to make this work. "You're a peach, Luanne."

"Save your flattery for someone your own age. Not good for my health to have you charming my socks off."

"As if I could even so much as turn your head away from that beautiful wife of yours." Natasha rested her chin on her hand and batted her eyelashes at Luanne. She turned to Dinah. Luanne rolled her eyes in response.

"Okay, Dinah, Star Recovery is offering mobile crisis units. What you got for me?"

"I think you've got it backwards, kid. You should be wooing us. All you're offering is a date with the cops. Not much of a deal."

"That's because you've never met Tommy." Natasha clapped her hand over her mouth.

Luanne whistled low. Dinah looked delighted. It was like she'd just over-shared with her gossipy aunties.

"What color would you say her face is exactly, Luanne? Fuchsia? Magenta? I want to fuck my partner pink?"

"Leave her be, Dinah. When have you ever seen her like this?"

"Never, that's why it's so fun." Dinah rubbed her hands together.

"If this Tommy's able to turn her that shade of red, the best thing we can do is stay out of it and let Natasha figure out why no one else ever has." Luanne nodded like the issue was settled.

"You two do know I'm still sitting here, right?" Natasha waved her hand to get their attention.

"Hush." Dinah gestured dramatically.

Natasha drummed her fingers on the table. "There's nothing for you to dissect or analyze about Tommy and me. She's my partner, in the work sense, and most of the time she barely tolerates me. Our compatibility is questionable nine to five, so why would I take a peek at five to nine?"

"When you figure that out, you circle back to us. We'll be waiting."

Dinah still looked too excited for her own good. At least she wasn't talking too loudly, or at all, about Tommy. That was something Natasha was sixty-five percent sure she didn't want to think about.

The meeting had taken longer than Natasha had anticipated. Now it was dark and she'd had a triple espresso for dinner. She thought about calling a rideshare to get home faster, but she had nothing pressing waiting for her so she walked.

Despite the teasing, the meeting was productive. After giving her grief, Dinah had also mapped out a tentative plan to help anyone Natasha came across with Tommy in need of the kind of services the behavioral health clinic provided. It was a start. If she could make it work it would help a lot of people.

But would the other half of the equation buy in? Who was the other half of the equation? Tommy was the obvious answer, but what if she wasn't enough? Natasha thought about the way Tommy had lit into Justin after things went so poorly with Frank. Justin probably thought Tommy was more than enough.

She'd underestimated how Tommy would respond to Frank's needless suffering. It wasn't fair to Tommy, but it was also lazy on her part. She'd been fighting lazy stereotypes and snap judgments about the career aspirations and intellect of a rich blond girl her whole life. She could do better. It took effort not to dwell on other ways Tommy had surprised her. Like her kindness, humor, integrity, and really great ass.

Damn it. Tommy was her partner, not Ms. July from the hot cops calendar. Although she could've been. Natasha shuddered at the thought of Tommy wearing nothing but a few tastefully placed fireworks. Explosions for sure.

Damn it.

Natasha almost trampled the Zookeeper's shins before she noticed her sitting on a park bench with her legs outstretched. A closer inspection revealed she was sleeping, or passed out, not dead.

There was no one else around. It was strange the Parrot Master wasn't close. The Zookeeper and Parrot Master were a bonded, if odd, pair. Natasha slid onto the bench. She put her hand on the Zookeeper's shoulder and slid back about a foot while she awoke.

She jerked awake and looked around wildly. She slumped back when she saw Natasha.

"You are not my first choice to stumble upon me in my current predicament, Nat."

"You wound me, Zoo. Should I call in a replacement? Where's Parrot Master?"

"He's running the business. We're okay. I know you're too polite to ask. I'm the one struggling, not the two of us." The Zookeeper stood up, shook out her legs, and started walking.

Natasha jogged after her. She wouldn't say she and the Zookeeper were friends, but they were past acquaintances. They fell in a weird zone. But Natasha was worried about her and she cared enough to follow now.

"Officer Finch treating you okay?"

"What? Tommy? She's fine. You should probably make sure she thinks I'm treating her okay. Actually, don't. I feel like I know the answer."

The Zookeeper stopped and turned to Natasha so quickly they almost collided. "If she gives you any trouble, you let me know. I have unlimited resources to jam up a cop and I'm well versed on the law. I can make it stick."

Natasha opened her mouth, closed it, held up a finger, then put it down. She tried again. "Please do *not* plant drugs on my partner under *any* circumstances."

The Zookeeper looked noncommittal. "It would only be warranted if her own stupidity or boorishness dictated. No one to blame there but herself."

"You said you're struggling. Anything I can do?" A subject change seemed in order.

"I'm going to assume you're asking as a friend and I'm not going to get a bill for services rendered at the end of this chat." The Zookeeper was walking again, moving quickly down the sidewalk.

"I'm asking a friend how they're doing. Nothing more."

The Zookeeper nodded. "I think I might be in some trouble. I don't know how to get out of it, and I have people depending on me."

Natasha knew about the group of mostly women and young people the Zookeeper looked after on the streets. She shepherded them to safety from sex traffickers or other ills that befell the vulnerable when she could. The motivation was convoluted, given the Zookeeper's source of income was dealing drugs, but Natasha couldn't deny the difference it made to the women she protected.

"Tell me what's going on." Natasha put her hand briefly on the Zookeeper's shoulder.

The Zookeeper stopped and let out a breath. She raised her hands and ran them through her hair while looking to the heavens. "I broke my unbreakable rule. I tried some of our damn product and now I seem to be in the grips of something I'm ill-equipped to handle."

"Drugs? We're talking about drugs, right?" Natasha needed to take this seriously, but it was weird talking to a drug dealer fretting about a budding addiction and the impact on her life.

"Obviously. I got drunk at one of our parties. I don't know what convoluted thoughts led me to this place, but I'm stuck here now."

"Alcohol thoughts lead to plenty of unpleasant places. What can I do to help? You know there are resources and treatment options?"

The Zookeeper waved her hand dismissively. "I'm well aware. One of my former flock works at Star Recovery now. I don't believe a drug dealer would be welcomed particularly warmly there."

She probably had a point. "That doesn't mean they wouldn't help you. Does Parrot Master know?"

The Zookeeper nodded and started walking again. Had Natasha said the wrong thing?

"He knows. He loves me through any fire. But I'm doing this myself."

"Doesn't have to be that way."

"You're a cop now so you can protect my flock if anything happens to me. I have no plans of abandoning them, but this life is fickle. Should it turn on me, I would like to know they are being watched over in a manner I would approve. Do you agree to my terms?"

"Those aren't terms, Zoo, that's a favor. And I'm not a cop. I don't think I could do what you wanted even if I tried. Do you have a backup plan for someone to look after them, day-to-day, like you do?"

"That's what I'm asking, for *you* to try. That's how it works. See something that needs doing, try to do it. See something that needs changing, try to change it. Simple as that."

Natasha turned to tell the Zookeeper she was full of it, but she was gone, loping across the park, already too far away for Natasha to catch up. There wasn't anything left to say anyway, apparently.

She thought about her job, her co-workers, and Tommy. See something that needs changing and change it? Simple? She hadn't found anything simple about it.

CHAPTER THIRTEEN

It was the end of their shift, but neither of them had managed to close out the day and get out the door. In the course of "heading out for the night" Tommy had somehow ended up sitting on Natasha's desk. As soon as she sat down she realized it was a mistake. From her current angle, Tommy had a much too pleasant view of Natasha's chest and the hint of her bra. Was it black lace? She should report herself for sexual harassment in the workplace.

"Explain it again?" Tommy focused on Natasha's face. It felt too intense. Why was she making things weird?

"Did you hear anything I said?" Natasha poked Tommy's shin with the tip of her shoe.

Tommy felt her cheeks heat. "Uh, maybe you should start from the beginning in case there were bits I missed."

"I was telling you how the mobile crisis unit at Star Recovery would've saved us about two hours today. If we can work out the logistics, it's going to be a beautiful partnership."

"Two hours seems like a stretch since we were only on scene with the woman for forty-five minutes, but your point is taken. You already won me over. I told you that the first time you brought it up. I'm not the logistics person."

"Well then, get your butt off my desk so I can get the right butt onto it. If you can't help me I need to switch you out for a more useful model." Natasha poked Tommy again with her foot, pretending to kick her off the desk.

"I don't think the butt you need comes to you." Tommy held on to the desk tightly, refusing to budge. "It hasn't been that long since you proposed all of this. It needs time to work through the bureaucracy."

This after-hours banter with Natasha was nice. The pressure of finding common ground without losing their ideals was gone with the punch of the timecard. Now they were two co-workers who seemed to get along rather well without all the added pressures.

Tommy saw Natasha look toward the captain's office door. Tommy knew Captain Gillette was still in her office. She always worked later than most of the day shift. What she didn't know was what Natasha was thinking.

Natasha was out of her chair and headed to the captain's office before Tommy could get off the desk to stop her. She chased after her, trying not to look desperate.

"Natasha, this isn't a good idea." Tommy was debuting her stage whisper without a dress rehearsal.

"Don't worry, Tommy, I know what I'm doing."

"No, you don't." Tommy stopped power-walking behind Natasha and stared at her.

Natasha stopped just outside Captain Gillette's office and turned to her. Natasha's smile was blinding. "I know. I really don't. But it'll be okay."

Tommy watched Natasha knock on the door and ask if the captain had a minute before she could do anything else to intervene. Why did Natasha always assume things would work out? Maybe they usually did.

It seemed like Natasha was in that office forever. Tommy paced around Natasha's desk waiting. She didn't have to stay, but Natasha was her partner and whatever the captain did, said, or decided would impact both of them.

She still couldn't believe Natasha had just waltzed over and demanded a meeting. The captain was approachable and had an open-door policy, but Natasha was asking for a lot of change and she was springing it on the captain after-hours with no warning and with no regard for the channels her proposal was already creeping along. If Tommy thought about it though, it tracked. Natasha wasn't pushy or rude, but she expected things to get done. If they didn't, she seemed willing to do them herself. She stood her ground and advocated for the people and things she cared about. And that was why the two of them had been butting heads constantly since Natasha started working at the station.

But that wasn't really true. Somewhere along the way they'd started arguing less and collaborating more. Their days had settled into a solid routine, and it wasn't often they disagreed. Did that mean she was losing her edge as a cop? Or maybe that she was becoming a better one?

Her phone buzzed with a text from Harry. Her sister wanted to know where she was since she was ten minutes late meeting her. She told Harry she got caught up just as Natasha strolled out of the captain's office.

Tommy looked for signs of trauma, but Natasha looked like she'd just gotten back on the beach after the best day of surfing in her life. Even in the middle of a police station, Tommy always thought Natasha should be toting a surfboard. She just had the look.

"Well, I didn't get everything I wanted." Natasha's grin was so wide Tommy knew she'd gotten almost everything.

"So you still don't get to carry a gun?"

"Oh, God no. If I had a gun, what excuse would I have to keep you so close?"

"So what did your considerable charms win in your negotiation?" Tommy couldn't help but puff out her chest a little at Natasha's insinuation she wanted Tommy's protection. It annoyed her a little that she was so easily flattered.

"Charm had nothing to do with it. You might find my allure resistible, but I can level up when I need to."

"I will concede your ego is hard to ignore." There was no bite to her words. "I'm afraid to ask what next level looked like. Should I bring the defibrillator to the captain?"

"Are you accusing me of using sex appeal to get what I want?"

Tommy sputtered and started backpedaling. At least her mother would kill her more quickly than the slow death spiral her career would take once Natasha complained to human resources about her behavior.

"Tommy, relax." Natasha slipped her hand into Tommy's quickly, squeezed, then pulled away. "I was teasing you. I know you're nothing but a perfect gentleman."

Tommy looked at her hand, then at Natasha. Earlier, she'd been objectifying Natasha like a horny teenage boy, but that brief contact had triggered something else. It felt…nice. She wanted an excuse for Natasha to take her hand again, which was ridiculous. She and Natasha were tolerating each other now, but there was still a lot unresolved, professionally, between them. And "unresolved professional" time was the majority of their time together. Tommy had career aspirations that diverged from the path Natasha was walking, and even if all that could be reconciled, there were strict rules about partners dating. The two of them was a non-starter. What was wrong with her tonight?

Another text from Harry lit up her phone. She'd never stood up her sister before. She toyed with her phone for a second. "Do you want to get a drink?"

Natasha looked shocked. "Did you just ask me out? Is there a manual or a troubleshooting guide I can consult? Maybe a reset button? I think you're malfunctioning."

"I just asked my partner to get a drink after work." Tommy crossed her arms over her chest. "You're not technically police, but I think Chet will still let you in the bar."

Natasha's eyes lit up. "This is so much better than a date."

"Excuse me?" Tommy stopped mid stride and turned to Natasha. It seemed like she should be insulted.

"If you asked me out, you probably just wanted to get in my pants. Asking a co-worker to get drinks after work means you actually like me. You don't go out of your way to spend time outside of work with co-workers you don't like."

"I barely tolerate you." Tommy's scowl failed her.

"True. Doesn't mean you don't like me." Natasha pulled Tommy to the door. She looked like she was skipping every few steps. "Hurry up. I want to meet Chet."

Tommy was going to pay for her impulsivity the moment she walked in with Natasha and she knew it. She should be able to bring her partner to get drinks after work, but Harry would read into it, even though she shouldn't. Probably. Sisters were annoying like that.

"As long as you give me all the details of whatever next level thing got you everything you wanted from the captain. And so I'm prepared when you try to use that version of you on me."

"It's so adorable that you think I'd have to." Natasha gave Tommy another nudge toward the door. "But, in the captain's case, I used cold hard logic. She wants me to succeed. We both have a lot on the line. Getting this set up will help and it will also save money. Whatever arrangements we make with Star and the clinic are going to be cheaper than calling out an ambulance or utilizing your amazing taxi skills."

"Impressive. I can see why you won her over. Who knew logic came after charisma for you?"

"Believe it or not, I'm not just a dumb blonde with nothing but good looks and sex appeal to offer the world." There was deep hurt in Natasha's tone and on her face.

"Hey, I'm sorry if I make you feel that way. You wouldn't keep me so damn off balance and have me constantly reevaluating the way I do my job if you were just some dumb blonde. As a side note, it's really annoying to be second-guessing something I've been groomed to do since I was born."

"I wasn't talking about you, Tommy. I told you before, you're a perfect gentleman." Natasha patted Tommy's cheek. "What if you'd become a kindergarten teacher or tattoo artist? Or a gardener? Ooh, or a model? Would you have been allowed to stay in the family?"

"A model, no. Because I'd be waiting tables, unemployed and begging my parents for rent money. That's where they would object. The family business allows for a black sheep to keep things interesting. But it turned out no one wanted the job."

Natasha made a "pfffff" sound. "You would not be an out of work model with a face like yours. And if you were waiting tables, the tips you'd get definitely wouldn't require begging for rent money."

Tommy knew her cheeks were reddening even though she was trying to squelch the reaction. "What would you know anyway?" She pulled open the door to the bar and ushered Natasha inside.

"I've been trying to tell you, there are lots of things I know that you don't. But that's for another time. I believe you were about to buy me a drink."

Tommy shook her head and smiled. She watched Natasha move into the bar like she owned it. Tommy figured she probably would by the time she left. It wouldn't do any good, but she called after her, "That's not how I remember the invitation."

Natasha turned and smiled. It was her genuine, light up the room smile. It was a smile that swirled around Tommy and stole her breath. That probably happened to everyone in the path, right?

"What did you say to her to deserve that?" Harry slid next to Tommy. "And why's she here?"

"Because we're grabbing drinks after work and she's my partner." Tommy took a step away from Harry, toward the bar.

"Hey, lower the hackles. I haven't even gotten to the annoying questions yet."

"Can we skip them? It's been a long day." Tommy tried to get Chet's attention for a beer and saw Natasha head to the pool table to talk to some of their colleagues.

"That's your fault. It would've been a normal length day if you'd shown up here when you were supposed to."

Tommy glared at her.

"Fine. One question. Are you doing anything I'd be doing?"

Tommy threw her hands up. That was the thing that finally got Chet's attention. "No. Ask her yourself. She'll tell you I'm a perfect gentleman."

Harry looked suspicious. "I think you're supposed to be a good partner or a serviceable co-worker. Gentleman isn't how I'd describe anyone I work with."

"That's because you work with scoundrels." Tommy took a sip of her beer.

"Tommy, be careful."

"Harry, relax. I'm not going to make the mistakes you've made. If Natasha were a guy you wouldn't think twice about my bringing him tonight."

Harry poked Tommy in the shoulder. "If Natasha were a guy, would you have invited him? I'm your big sister. It's my job to worry, even for nothing."

Tommy considered Harry's question. Would she have invited a male partner to the bar? There wasn't any way of knowing for sure, since she hadn't been partnered since she'd finished her probationary period, but why not? The feel of Natasha's hand in hers came to mind. Had she invited Natasha because their hands felt nice together? That couldn't possibly be true.

A commotion at the pool table pulled Tommy from her musings. Harry had moved down the bar to talk to another group so Tommy moved toward the excitement. When she pushed through the crowd, half her station was positioned behind Natasha, looking ready to rumble. On the other side of the table was a lone firefighter. His face was red with anger and his stance was combative.

Tommy was proud of the station for seeing Natasha as one of their own and backing her. Until this moment she'd have given it fifty-fifty odds.

Despite being the epicenter of whatever trouble was bubbling, Natasha looked as calm as a gently rolling wave. Tommy stepped between the angry firefighter and Natasha. She wished she had some bomb defusal skills. What if she cut the wrong wire?

The minute she set foot between the two factions, everyone began yelling their tales of mistreatment. Tommy could only hear one or two words out of each shouted passage.

"What's going on here, Natasha?" Tommy leaned close to Natasha's ear.

"Pool minnow over there lost a bet to the biggest shark in the sea. Now he's pissed he had to pay up and is saying I cheated."

"How much did you take him for?"

"Two hundred. I do *not* cheat."

"What the hell were you doing betting that much on a game of pool? Never mind. I don't suppose tossing him a few bucks back would work for you?" Tommy eyed the crowd. The tension was seeping into every crack in the room.

Natasha looked incredulous. Tommy nodded. She wouldn't have given it back either.

Tommy turned to the firefighter. He looked drunk.

"Look, man, you're about to piss off a lot of people. How about you head home for the night? Can I call you a ride home?"

"Not until that cheating bitch gives me my money back."

Tommy clenched her jaw. She took a deep breath and tried again. "I think the crowd's backing your opponent on this one. She says she didn't cheat. It's time to go home, man."

"If she didn't cheat, how did some dumb blond whore beat—"

Tommy lunged forward and would've knocked the man's nose far enough back that he'd be smelling his ass for the rest of his life, but someone grabbed her arm. When she turned, Natasha had both hands looped around her bicep. The grin on her face wasn't the megawatt one Tommy was used to. This one felt intimate and personal.

"Like I said, a gentleman."

Tommy lowered her arm and Natasha let go. The connection was broken as soon as their bodies lost contact.

"Out you go."

Tommy turned to see Chet the Younger and Harry depositing the drunken firefighter on the sidewalk. A cheer went up from the cops behind Natasha.

"I thought you said you weren't doing anything I'd do." Harry patted Tommy on the shoulder as she moved back to the bar. "We'll talk about this later."

Bar fights were more Harry's domain, at least they had been in her younger years. But this was different. She was defending her partner. That asshole had called Natasha…Tommy didn't want to think about it. She turned to look for Natasha, who was at the bar.

"You okay?" Tommy slid onto the stool next to Natasha.

"I'm two hundred dollars richer, felt like a part of the station for the first time ever, and had my own personal bodyguard. I've had worse days."

"You said you kept me around to protect you." Tommy leaned on the bar.

"I did say that, didn't I? But I didn't say I would start bar fights to make you prove it."

Natasha took a sip of some drink served in a real glass. Maybe it required one of the fancy vodkas Chet had on display.

"He shouldn't have spoken about you the way he did. He deserved to lose a few teeth. Why'd you stop me?" Tommy peeled the label off her empty bottle.

"He wasn't worth it. I've dealt with guys like him my whole life, the ones who think they have something that makes them better than everyone else. Money, a fancy last name, a job handed to you by Daddy. I don't get the sense bar fighting is something you do much of, so why waste stepping outside your comfort zone on someone like him? If you're going to do it, let's make it really count." Natasha nudged Tommy with her toe.

"As a thought experiment, what do you imagine outside my comfort zone looks like?" Tommy sat back and stretched.

"Wear scuffed up boots to work one day this week."

"Absolutely not."

"Let me drive tomorrow."

"No way."

"Let me out of the car on a call that doesn't fit the strict criteria you've been given."

Tommy hesitated. If she were honest, she'd wondered if Natasha could be helpful on other types of calls. Now was her chance to find out. Before she could make a decision, Natasha challenged her further.

"Ask for only our kind of calls for an entire shift."

"Fine."

Natasha did a sitting bouncy, shimmy dance. It was adorable. Tommy wasn't even sure what she'd agreed to.

They sat together at the end of the bar talking for the rest of the night. After Natasha's successful pool sharking, other members of the station were more willing to come up and chat, but neither of them strayed back into the crowd. Tommy enjoyed the teasing from the other officers when they came to talk to Natasha. Some busted her balls about being held back by her partner. Others patted her on the back for throwing down for the station.

Everyone who came over however was suddenly curious about how Natasha and Tommy worked. There were a few who seemed open-minded about Natasha's contributions. "Is she making your job easier?" "Is she making you a better cop?" "Is it hard to change the way we've always done things?"

More consistently however, her fellow officers let their obvious insecurities spew out with questions like, "Is she taking over your job?" "Do you remember how to be a cop?" "Is she making you soft?"

"How will you ever make detective now?" Tommy wondered if her own discomfort had been so obvious when she and Natasha were first partnered. Probably. But now, having it openly questioned by her co-workers made it seem important and worthwhile, something she'd not recognized before.

Tommy looked at Natasha, who was surveying the bar crowd. Yesterday, she wouldn't have believed she'd be involved in an almost bar fight after spontaneously inviting Natasha out after work. Was change hard? Maybe not as hard as she thought.

CHAPTER FOURTEEN

Natasha pulled the brownies out of the oven before sliding the sheet pan with dinner in. If the oven went up in flames now at least she wouldn't go hungry, or miss out on dessert. She pulled out two wine glasses, grabbed a white from the fridge, and checked her watch. At exactly seven, the door to her apartment opened and Kayla breezed in.

Kayla pushed past without a word and leaned over the brownies. "Tell me."

"Nutella." Natasha poured the wine.

"And you think I'm going to want to eat any of the food you've got cooking there, knowing these are waiting for me?"

"Who says I'm making any of that for you? You invited yourself over, if I remember." Natasha's straight face lasted less than a second.

Kayla hopped up on a stool at the kitchen island and helped herself to one of the glasses of wine. "While we wait for dinner, fill me in on life as a police officer sidekick."

"That's not what I am." The glass Natasha was putting away clattered dramatically when she set it down with more force than necessary.

"Whoa, I'm sorry. I accidently pushed a button I didn't mean to. Can we start over?" Kayla reached across the island to try to jab at Natasha. "Tell me about Officer Hottie. You know the two of you are my favorite soap opera."

"Can we come up with a different name for her? Maybe you could try out, I don't know, Tommy?" Natasha yanked open the oven to check on dinner which wouldn't be ready for at least another fifteen minutes.

When Natasha turned back around, Kayla was staring at her. Natasha had always thought of it as Kayla's "you have some explaining to do" look, even though after all their years of friendship she still had no idea what she was actually thinking.

"Did you learn something untoward about her? Has she lost her sexy shine? Did something happen at work? Have you decided to become a door-to-door salesman of snake oil cures and tinctures?"

Natasha tried not to spit out the sip of wine she'd just taken. "What? No. Nothing like any of that. There's nothing wrong."

Kayla looked at her again, clearly waiting for a real answer.

"Fine, calling Tommy officer hottie feels objectifying and shallow. I know her now, and she's, I don't know, a good person."

"So you can't talk about how hot she is because she's a good person?"

"Her being sexy and being a good person are all jumbled up now. I told you how she was ready to throw a punch because a drunk guy spouted off at me."

"You mentioned you instigated a bar fight."

"Not at all what I said, but that's not the point. How many women have defended you from an asshole hurling insults lately?"

Kayla held her hands up to form a big zero. "The real question is why she did it. Because you're her partner? Because she's got the hots for you? Because she's a white knight looking for damsels to rescue?"

Natasha shrugged and turned to pull dinner out of the oven. It bought her some time. Kayla looked expectant when she turned around.

"I don't know why she did what she did. Maybe she'd do it for anyone. I suspect she would. It seems like who she is. I didn't need her to rescue me from that idiot, but it still felt nice for her to have my back. And yes, it makes her that much hotter now that I know her better."

"Great, so she's hotter now. Hop in bed with her and get it out of your system."

"No."

Kayla stopped with her wine glass halfway to her mouth. She put it back down. "Just no? That's all you're going to say?"

Natasha dished up the food and slid a plate to Kayla. Natasha started eating, but Kayla didn't take her eyes off her.

"What? I'm not going to sleep with her to get her out of my system. I believe we've talked about the 'no fucking your partner' rule. Yes, that's all I'm planning on saying about it."

"How many times have you said shit like that? I can always get you to talk."

Natasha laughed. "It's true. You'd make a good interrogator. You're decent at making me feel better when I'm a grump too, but don't tell your already oversized ego."

"So we can chat like friends now instead of whatever this tense form of communication is?"

"If you insist." Natasha pointed to Kayla's food. "But eat that or I'm keeping all the brownies for myself."

For the rest of dinner, they caught up on Kayla's day-to-day. It wasn't hard to tell Kayla wanted to ask Natasha a zillion questions, but she held them in. They had a well-worn pattern. When Kayla needed something, she waited until after dinner and dessert so she could lay on excessive compliments. Then she'd make her ask.

"I have an early morning tomorrow, Kay, so you don't have to wait until after dessert to ask whatever's making the ants in your pants dance. Spit it out."

"I don't even get the satisfaction of a good comeback to that. Telling you 'you wish you could see what's in my pants' makes me feel dirty inside." Kayla shivered.

"And now you know why I can't think of simply fucking Tommy to get her out of my system."

"Because she's replaced me as your best friend?"

Natasha glared at Kayla.

"Because you've friend-zoned her?"

"No. I didn't friend-zone her. Maybe that was a bad parallel. I'm working my ass off trying to build something from scratch, something I believe in, and I need Tommy's help to do it. There's no way I'm going to throw that away. Besides, I don't think that's really Tommy's thing anyway. She's looking to climb the career ladder, not into every bed she can."

"Sex with smokin' ladies? Yeah, I can see how that would be a turnoff."

Natasha started to protest, but Kayla held up her hands and waved her off.

"I'm sorry. I'm not trying to be flippant. It seems like you have given it thought. Has she gotten under your skin?"

"I don't know. She's sweeter than I expected from looking at that butch shell wrapped in a uniform. She's stubborn and pig-headed about rules and cop things, but she's also been more open minded and flexible than I thought she would. And she *sees* people. Remember that guy I told you about who ended up getting restrained and taken to the hospital because of that idiot kid cop?"

Kayla nodded. "The kid cop who reminds you of Preston?"

Natasha rolled her eyes and made a gagging gesture at the mention of her brother. "Forget about Justin. Tommy saw the homeless man as a person. It sounds stupid, but guys like him aren't usually seen at all and when they are, they're less-than to most people. Mental health, substance use, it's easier to look the other way."

"I know, honey. That's why you're doing the job you're doing. And why I see Officer Sexy's going to have to keep her hands to herself." Kayla wandered into the kitchen and grabbed the entire pan of brownies and two forks.

"I told you, stop calling her that." Natasha took a fork.

"Because it's not true, or because she's more to you now?" Kayla wagged her fork at Natasha.

"For all the reasons I just outlined, the only feelings I'll have for Tommy are strictly professional. Calling her Officer Sexy doesn't help that." How was that for a lame argument?

"Good thing feelings never misbehave. If you're not going to be honest with me about Tommy, tell me about the mobile crisis set up. That starts soon, right?"

"It's taken forever to get in place, but tomorrow's the day."

"From what you said, you fast-tracked it quite a bit. A few months to get an entire logistical nightmare in place is lightning fast, especially when you're talking about local government."

"I guess. Sometimes it would be easier if I could still throw around my parents' last name. Barriers do magically fall away for a Blackstone."

"Speaking of, do they know you're spending their money funding a mobile crisis unit at a recovery center?" Kayla jabbed her fork in the brownies and took a huge bite.

"Have you seen it splashed across the news and all over social media?" Natasha put her bite of brownie down and ran her hands through her hair.

Kayla picked up Natasha's fork and waved it under her nose. "They do love to make everything about themselves, don't they? So let's not make this about them. What are you doing to celebrate Star joining the team with you and Officer Up for Grabs Because Natasha's not interested?"

"Sometimes you're really the worst, you know that, right?" Natasha pulled the entire pan of brownies out of Kayla's reach. "When we were at the bar and Tommy tried to throw a punch in my name, she promised me an entire day requesting only mental health or substance use calls. I've been sitting on it, which I can tell has her more and more on edge. Tomorrow I'm finally cashing in. I want to take our new community partnerships for a test drive, and I can't do that if I only have one or two cases."

She was excited about work in the morning. She told Tommy earlier in the week she was making her pay up on the promise as soon as Star and the behavioral health clinic were up and running. They'd gotten sign-off up the chain of command to send any and all appropriate calls their way.

Tommy had looked somewhere between excited and horrified. Natasha would give her a nudge in the right direction in the morning. Maybe they could get lunch at Lenny's to take away any residual sting.

"Whoa. What were you just thinking about?" Kayla waved her fork in front of Natasha's face and pulled dessert back her way.

"Work, why?"

"I don't get all dreamy like that when I'm thinking about work. Whatever put that look on your face, think about it more. That kind of happiness looks good on you."

Kayla helped with the dishes and then headed home. Before she fell asleep, Natasha thought about what Kayla said. Why had thinking about Tommy made her happy enough for Kayla to notice? She'd been thinking about lunch at Lenny's food truck, not anything romantic.

Tommy was different at work than she was off the clock. Their interactions had been different. Like at the bar, where she'd felt almost like she was out with a friend. Natasha put her head in her hands. Maybe Officer Sexy was going to be harder to banish than she'd hoped.

CHAPTER FIFTEEN

Tommy was as nervous for her shift as she'd been on her first day on the job. The nerves were ridiculous. She scolded herself the entire drive to the station, which only made the jitters worse. What was there to be nervous about? She knew why she was feeling on edge, but it felt foolish to admit.

Today Natasha had called in her favor and the two of them were only taking "Natasha calls." Tommy had tied herself in knots the night before trying to picture what the day would look like. Would Natasha run point? Was Tommy's role a uniformed bodyguard? At the end of the day would she still recognize herself as part of the force?

She'd spun herself so far afield, she'd called Harry. Given how late it was and that she'd woken her sister up, Harry's advice had been brief and to the point.

"Jesus, Tommy, are you okay with the one or two calls you do a day with her now? If so, then tomorrow will be just like those, except all day. Go to bed. You're overthinking shit."

Harry had done enough to get her out of her own head and off to sleep, but now she was concerned again. She rarely second-guessed or fretted, so the fact that she was doing both now was another source of distress. She ran her hand through her hair but stopped when she caught a glimpse of herself in the rearview mirror. Her hair was sticking out in every direction. How many times had she done it already?

She headed to Natasha's desk to check in on their plan. Hopefully, Natasha wouldn't notice her inner turmoil or crazy hair. When Tommy turned the corner and caught sight of Natasha, her breath caught. Tommy was well aware of how beautiful Natasha was, but today she looked stunning. It wasn't just her physical appearance. She was radiating exuberance. It was contagious, and Tommy felt less tense seeing how happy Natasha was. Tommy assumed she was excited for the day ahead for all the reasons Tommy was twisted like a pretzel.

"Finch, you planning on joining us?"

Tommy hadn't seen Lieutenant Smith standing next to Natasha's desk.

Oh shit. How long had she been standing there staring?

"Yes, ma'am."

Tommy hustled over and stood at attention, which wasn't how she normally interacted with Lieutenant Smith. Everything was out of whack with her this morning.

"At ease, Tommy. You all right this morning?"

"Yes, ma'am. What can we do for you?" Tommy relaxed and moved next to Natasha.

"You're to check in after every call today. I know we've got new community partners coming online today, and I'm sure the temptation will be high to let them show us how valuable they can be. I want updates on how they're being used and which cases are being diverted out of our hands."

Tommy moved a step closer to Natasha. "Have you been dissatisfied with the way Natasha and I have handled our cases thus far?"

"That's not the point, Finch. Don't give me a reason to be unhappy. And don't forget you're a cop first out there. Natasha, no offense, but you seem like the type that's always looking for the buried good in people."

Natasha tilted her head and studied Lieutenant Smith. "It concerns me, Lieutenant, that you don't. But you don't have to worry, there isn't a minute that goes by in our time together that Officer Finch lets me forget she's a born-and-bred police officer."

Lieutenant Smith walked away without another word. Tommy hadn't been aware of how tightly she'd been holding her shoulders until they relaxed, and she felt like a puddle slipping onto the floor.

"I think she likes me." Natasha nudged Tommy.

"Does she always treat you like that?"

"Down, boy. She treats me like she treats everyone else around here." Natasha patted Tommy's arm. "Part of my job is winning over the station. Pete was a gimme. You're a work in progress. The rest are tougher nuts to crack, but they can't resist forever. I already got most of them ready to fight with me at Chet's. We're making progress."

"We're going out today on all 'Natasha calls,' so I can't be that much of a work in progress." Tommy crossed her arms. "And if that bar fight had actually happened, you and Lieutenant Smith would've been a lost cause. She doesn't like getting calls about her officers causing trouble out in the community."

Natasha crooked a finger and headed for the door. Tommy pushed off the desk, adjusted her duty belt, and followed. Somehow, when she was with Natasha she always felt a few steps behind.

Once they were on their way, Natasha leaned against the passenger door and looked at Tommy. "You know you can't call our work today 'Natasha calls' and be one hundred percent on board with what we're doing together, right?"

Tommy glanced over at Natasha. She was still so beautiful Tommy lost her train of thought briefly. She needed to pull it together. Why was today any different than other days with Natasha? "You're with me when we go on calls like today's. Thus 'Natasha calls.' What should I call them?"

"Did they have a special name before you met me?"

"No, of course not." Tommy kept her eyes on the road. "But I didn't have a special role on those calls before either."

Natasha ran her hand through her hair and let out a breath. "And what's your special role now?"

Tommy gripped the wheel. "I still don't know."

She stole a glance to her right. Natasha looked frustrated. She was still looking at Tommy, but she wasn't saying anything. It made Tommy squirm.

"I'm not trying to be difficult." Now it was Tommy's turn to pass her fingers through her hair, again. "I was nervous coming to work today. I wasn't sure what the day would look like for me."

"Jesus, Tommy. What the hell did you think was going to happen today that hasn't happened every other day we've been on the job?

Except today it happens all day, instead of just here and there. We haven't had a problem figuring out roles any other day. We just do our job."

"You sound like Harry."

"I can't imagine that's going to happen often. You might not want to tell Harry." Natasha made a motion like she was zipping her lips. "You're a good cop, Tommy, just like you told me you were when we first started working together. I see that every day. It's possible we're even starting to find a bit of rhythm as partners. So what's really got your Jockeys in a jumble?"

Tommy muttered, "it's not important" under her breath. There was no way Natasha would understand.

"Oh no, Finch, don't pull that crap with me. We're partners. Something's different today. Talk to me."

Tommy pulled to the curb. They were headed to a follow-up on a call they'd taken the week prior, but it was still a little early to drop by.

"Fine. I still don't know the rules when we're working together. When I'm out alone, I know my job inside and out. When I'm with you, everything feels like quicksand under my feet. We've been figuring things out as we go, and yeah, it's working pretty well, but there's no rulebook that I've been trained on. That's a scary feeling for someone like me. And today is an entire day of it."

Natasha smiled, slow and lazy. "That's what partners are for. When you feel like you're sinking, take my hand." Her cheeks pinked slightly. "Metaphorically, of course. I'm sure Lieutenant Smith wouldn't approve of us strolling the streets hand in hand."

Tommy shook her head. "It's almost worth doing it just to see the look on her face."

"We'll keep it in our back pocket for a slow day, to liven things up."

The suggestion of holding hands with your partner wasn't supposed to elicit butterflies. Natasha must have mistaken Tommy's silence for continued uncertainty.

"Do you trust me?"

Tommy didn't hesitate. She looked Natasha in the eye. "Yes." The easy way the word slipped out surprised her.

"Then everything will be fine." Natasha turned back to face the front.

Tommy shook her head. She felt lighter. "How are you so sure?"

"Because I trust you too."

They'd come a long way in a short time. Tommy wanted to ask a million more questions. She still didn't have answers to any of the big ones that had held up her enthusiasm for this venture in the beginning, but she had Natasha's trust. And Natasha had hers. There was a lot they could do now that they had established that.

The first couple of hours of the day were following up on callouts from the prior week. Some folks needed a recheck, some complaints were resurfacing. Tommy thought it would be harder to follow Natasha's lead, but both Harry and Natasha had been right, it felt like any other workday.

As they were getting ready to sign out for lunch, a call came over the radio. It wasn't specifically meant for them, but it was near their location and on a street known for drug activity.

"Get your ass in gear or I'm driving after lunch." Natasha motioned to hurry them along.

Tommy nodded, thankful Natasha was on board, and flipped a U-turn to head toward the call location. Tommy assessed the scene as they pulled up. She was out of the car almost before she was able to get it in park. She called for backup as she ran.

A man had someone, a woman or teenager, pinned to the ground, and was punching them repeatedly. Tommy identified herself as she approached. She unclipped her taser. She'd pull out her service weapon if needed, but she didn't want to shoot anyone.

As soon as he was aware of Tommy, the man scampered. Tommy yelled over her shoulder for Natasha to wait in the car and then took off in pursuit. She hoped Natasha listened. She hadn't been able to clear the scene, and Natasha was defenseless. She slowed for a beat and then charged ahead. Her duty was to catch the assailant in front of her. But part of her was pulled back, worrying about Natasha.

Tommy chased her man over what felt like half the city. She called in updates on their location as often as she could, but they zigged and zagged through parking lots and alleyways, so getting backup in place was challenging. Finally, she was able to herd him toward a patrol car one street over. She let the other officer make the arrest. She needed to catch her breath.

She was anxious to get back to Natasha and caught a ride back. She told herself it was because she was her partner, as well as the fact that she was a civilian and Tommy had left her without protection. Surely that was all it was.

When she got back to her patrol car, Natasha wasn't inside. She looked to where she'd first encountered the man she'd chased through the neighborhood. Natasha was with the person Tommy could now see was a young woman whose face was bruised and bloody. Justin was hovering nearby. There were also two people Tommy didn't recognize who hadn't been there when she'd taken off. At least she didn't think they had been. Tommy's stomach knotted. She didn't wait in the car. What if she'd been injured?

She jogged over to Natasha. Justin acknowledged her as she approached and took a step back. She gave him a quick nod. She'd thank him later for securing the scene and watching Natasha's back.

"How you doing, partner?" Tommy crouched next to Natasha.

Natasha looked Tommy over intently. Tommy wasn't sure what she was looking for, but Natasha looked relieved to see her.

"Officer Finch, this is Shay. Justin took her statement already, but the man you saw assaulting her is her ex-boyfriend. If you were able to track him down, she'd like to press charges."

"Nice to meet you, Shay. I'm glad you were able to talk to my colleague. We did arrest your ex-boyfriend. Have you received medical attention? Do you have somewhere safe you can go?"

Natasha patted Tommy's arm. Her hand was cool on her skin. Her touch felt nice. Probably a little too nice.

"Shay asked that we not call for an ambulance. But she is okay with going to Star Recovery and learning more about their services. They have onsite medical services. Is that still okay with you?"

Shay nodded. She looked at the two people Tommy didn't recognize, and Natasha waved them over.

"Shay, you're in good hands with the Star Recovery team. They can help you make the changes we talked about. I believe in you."

Shay nodded again and left with the folks from the mobile crisis unit. Tommy checked in with Justin and met Natasha back at the car.

She updated Lieutenant Smith as required. Tommy was ready to pull away from the curb and get back to work when Natasha stopped her.

"You're bleeding."

Tommy looked at Natasha's hand on her arm. It was all she could feel. She forced focus. Her hand. She'd scraped it during the pursuit earlier. She looked now. A couple of knuckles were bloodied and there was a cut on her middle finger. She wasn't going to bleed to death, but her hand did look a bit of a mess. "There's a first aid kit in the back, I'll go grab some supplies."

Natasha waved her off. "I'll get it. You sit tight."

Tommy wasn't sure how to respond. She was perfectly capable of getting a couple of Band-Aids. When Natasha returned, Tommy tried to take the supplies. Once again, Natasha shooed her.

"Natasha, they're just scrapes, I can put on the Band-Aids." Tommy reached for the supplies again.

"I'm sure you think you can but a one-handed job isn't going to be as good as what I can do using both hands. Let me take a look."

Natasha took Tommy's hand and inspected the wounds and Tommy saw a slight tremor in Natasha's hand.

"Natasha, what's going on? I'm fine. They're scrapes."

Natasha ripped the wrapper off one of the Band-Aids and shoved it roughly on Tommy's hand. "I know that, Tommy. But what if it was worse? What if I watched you run after that guy and I was waiting for you to come back and you were bleeding to death in an alley a couple of blocks away because that asshole had a knife or a gun?"

Tommy intercepted the next Band-Aid and squeezed Natasha's hand gently in both of hers. "Hey, that's always a risk. Any officer who says they're not scared of something just like what you described is lying. But thanks to our training, our equipment, we're as prepared as we can be."

She let go of Natasha's hand and scrubbed her face. "What scared me shitless out there was leaving you behind. I hadn't cleared the scene, you had no way of protecting yourself, and I left you vulnerable. I almost turned back."

"Tomasina Finch." Natasha had fire in her eyes. She jabbed a finger in Tommy's chest. "You listen to me. I will make myself the scariest thing on these streets if you start treating me like a damsel in distress and stop doing your job to stand by my side at all times making sure no harm befalls me. Are you hearing me loud and clear?"

"Crystal." Tommy couldn't hold back her smile. Oddly, she liked being bossed around by indignant Natasha. "But I'm going to worry any damn time I please. Especially any time I have to leave you in a vulnerable situation."

"And I like that you worry. But you can't stop doing your job, and I know the risks I'm taking by doing mine, too. Didn't you fret yourself into an ulcer about this very thing this morning?"

"I don't know what you're talking about. Can we get back to work?"

"Not yet. Whoever took care of your hand did a terrible job. Let me get those taken care of, and then we can go. My personal bodyguard can't look like this the rest of the day." Natasha made quick work of the new first aid.

Once they were signed back in another "Natasha call" came immediately. So it went the rest of the day. Although Tommy didn't have to leave Natasha at a scene alone again, it nagged at her the rest of the shift. She'd make the same decision she did today, but what if Shay had been less friendly? What if Justin didn't arrive as quickly as he did?

She played out the day's scenario and others over and over. Every iteration made her uncomfortable. She hadn't been sure how to react or who to protect before she'd gotten to know Natasha, and all of this had felt more hypothetical. But now, her first instinct in every imagined situation was to jump to Natasha, to shield her, to protect her. Maybe that's what a good partner should do. Or maybe she was in danger of losing the details of each situation in her blind desire to see Natasha unharmed.

By the end of the shift she felt hopelessly lost. This wasn't something Natasha could help her sort out. She'd ask Harry for advice. In all her musings when Natasha was first assigned to her, she'd never expected to grow to care for her. Today caring had cost her half a step and a few seconds of time and it hadn't changed the outcome of her pursuit. The real question though was what could caring cost her in the future?

CHAPTER SIXTEEN

Natasha paused on her way out of the station. She looked over at Tommy chatting with a couple of other officers. She should walk out the door...

Tommy looked surprised to see her still at her desk when she wrapped up her conversation and walked by.

"I thought you were leaving for the night." Tommy leaned against the desk.

"You're still here."

"Ramirez had a question. Actually, if I'd known you were still around, I would've sent him to you. First time that's happened, someone coming to ask me about what we would do in a specific situation. Seems you're having an impact."

Natasha was surprised. Pleased, but surprised. Weeks had gone by without a lot of indication that the other officers were taking notice of the work she and Tommy were doing. It felt like only recently had Tommy truly gotten on board and that was under protest.

"How late is Lenny open? Impactful work is hungry business."

"He's open another few hours. Dinner service is new for him, you're in luck. You really going to drive all the way over there by yourself for a food truck meal?"

Natasha swallowed. Annoyingly, and inappropriately, her stomach flipped. "I was hoping to have some company. You busy?"

A slow smile spread across Tommy's face. "Nothing planned for tonight. Lenny's truck sounds great."

Natasha stood up. She nodded and shoved her hands in her pockets. Tommy hadn't asked if they were going to Lenny's as partners grabbing a bite after work or something else. Maybe she assumed one way? But which way? Natasha meant the invitation as partners, right?

Tommy looked a little uncomfortable too.

"Wait a minute." Natasha pointed a finger at Tommy. "Was it your plan all along to never feed me lunch today so I'd be so hungry I'd buy you dinner after work?"

"Worked, didn't it?"

"Not yet it hasn't." Natasha wagged her finger. "If I get a sniff of you withholding Lenny's so I never ask for another full day of 'Natasha calls' again, there will be hell to pay." Natasha stretched. She swore Tommy looked her up and down before quickly looking away.

"We never miss lunch when we're working my kind of calls."

"That's a lie, but you're cute, so I'll let it slide. But the fact remains, I didn't get lunch and now I'm starving. Come on, I'm driving this time."

Lenny's food truck was parked along the river bordering the western edge of the city. They ordered and wandered down toward the water, onto a multiuse recreational path that meandered with the water.

"I'm disappointed in you." Tommy took a seat on a park bench and handed Natasha half the stack of napkins. "I was expecting a world record hot dog eating performance after you skipped lunch."

"I know. It's unlike me. Maybe it's your fault. You're throwing me off my game." Natasha bumped shoulders with Tommy.

Tommy looked thoughtful. "You know I don't say this lightly, but I actually think we made a pretty damn good team today."

Natasha checked Tommy's forehead for fever. Tommy swatted her hand away. They both laughed.

"You're right, we did. And the world didn't end after a full day of 'Natasha calls.' Imagine that." Natasha licked her fingers after finishing her third hot dog.

"Shh, my partner gets pissed when you call them that." Tommy finished her food and stretched her legs in front of her.

"Geez, what's her problem?"

"She's right. There are no 'her calls' and 'my calls.' I'd tell her myself, but I'm not sure if she's here tonight." Tommy's body remained calm, but Natasha could see she was tense.

Natasha had caught Tommy checking her out a time or two, but hadn't considered that Tommy might also be struggling with real feelings for her. She wanted to be someone else for the evening and see where the night led them, but the repercussions in the morning would follow whoever she chose to be tonight. The partnership she and Tommy were forging had the potential to change policing in the community for the better. That wasn't worth throwing away for an orgasm.

Natasha cupped Tommy's cheek and let her fingers trail off her chin. "I think your partner probably should be here tonight."

Tommy blew out a breath and leaned her head back. "You're right. I'm sorry. I don't know what I was thinking."

"Exactly the same thing I was, hot stuff. There's a bit of a thing here." Natasha pointed between herself and Tommy. "But Ramirez also asked you for help with our kind of work today. Did you ever see that happening?"

"I've had my career mapped out since I was six. You aren't on the map. I can safely say I never pictured a day like today ever happening." Tommy helped Natasha up and they strolled down the path.

"Exactly. If I can change *your* mind, think of the possibilities."

"Hey." Tommy pouted.

Natasha had an unexpected urge to kiss her. This was getting out of hand and needed to be faced head-on. "I swore I'd never let this happen, but I like you, Tommy. Despite myself. You're a little irresistible. But I feel like I need to like the work we're doing a little more. I can see the real, lasting change we can have at the station and out in the community. I'd feel like a coward if I took the off-ramp to your bed."

"So when you invited me to dinner tonight, it was as your partner, grabbing food after work?"

Natasha hesitated. It would be easier if she said yes. It would be more complicated if she started lying to her partner. "Honestly, I'm not sure."

Tommy nodded. "That's okay. I'm not sure which invitation I said yes to, and that scares me a little. I'm Alice Finch's kid and I don't want anyone to say I achieved what I do in this department because of her. Flaunting the rules and sleeping with my partner isn't going to convince anyone."

If only Tommy knew that Natasha knew exactly what it meant to be seen for no more than your parents' last name. She felt a bit guilty keeping her Blackstone lineage a secret from Tommy, but in her experience, nothing good came from claiming it. She was a Parsons now and had no intention of ever going back.

They walked in silence a while. Natasha expected to feel uncomfortable but didn't. In the time she'd known Tommy she'd begun to feel at ease around her. She wasn't sure when the transition happened. No, it was more than that. She felt secure with her. Safe physically, but also free to do her job, which was strange in light of the near panic attack Tommy had this morning. The fact that they'd boldly acknowledged an attraction was interesting, and maybe would be the cold shower they both needed. Or it could light a spark neither of them could hope to contain.

"Did you always want to be a social worker?"

"Now how did you know I was thinking about work? What if I was picturing that lady over there naked?"

"She's not your type. It would've been that one over there." Tommy inclined her head subtly. "And you weren't looking over there."

"Impressive, Officer."

"And you were thinking about work because you always think about work. You're dedicated to your job, like I am. It's one of the things I admire about you."

Usually, Natasha had a witty comeback or a joke at the ready, but she didn't this time. Tommy's admiration mattered.

"No, I didn't have social worker on my radar at all, actually. I didn't have much of a plan until college. My parents didn't expect me to do anything except run the family charity, show up at the right social events, and not embarrass myself or the family. I've disappointed them on all counts."

"How could you possibly be a disappointment?"

Tommy looked so affronted some of Natasha's usual melancholy when thinking of her family drifted away. "Can you imagine a rich socialite doing any of the things we did today and maintaining their status in the highest echelons of society? I'm not even the black sheep of the family. I'm the lamb they dressed up as a goat and then pretended it didn't belong to the flock."

Tommy stopped walking. Natasha didn't realize for a few steps. When she turned around Tommy was ten feet behind her.

"I'm having trouble wrapping my head around a lot of this. Did you say rich socialite? And most importantly, who wouldn't want you around?"

"You, the first day we met, if my memory serves." Natasha walked backward while Tommy caught up.

"Point taken. No one's perfect."

"Tommy, my family are rich assholes who give rich assholes a bad name. You asked me why I became a social worker. My family has nothing to do with that."

Tommy caught up. It looked like she was going to take Natasha's hand but then pulled back. There was no reason Natasha should feel let down, but she wished Tommy had forgotten their previous conversation.

"Do you still keep in touch with them?"

"My family? As little as possible. But I have family obligations that are sometimes difficult to refuse. I thought you wanted to hear about how I became a social worker."

"I want to learn more about you. But yes, please, social worker origin story." Tommy rolled her hand and did a small bow like she was ushering in a royal performer.

"You're a pain in the ass, you know that?"

"I do. Thanks for noticing."

Natasha noticed a lot about Tommy. Probably more than she should. Tommy was smiling, so the dimple on her left cheek was visible and made the laugh lines around her eyes dance with mischief. Natasha always struggled to ignore how enticing Tommy looked in her uniform, and since they'd named the feelings between them, she was finding it especially challenging to keep her lascivious gaze and hands to herself.

Natasha rubbed her eyes and refocused. "When I went to college, I made a close group of friends. Aside from Kayla, they were the first friends I made on my own, without my parents curating the friendship. One was a man named Joseph. He started withdrawing from the group slowly. He changed some of his patterns of behavior over the course of a semester, and it turned out he'd started using drugs and drinking way too much. I still don't know the extent of his substance use. We were all worried about him."

Tommy nodded. "I can understand why you'd be concerned."

"Then, Joseph started hallucinating and having delusions. At first, his delusions were just plausible enough we laughed them off. He was convinced his roommate was plotting to get him kicked out of the apartment. That kind of thing. His roommate was a weird guy, so who knew?"

Tommy motioned to another bench, facing the water. Natasha sat closer to Tommy than was necessary, but Tommy was so strong, and solid, and secure, she wanted to be close to her while she talked about Joseph. Tommy seemed to understand. She put her arm over the back of the bench. It wasn't around Natasha, but it encircled her all the same.

"What happened after his delusions and hallucinations started?"

"They escalated. We couldn't ignore what was happening. We talked to his parents, to the school psychologists, anyone we could. But he didn't think anything was wrong so he was resistant to treatment. I would've…money was no object, but he wouldn't go to any treatment. Meanwhile, his hallucinations were dangerous to himself and one of our group. It came to a head one night and the police were called. I wish it was Pete, or you that had answered the call that night."

"Did he survive the encounter?" Tommy's voice was quiet.

Natasha shuddered. How easily the situation that night could've turned deadly.

"Yes, but he went to jail, not to get the treatment he needed. We begged them to take him to the hospital. *I* begged them. I talked to a social worker after, and I thought if she'd been with Joseph instead of at the hospital with me, maybe he wouldn't have ended up where he did."

"Tell me the rest."

Natasha shuddered. "That whole event was what led me to social work, specifically to social work on the street or in clinics with people in crisis. If there's a Joseph out there I can help, I'm going to."

Tommy's arm draped around Natasha's shoulder for a moment before Tommy moved it back to the top of the bench. "What about your Joseph?"

When Natasha opened her mouth to explain it felt like the entire dictionary lodged in her throat. She cleared it, took a deep breath, and tried again. "My parents paid for him to be admitted to the best treatment money could buy, his charges magically disappeared, and any chance that his name and mine would be associated in the future were wiped clean by as much money as it takes to buy silence."

She reached for her soda and took a drink. The words tasted foul even after all these years.

"Jesus. I'm sorry." Tommy blew out a breath. She was quiet a moment. "Wait, you said you went to the hospital and spoke with a social worker. You were the one in danger, weren't you? Did he hurt you?"

"I went as a precaution. I was…mostly fine." The fear from that night resurfaced and flooded her. She'd been horrified with how the responding officers had treated Joseph, but there was a good reason they were called.

"Hey, you okay? Why don't you tell me about the officers who triggered your wrath? So I know what not to do on our 'Natasha calls' tomorrow."

Natasha leaned her head back and looked at the sky. Her head was resting on Tommy's arm, but that was just a coincidence. It felt good to have Tommy holding her up. That's what partners were for, right?

"They shouted at him, and the more agitated he got the more they yelled. They used their Tasers. After he was subdued and handcuffed, facedown on the ground, one of the officers continued to periodically kick and punch him. I got the feeling they thought they were doing right by me somehow, but that's not what I needed. I needed their empathy for me and for Joseph."

Tommy tensed next to her even though she didn't let the tension radiate out to the arm under Natasha's head. Natasha liked that she knew Tommy well enough to know she was angry.

"I can't picture you treating another human being like that." Natasha still had her head resting on Tommy's arm. She turned her head so she could look at her.

Tommy rested her chin on her own shoulder. Their faces were only inches apart. The night felt like it belonged to only them.

"I like to think I wouldn't have done any of the things you described. My training and my conscience tell me I wouldn't. But I'm a product of society like anyone, full of biases and flaws, but my heart aches that it happened to you and your friend Joseph."

"So, what, you throw your hands up and there's nothing to be done? Maybe you'll do the same thing they did, who knows? I know you better than that. I work with you every day. You're *not* those two officers who beat Joseph after he was handcuffed." Natasha poked Tommy in the chest.

Tommy rubbed her sternum. "Ow. Of course not, but it's my job as a police officer to look at the biases I hold and the ones that are built right into the systems I'm a part of. Our society is good at cooking them into us and telling us who to be scared of, who to think of as less than human. Sometimes we don't even realize we have those beliefs. Some people never think twice, but I've been given a badge and a gun. I need to know where my weak spots are. I don't ever want to make an arrest, use force, or pull a trigger because I'm devaluing another human being."

"You're something special, Officer Finch." Natasha traced her finger along Tommy's cheek.

Tommy shook her head. "Trying to do your job well and serve the entire community fairly isn't special. Or it shouldn't be thought of that way. My joining protesters in their horror and anger and affirming that Black Lives Matter shouldn't earn me a spotlight or oversized praise."

"You're so much more than I assumed when we first met. After you accused me of being a PR stunt."

Tommy rolled her eyes. "Do I want to know?"

"This softer, passionate side of you? The one that cares so deeply? I wouldn't have guessed she existed. I knew you were a good cop, everyone at the station thinks you walk on water. Listening to you explain what it means to be a good officer, that's…I like it."

"They have to like me because of my last name." Tommy inched closer.

"Bullshit and you should know it."

They were so close Natasha only needed to move forward a few inches and she could kiss Tommy.

Why did you have to tell her you were just her partner? She looked at Tommy's lips. Hers tingled. She should move back, out of kissing range, but she was excited by where she was.

"I want to kiss you right now but my partner's here. She's devoted to her job and wouldn't like it if I followed through." Tommy spoke softly and toyed with Natasha's hair.

"Your partner must have lost her damn mind."

Tommy smiled. "She's probably right, I told her she was right, but hopefully she won't mind if I tell you how beautiful you are. I've been thinking it all night. Feels rude not to say it."

Natasha got up and put some breathing room between them. "Tommy, you can't say you want to kiss me, then tell me I'm beautiful, and expect *me* to be the one to slam on the brakes. I've already told you there's a thing here." She pointed between them.

Tommy stood up and caught Natasha as she paced by. "I'm sorry. You're right, that's not fair. I got caught up in the moment."

Natasha hesitated. Then she put her hands on each side of Tommy's face and pulled her close. Right before their lips connected, she said, "How's this for getting caught in the moment?"

The kiss was exquisite. Tommy's lips were soft and she let Natasha lead. Everything came down to the feeling of her mouth.

Someone whistled and said, "nice catch, buddy," Natasha was aware of the fact that they were standing kissing in the middle of the walking path. And that she was kissing her partner. She took a step back.

"God, I hoped you'd be bad at that."

"Uh, thank you, I think."

Tommy had a goofy grin on her face and Natasha wanted to kiss it off her.

"I know I started it, but I'm ending it. I was serious when I said there's a thing between us. And it's…it's…"

Tommy took Natasha's hand and kissed the top of it. "You don't have to explain. I see the potential in what we're doing together too. We have plenty to work out in that relationship without adding this complication. And I was serious about keeping my head down and proving myself."

Natasha pulled Tommy in and kissed her quickly, one more time. "That's for saying the right thing. Now we're back to business."

"Whatever you say."

"You're catching on. I knew you were trainable."

On the walk back to the car they returned to work talk. It felt like a much safer subject than what had just happened.

"Do you feel more comfortable having a civilian riding with you now?" The urge to take Tommy's hand was strong, but Natasha kept hers to herself.

"I feel more comfortable with you. Some of the issues that led to my temper tantrum the first time we met are still unresolved. But Pete told me he trusts each of us individually and as a team to figure it out."

Natasha saw the parking lot ahead and slowed her pace. "Pete's a smart guy. Today felt like a tantalizing snapshot of what we can accomplish together."

Tommy raised her eyebrows.

"Not that."

Tommy laughed. "How would you feel about another full day of 'Natasha calls' next week? It's hard to know where we're going to run into problems, and I'm going to need some more hand-holding to get this sorted out without more exposure."

"Are you doing that on purpose?"

Tommy looked so confused Natasha let it slide. Apparently, she was the only one who'd been thinking of hand-holding and exposure.

"You know I'm on board."

After Natasha dropped Tommy off she drove home with her mind whirring. It felt like she was back on the playground merry-go-round at the park she and Kayla used to sneak into when their parents thought they were ballroom dancing. The more force they applied the faster it spun, around and around and around. Kissing Tommy. More "Natasha call" days. The satisfying work of the day. Memories of Joseph. Tommy, Tommy, Tommy. That merry-go-round, like this one, was thrilling but if spun fast enough you risked losing your grip and flying off completely. But maybe that wasn't a concern for tonight. Maybe it was enough to let her thoughts go round, speeding up and slowing down without a care for the dizzying vertigo that could follow.

CHAPTER SEVENTEEN

Tommy pushed her food another lap around her plate. She couldn't remember a time she'd not eaten her mother's cooking. Her thoughts were a tangle of Natasha, work, and that damn kiss. Her brain seemed to be hogging all the signals and everything else was shut down. If Natasha could do this to her after one kiss... good Lord.

After dinner, her mother called her and Harry over. "You two are relieved of dish duty this evening." She handed both of them a beer. She gave Tommy an apple and a bag of potato chips. "In case you get hungry."

"I'm sorry, Mama." Tommy hung her head.

"Shush. But maybe tell your father the peas were good. He discovered vegetables can be microwaved in a bag and he was quite proud of them."

"I'll be sure to mention them. Thanks, Mama." Tommy took the offered food.

"Instead of dishes, you two make sure to bring in the patio cushions and stack the chairs for us when you're done out there. And, Tommy, if Harry's counsel isn't enough, I'm always here to talk."

Tommy hugged her mother. She wasn't a child anymore, so a hug couldn't cure everything, but it was still effective more often than not.

Outside, Harry grabbed the bag of chips and opened them. She popped the tops on both beers and set one in front of Tommy. Before she could ask, Tommy blurted, "I kissed her."

Harry stared at her.

"Actually, she kissed me. But I told her I wanted to kiss her, so I'm probably, technically, the initiator."

Harry took a long pull on her beer. She shook her head. "Tommy, what the fuck? I told you not to do what I've done. You said you had this under control."

"Well, clearly I don't. Are you going to lecture me or help me?" Tommy snatched the chips back.

"Who says I can't do both? But first, is the kiss the only thing that had you turning up your nose at a delicious chicken marsala?"

"No, work's complicated too."

Harry jabbed a finger in Tommy's face. "That's what happens when you kiss your fucking partner."

"It was complicated before that." Tommy stared across the dark yard.

"All right. So where should we start? Kissing, work, or the middle of the Venn diagram where they overlap?"

"I don't care. You pick. I don't want to talk about any of them. But I'm hungry and don't want to miss any more meals."

Harry picked a chip out of the bag and waved it in front of Tommy's nose. "This is what your life will be if you don't get your head out of your ass. Potato chips and beer with your sister. Are there worse things? Of course, but I have higher hopes for both of us. Now tell me about the kiss."

"I don't know. It sort of just happened. We went to Lenny's and ate down by the river. We were talking and you know how beautiful she is."

"Tommy, how many times have you seen beautiful women get me into more trouble than I can get out of? I warned you about thinking with that." Harry pointed her beer at Tommy's crotch.

Tommy swatted Harry's long neck away. "You've only chased women to get laid. Did you ever have feelings for any of them?"

Harry shrugged and gave her a half smile. Then she got serious. "Wait, are you saying this was more than scratching an itch?"

Tommy shifted from foot to foot. "Yes. No. I'm not sure. Something happened on one of our calls."

"We're cops, Tommy, something happens on all of our calls. Part of our training is making sure we keep our heads. In the moment and after the fact."

Tommy glared at Harry who didn't seem to notice. She explained the domestic incident she and Natasha broke up and how she'd chased the perpetrator halfway across town.

"When I took off after the guy, I left Natasha behind, and I *hesitated*. I hadn't had time to check the scene for weapons and she was unarmed. The thought of something happening to her almost made me go back. That shouldn't have happened."

"She's your partner, of course you're going to worry about her safety." Harry mimicked Tommy's posture and gazed across the yard.

"I don't think I would've slowed down, even a step, if it was any of the other officers at the station."

"They're all armed and capable of defending themselves. Not that they don't need your backup, but it's different with an unarmed civilian counting on you."

"I'd agree with you if I didn't kiss her later that night. We both agreed no more kissing, but I don't know how I'll react the next time she's in danger. And I still want to kiss her."

Harry didn't say anything for a while. It was enough time for Tommy to revisit the moment of panic when she realized how vulnerable Natasha was. And to think about the kissing. It felt like Natasha had turned Tommy's life upside down, shaken out all the contents, and left them scattered for Tommy to pick up and reorder. The worst and most exciting thought was that it didn't feel like the upheaval was over yet.

Finally, Harry turned to Tommy. "Wasn't this one of the things you were worried about when you were first partnered up? You didn't know what to do when she needed your protection and you also had your real job to do."

"Protecting her is part of my real job." Tommy frowned at Harry.

"Whoa, whoa. You know what I mean."

"No, I don't."

Harry put her arm around Tommy's shoulder and pulled her close. "I'm not trying to give you a hard time. Help me understand."

Tommy scrubbed her face with her hands. She rested her head on Harry's shoulder. "When I was partnered with Natasha, I hated the idea down to the last cell in my blue blood. Who was this outsider to tell me how to do my job? What if I had to protect her and not someone in the community? How would she watch my back? What if I'm convinced someone should go to jail and she thinks they should go to treatment? What if I get stuck on dead-end cases forever and can't pursue my career so she can bolster hers?"

"That's quite a list. No wonder you left her behind the first day."

Tommy popped a chip in her mouth and leaned against the deck rail again. "Now though, the work we're doing is good. I still have reservations, a lot of the same ones actually, but I can see the good we're doing. But a few things have been eating me alive. What kind of cop am I if someone else is doing most of the work when we're out on 'Natasha calls'? What happens when we disagree on what should happen?"

"You're worried that when you move on and make detective you won't be seen as deserving because you've been the understudy to your social worker? Or when you're chief of police someone's going to refuse to follow your orders because you learned additional empathy from a master teacher?"

"I don't feel like you're taking me seriously." Tommy moved the chip bag out of reach when Harry tried to help herself to another.

"Have you ever considered that maybe you take yourself too seriously?" Harry held Tommy tight. "You've always been hung up on living up to Mama's legacy. Figure out who you want to be and create your own. Why can't your work with Natasha be a scintillating, G-rated chapter?"

"I don't want to get something I don't deserve because of my last name." Tommy looked at her hands.

"Tommy, look at me." Harry waited for Tommy to comply. "If anyone in this family is riding Mama's coattails, it's me."

Tommy started to laugh but stopped when she saw Harry was serious. "You're the best cop I know, and Mama has nothing to do with it, which I will never admit I just said, even under oath."

"Then get out of your head and stop worrying so much about what everyone is thinking. Now, what's the other thing that's eating you up? You said there was a list."

"You know, you're a pain in my ass ninety-five percent of the time, but I got lucky in the sister lottery." Tommy leaned against Harry again. "Now earn your praise and tell me how the hell I'm ever going to know for sure if I'm protecting her because she's my partner or because I can't stop thinking about kissing her?"

Harry laughed.

It wasn't the reaction Tommy was expecting and she pulled away.

"I'm not making light of any of this, I promise. But I can't think of a time you were this wound up over a woman, and it's your partner. The partner you hated the thought of enough to leave behind your first day together."

Harry was right. Tommy smiled. "I can't help it. She's…I don't know how to describe her."

"I've met her. No need. For the serious stuff, Tommy, only you can know your motivation for sticking with Natasha. But no one is going to fault you for having your partner's back. The more you treat her like your partner, the more everyone else at the station will too."

Definitely no more kissing then. Tommy's insides knotted at the thought of anyone else getting close enough to Natasha to steal a kiss. Not that Natasha would let them. She hadn't let Tommy until she was good and ready.

"Stop thinking about kissing her. I'm not done with the rest of it yet." Harry swatted Tommy on the back of the head.

Tommy pretended to be offended.

"Senior's always told us when people call nine-one-one they're calling for help, not the police, fire department, or paramedics. They just need help, and they don't care who shows up to give it. What does it matter if you know the answer or Natasha does? You both show up, and as a team, you can help. Isn't that all that matters? And Jesus, Tommy, of course you're going to disagree. You think you'd get along all the time if you were partnered with that knucklehead kid you're always telling me about?"

"What happened to you? I thought you were against the idea of someone like Natasha. Weren't we out here on this deck talking about how no one should be telling us how to do our job?"

Harry shrugged. "Sure. But I can change. I've listened to you talk about your work with Natasha. You seem driven with purpose when you describe it. And all of us Finches have been taught from early on that being a good cop isn't a static thing. If there's a better way to do the job, it's time to change. The world seems to be telling us there's a better way."

Tommy pondered that. She'd told Natasha essentially the same thing down by the river.

"Besides, I can tell it matters to you. And the way you light up when you talk about her? I thought it was related to the job, but now I know better."

"Shut it." Tommy took a swipe at Harry but missed. "You never answered my question earlier. Did you ever have feelings for any of the women you got yourself in trouble with?"

Harry looked serious. "No. But that was the point. I chose women who weren't looking for that either. But even then, I made some terrible decisions."

"What's wrong with finding what Mama and Senior have? Or Cody and Priya?"

"Nothing. I just don't know if it's for me. My career's important to me. That's the relationship I have right now."

"That's lame. It's important to me and Cody too. And look at Mama. Having all of us didn't stop her. I think you're scared."

"We were talking about you." Harry smiled around her beer bottle.

"Nah, you fixed me. No kissing. Worry less. Treat her like my partner. Be a better cop. I'm cured of all that ails me. Plenty of time for you."

Harry looked at her and raised her eyebrows. "Think about kissing her right now. Remember how it felt. What happens to your stomach?"

"Fuck you."

Harry blew her a kiss.

They stayed on the deck another hour talking about nothing in particular. While they cleaned up the deck furniture as instructed, Tommy thought about what Harry said. People needed help and they didn't care where or how it arrived. She took her job to serve and protect the community seriously and Natasha had made that easier. Wasn't that all that should matter?

CHAPTER EIGHTEEN

Natasha stared at her computer. Maybe if she looked long enough the paperwork would write itself. How could two months have passed since the community coalition had truly begun? She looked for Tommy. She'd been stealing looks since they returned from their time on patrol. It didn't seem possible that an entire day in the car together hadn't been enough of her.

You have to get yourself together. She and Tommy might have agreed to no more kissing, but that wasn't stopping her from thinking about it, frequently. She'd caught Tommy looking at her a few times too. And there were touches. Nothing big, but times they seemed to last a little longer than they needed to. Or when they were walking back to the car, and Tommy opened the door for her and their hands happened to brush past each other. Maybe they were coincidences. Maybe they didn't set Tommy on fire the way they did her. She liked to think Tommy was still thinking about their kiss, at the very least. Everything would've been easier if Tommy had been a terrible kisser.

"Hey, you packing up soon?"

Natasha nearly jumped out of her chair. All day she'd been aware of Tommy's movements, and in the midst of a daydream, she'd snuck up on her.

"Sorry to scare you. I thought you saw me. You were staring right at me."

"Lost in thought. Trying to finish up these reports for our community partners. They want to know how the first couple of months have gone."

"So eager to get into your paperwork you didn't even take your vest off? Starting to like the way 'Police' looks on you?" Tommy hooked her thumb through the shoulder of Natasha's vest.

Natasha brushed her away. She'd gotten so used to the vest she'd forgotten she was still wearing it. Not something she thought possible the first time she put it on.

"Paperwork always waits for you, you know. Hungry stomachs won't. Plans tonight?" Tommy seemed to have found something very interesting on her shoe and was giving it her full attention.

"No. But that look on your face says you have some and you're not sure you should be inviting me. *Please* tell me I get to meet your mother."

Tommy didn't have a chance to answer. Broken glass and shouting from the front door of the station drew their attention. Tommy put her arm in front of Natasha, shielding her. It was sweet and also a little annoying. Tommy moved toward the door with her hand on her weapon. Natasha saw every officer in the station doing the same.

"Like hell, Tommy. I'm coming too."

She wasn't going to rush out the door first, but she wasn't interested in cowering under the desk while her partner ran toward danger. They were a team, and if there was a chance she could be helpful, she needed to be closer to whatever was happening outside.

When she got to the door it felt like things slowed so she saw everything in freeze-frame. She saw officers shouting, their guns drawn. A man with wild eyes wielded a pipe with one hand. A sidewalk was crowded with gawkers. Broken glass was glinting like fresh snow on a blue sky day. Another pipe swing toward the crowd.

Tommy's voice snapped the motion back to full speed. Hers was the one calm entry in the shouted orders to drop the pipe and submit. Tommy's voice also mobilized Natasha. She knew the pipe wielding man and that he wasn't aware enough of the shouted orders to comply. She knew this man and she wasn't about to watch him die.

Please keep them from shooting me, Tommy. Natasha bolted from the door of the station. She called for Tommy as she put herself between a sea of raised weapons and the man with the pipe.

"Don't shoot! Tommy, he's one of ours. I can help him. Trust me." She stood with her arms outstretched, one facing the man with the pipe, the other facing the angry officers. She kept her focus on Tommy.

Tommy searched her face. Natasha didn't look at any of the danger around her. Tommy was all that mattered. She didn't feel fear, although with guns pointed at her she should have. She kept her eyes on Tommy. She'd protect her.

Tommy spoke to the officers around her. She never took her eyes off Natasha and the man with the pipe. "Everyone relax. Go ahead settle him down. I'll cover you."

Natasha turned fully to the man. Tommy was watching her back. She put her arms out to the side and took a slow step toward the man. She thought she remembered his name was Sean. He barely glanced at her as she approached.

"Sean, I'm here to help." Her heart was beating so fast she was sure ten beats pounded between every word.

Sean didn't answer or look her way.

Her instincts and adrenaline were screaming at her to blurt out more, to shout at Sean or try to make him understand the urgency of his situation, but that wouldn't help. She waited to give him time to process. "I need you to put down the pipe."

Again, she waited. This time he looked at her for a moment.

"Sean, I'm here to help you. Pipe down first."

Despite swinging a pipe, breaking a window at a police station, and nearly getting shot, he wasn't displaying any emotion. His face was blank.

"I understand what you're saying. I'm scared." Sean swung the pipe again. It whizzed to the left of Natasha.

She heard the officers behind her shuffling agitatedly. She motioned behind her and shook her head. Sean wasn't swinging at her.

"Why are you scared, Sean?"

"Why am I scared? Well, see there are stars, stars I can see out my window, and they shoot. The stars they shoot in the sky and I…I…I'm seeing sunsets in the morning light. Not beautiful like they should be, ugly, with…with…black and gold crowns." Sean swung the pipe again, behind him this time, but close to the crowd again. "Get away from me."

Hallucinations might make this harder. "Sean, why are you scared?" she asked again, to get him talking.

He looked at her and seemed to see her for the first time. "I'm scared of everything in my head."

Natasha's heart clenched. She took a tentative step forward. She didn't want to scare him, but the tentative connection they'd created might strengthen with proximity. "Please put the pipe down."

Sean took another swing, this time in Natasha's direction and because she'd moved closer, it came uncomfortably close. She heard Tommy swear behind her, but again she motioned to the officers to settle down. She needed to keep Sean talking.

"I can see the aura, but I can't let it get too close. It tries but I can fight. I'm a fighter for the world. Like the whales. I see how they get hunted, but I'm not a hunter, I'm the light."

Natasha took a deep breath. She wasn't giving up on Sean. "Look at me."

She waited and waited. She could feel the crowd take a collective breath and hold it. Finally, Sean looked and seemed to see her.

"May I have the pipe?" Natasha pointed at the pipe and reached out her hand.

Sean looked around wildly. He looked at the pipe, then back at Natasha. "Will you fight?"

"I will fight *for* you."

Incrementally, Natasha saw Sean relax. With each unclenched muscle the air molecules crept back into the vacuum surrounding them.

The air flowing more freely into Natasha's lungs was laced with fear. Each deep breath brought a jolt of terror down in deep recesses she never thought would be opened again. But now wasn't the time for fear. She still had to finish her job. She'd hold her breath if she had to.

Sean reached out and handed Natasha the pipe. She felt everyone on the sidewalk let out their breath in unison.

Sean slumped to the ground. He pulled his knees to his chin and retreated into himself. Occasionally, he swatted angrily at whatever hallucination was harassing him and had necessitated the pipe. Natasha stepped back enough to turn to Tommy. Seeing her chased the fear away so she could stand firm again. She was like a flashlight shining under the bed after a nightmare. Natasha breathed deeply. The crowd behind the officers was much larger and an ambulance was on scene. It was hard not to fixate on all the smartphones held aloft capturing every movement. She wanted to cover her face, but the time for hiding from the spotlight was long gone. Hopefully, no one would recognize her, they usually didn't. Perception was part of the game, and Natasha didn't give off rich girl vibes, not anymore.

The paramedics took over Sean's care and Natasha retreated after she updated them on his condition. Two officers stayed to ensure their safety on Lieutenant Smith's orders. The rest of the officers shuffled back into the station.

Once inside, the station felt like a shaken beehive. Everyone wanted to talk to her or about her, about what happened or what they should do next time. The adrenaline was driving everyone to continue to rehash, plan, and speak. Natasha wanted to find Tommy, be close to her for a few minutes, and then go home. The adrenaline was gone, leaving her shaky and wiped out.

Who was she kidding? She wanted Tommy to take her wherever she'd been inviting her before Sean swung his pipe through the window. Then she wanted Tommy to continue fighting off the fear. What had she been thinking? She headed toward her desk, her legs wobbly.

"What the fuck were you thinking?" Justin shoved her in the back. "You couldn't miss the chance to show off, is that it?"

"Get lost, little boy." Natasha tried to push past him.

"Answer my question. What were you thinking? Hoping to be a hero like the real cops in this room? We would've handled that idiot. No one needs your soft on crime, shrinky dinky bullshit."

"So you could shoot a man who was scared and so lost in his own mind he probably didn't even see you guys? Justin, not now, man. Seriously, fuck off." Natasha balled her fists and dug her nails into her palms looking for something to ground herself. She wouldn't give Justin the satisfaction of seeing her cry.

"What's wrong? Truth hurt? What makes you think you can do my job better than I can? You have something to say, grow a pair and say it. Or are you just a pussy?"

That did it. "I've got a pair right here, you fucking idiot." Natasha grabbed her chest with both hands. "Do you—"

Natasha felt a hand on her shoulder. She looked behind her ready to swing at whoever was attacking from behind. It was Tommy. She looked furious, not at Natasha, but at Justin. It wasn't just Tommy. Nearly the entire station was gathered behind her.

"Of course you're going to defend your girlfriend, Tommy. Is she a good fu—"

"Enough." Captain Gillette roared above the angry crowd.

Everyone in the station, including Natasha, snapped to attention.

"Officer Jordan, you have the potential to be a good officer. If you open your mouth again, you will do nothing but hand out parking tickets for the rest of your career. Understand?"

Justin nodded, his jaw working hard as he stared at the ground.

"You're a rookie. I know you're eager to prove yourself. We've all been there. You'll have your chances. What you don't seem to grasp yet is the toll pulling the trigger would've taken on you and our community. Not to mention how it affects every officer in this department." Captain Gillette put her hand on Justin's shoulder. "I pray you never have to take a life."

"He had a pipe, ma'am, he was swinging it at civilians, and wasn't complying. We had the right to use any force necessary." Justin looked frustrated.

"He was floridly psychotic." Natasha broke her rigid posture to glare at Justin.

Captain Gillette shot her a look. Natasha shut up.

"Does anyone know how often those killed by police have mental illness? Or are under the influence of substances?" Captain Gillette looked around the room. No one seemed to know if the question was rhetorical.

Natasha knew nearly a quarter of those killed by police showed signs of mental illness, but she didn't want to incur the wrath of the captain by speaking up again.

"Twenty-five percent, folks. Our community is asking us, all of us, to be better." Captain Gillette motioned toward them all. "Being white and of sound mind shouldn't be the only way to guarantee surviving an encounter with one of us. Being *able* to use necessary force, Officer Jordan, doesn't mean you *should*. What Ms. Parsons did today was reckless and stupid, but the outcome is exactly why I brought her on."

Natasha was sure she'd have some explaining to do. Getting herself killed by friendly fire felt more real now than it had at the time. What if it were Tommy who'd pulled the trigger? She shuddered.

"Officer Finch, you've been partnered with Ms. Parsons for months now, correct?"

Tommy looked to Natasha. "Yes, ma'am."

"How do you feel about the work the two of you do?"

Tommy looked thoughtful. "I'm surprised how deeply satisfying it is. It was also humbling how ill-equipped I am to handle some of the types of calls we get every day. Before being partnered with Natasha I thought I had the skills and training I needed, but she's better at talking people down and making it so they get help instead of remain a problem we keep having to deal with. I've learned a lot."

It took a lot of effort to keep her face neutral. Natasha wanted to pull Tommy into her arms and kiss her soundly. It wasn't a good idea.

"You were skeptical at first, correct?"

Tommy's attention was entirely on Captain Gillette.

"Very. Natasha and I had quite a few obstacles to work out early on. There are still things we're navigating to strengthen our working relationship. Police and social workers approach the world differently. So far we've found that doesn't mean they have to be at odds." Tommy looked at Natasha and smiled.

Natasha's stomach did a backflip.

Lieutenant Smith leaned in and said something to Captain Gillette.

"Ms. Parsons, it seems you're *trending*. My office please. The rest of you are dismissed, but don't forget why you're out there, and who you're really working for."

Trending, fuck. Natasha started to sweat and not the satisfying post workout sweat Kayla always talked about. This was the ugly, smelly, instant pit stain sweat and Natasha was about to walk into her boss's office. Had anyone connected the dots? Would the captain demand an explanation? Did she need to give one?

Captain Gillette closed the door and motioned for Natasha to have a seat. "I don't know what to do with you, Natasha. I want to fire you for doing something so insane, but you probably deserve a medal. The rest of the world certainly thinks so." She showed Natasha videos of the encounter and trending hashtags.

Natasha didn't want to be a hashtag, but she said a silent prayer that the world was praising Natasha *Parsons,* for now at least. "I'm not interested in being a social media moment, ma'am. That man needed what I could provide, not guns aimed at center mass. I doubt he could process what was being screamed at him. All he could perceive was a threat, nothing more."

"I'm not disagreeing with you, but he was swinging a pipe at a crowd and wasn't relinquishing his weapon. Most officers are going to escalate to physical force. It's how we're trained."

"Then you need different training. He was obviously psychotic." Natasha crossed her arms over her chest.

"Then teach us." Captain Gillette sat back and mimicked Natasha's posture.

"Excuse me?"

"If we lack the training, then provide it. You changed Tommy Finch's mind, so clearly you're a miracle worker. The rest of the station shouldn't be too hard."

Natasha tilted her head and regarded the captain. Her face was impassive.

"You're right, Tommy's impossible. Almost everyone at the station had a chance to shoot me today and no one took a shot, so I'm sure they'll love spending more time with me." Natasha smiled.

Captain Gillette paled slightly. "No more reckless stunts, please."

"It wasn't reckless and it wasn't a stunt. Tommy was there, I checked in with her, and I knew she was watching my back."

"Why?" Captain Gillette looked baffled.

"Why what?" Natasha had to lower her voice. Yelling at her captain wasn't going to win her many points. She was already in the red.

"Why were you so sure Tommy was watching your back and you were safe?"

"Tommy's my partner. Everyone here thinks it's me against the police, but do you see this?" Natasha pointed to the vest she was still wearing. "I'm part of this team. You learn from me, I learn from you. What it means to have a partner and be a partner is one of the best things I've learned."

Before she dismissed her, Captain Gillette made sure she understood, no matter how popular she was on social media, more lone wolf actions like the one today were out of bounds.

Natasha left Captain Gillette's office and headed to her desk. She wanted to see Tommy, but she also had a strong desire to get out of the station. After putting her life on the line for her job, Justin's hostility, and being grilled by the captain, she wasn't sure she could take another tense encounter with a co-worker. She was relieved when it was Pete waiting for her, although she wished it was Tommy.

"You've always been your own breed, Nat. Do you see this gray hair?" Pete pointed to his head. "That wasn't there this morning. You did that to me."

"It looks good on you. Makes you look wise." Natasha pushed Pete's feet off her desk chair.

"Seriously, Nat. I could've shot you. Don't do that to me again." Pete's voice was quiet and his expression was as serious as Natasha had ever seen.

She didn't get a chance to answer him before a few other officers wandered over. She tensed after her experience with Justin, but they weren't looking for a fight. A couple thanked her for settling the tense confrontation non-violently. A few were interested in what she and Tommy did. Natasha told them she was going to see if she could demystify what she did and give everyone the skills to do what she did for Sean. The officers looked skeptical but not unwilling.

When she exited the station she was weary. It wasn't just her body. Emotionally, she was spent. Sean reminded her of Joseph and the night he'd been arrested. She was disappointed Tommy had slipped out without saying good-bye. That hurt. Maybe she didn't feel what Natasha did, or maybe she was just too pissed off at what she'd done to want to talk to her right now. Natasha should do exactly what they'd been saying was best and move on from the kiss, stop thinking about it, and focus on the work. Except Tommy was the only one Natasha wanted to see.

Natasha rounded the corner to the parking lot and stopped short. Tommy was leaning against her car, looking haggard and emotionally strung out. Natasha wanted to rush to her and pull her into her arms, but there were cameras everywhere. So she just walked over quickly and stood close enough to absorb some comfort.

"Jesus, Natasha. I could have…you almost…" Tommy scrubbed her face. "Mama's expecting me for dinner in fifteen minutes. Will you come with me?"

Natasha didn't hesitate. She didn't analyze. She wanted to be with Tommy and it looked like Tommy felt the same. Natasha nodded to the passenger side of her car. Tommy climbed in and Natasha pulled out of the lot. She stopped at a red light and her stomach fluttered with nerves. It seemed impossible that meeting Tommy's parents could battle for the most intimidating part of the day, but here she was, deep breathing at a stoplight.

Tommy slipped her hand into Natasha's and entwined their fingers. She looked at Tommy and they both smiled. Natasha raised their joined hands and kissed Tommy's knuckles. It was going to be okay. Probably. Alice Finch raised Tommy and Tommy liked her, so Alice would too. Most likely. That was dumb. It didn't always work that way. But it could. She should probably stop kissing Tommy, though. Alice might frown on that.

Natasha pulled to a stop in front of the house Tommy pointed to and took a deep breath. Tommy hopped out and came around and opened her door. She held out her hand and Natasha took it and stepped out of the car. After the months of teasing and cajoling, she was about to meet Tommy's parents. Holy shit.

CHAPTER NINETEEN

Tommy helped Natasha out of the car but didn't let go of her hand. She couldn't get the sight of Natasha suddenly lined up in her crosshairs out of her mind. All it would've taken was one of her colleagues getting spooked and pulling the trigger without Natasha out of the way. Tommy shuddered and pulled Natasha closer.

"What's wrong?" Natasha brushed her fingers over Tommy's eyebrow and along her cheek.

"There are so many ways things could've gone pear-shaped earlier, and I can't stop thinking about you getting shot. You put yourself in front of twenty armed cops so they wouldn't shoot someone else."

Natasha's back was against the car and she pulled Tommy to her. She took their hands, which were still joined, and put them over her chest. "Do you feel that?"

Tommy nodded. Natasha's heart was beating hard and fast under her palm.

"I'm alive and okay because of you. I knew you'd keep me safe."

Tommy kept her hand on Natasha's chest. Her heartbeat was comforting, and she leaned her forehead against Natasha's. Natasha rested her hands on Tommy's hips. Suddenly, Tommy realized the position they were in. Every nerve seemed to flood her body with pleasure signals at once.

"Does your heart always beat this fast?"

"You have me pinned against a car with your hand on my chest. Safe to say, that's all your doing." Natasha was flushed. "I know we said no more kissing…"

Tommy didn't need her to finish her thought. She tangled her hands in Natasha's hair and pulled her in. The politeness and hesitation of the first kiss were gone. This kiss was full of passion, hunger, and demanding give and take.

Tommy had never been kissed like this. She never wanted to stop. She vaguely registered a door opening and someone calling her name. Whoever it was could wait. All she cared about was Natasha's soft lips and her hands on her ass.

"Tommy, that you? You coming in? Oh."

Natasha pushed Tommy away gently, gave her one last chaste kiss, and stepped away from the car. "Hello, Harry. Nice to see you again."

"Natasha. You staying for dinner? Seems like you started with dessert." Harry still hadn't looked at Tommy.

"I invited her. I'll let Mama know." Tommy tried to catch Harry's eye.

"I'll do it. But don't take too long to get inside. Some of us are hungry. Besides, you two are famous and all anyone wants to talk about in there. If you're in there, instead of out here, they'll stop asking me questions."

Harry finally looked at Tommy, who wasn't sure how to interpret her expression. She knew all of Harry's major expressions, so it wasn't any of those. Disappointment didn't seem right. Concern maybe. Jealousy? Nah. They could talk about it later.

"Good thing that wasn't your mother." Natasha kissed her one more time once Harry was back inside.

"Are you ready to meet her?" Tommy kissed Natasha again. She was having a hard time stopping, even though she should. "Okay, I'm done now. You're a little addictive. I know we keep kissing when we say we're not going to, and we should probably talk about that, but do you mind if for tonight, we're just partners from work?"

Natasha smiled. It was the smile that left Tommy's insides twisted in knots. "I don't mind keeping this between us, even if it goes back to the way it was and doesn't happen again. But you need to stop looking at me like that. And what about Harry?"

"She won't say anything. She'll want a chance to talk to me one-on-one first."

"Okay, then let's go meet the family."

Tommy could tell Natasha was nervous. She wanted to take her hand and pull her close, but that's not how co-workers would behave. Tommy pushed open the door to her parents' house and stepped into the familiar chaos.

Her nieces and nephew barreled full speed at her but stopped short when they saw Natasha. The oldest marched up to Natasha and held out her hand. Natasha took it, and after a prolonged and aggressive shake, she was released. Each child repeated the gesture, copying their oldest sibling.

Tommy and Natasha made it as far as the dining room before her mother realized they were in the house. "Tomasina Finch, would you like to explain to me why I've been seeing videos of you and your—"

Her mother saw Natasha and put her hand on her hip. Apparently, Harry hadn't warned Mama about the extra guest.

"If you're both here, I can talk to you too." Mama pointed to Natasha.

"Are you going to yell at us as my mama or as our superior officer?" Tommy took a step closer to Natasha.

"Any reason I can't do both?"

"Your prerogative. But she's been yelled at a lot today, so maybe go easy on her?" Tommy nodded toward Natasha.

Mama's face immediately softened. "Oh my dear, I'm sorry I haven't been more welcoming. No one should be threatened with a dressing down the minute they walk into someone's home."

"That can wait until the dessert course. It's best paired with pie anyway." Cody walked in from the kitchen, his arms loaded with food.

"Whose side are you on, AJ?"

"Whatever side leads to the most entertaining fireworks. I'm not afraid to become a double agent."

They settled into dinner and talked of other things. Natasha seemed to be enjoying herself. She looked relaxed, happy, and charming as always. Tommy could tell her parents liked her. When Natasha caught Tommy staring she was ready with a quick smile.

It seemed like her mother was watching Natasha especially closely and Harry seemed overly focused on how Tommy interacted with Natasha, but the rest of the table welcomed her warmly.

After the kids were excused and ran off to play, an uncomfortable silence settled over the table. Priya was the one who broke it. "Was anyone hurt today? It's hard to tell from the videos online."

Natasha shook her head.

"No, thankfully, everyone was fine. Largely thanks to Natasha." Tommy's heart raced when she thought about Natasha jumping into danger.

"You've gone viral." Priya looked at Natasha. "There's a hot debate about what your superhero name should be. I'm partial to Captain Couture myself."

"I'm not a superhero. I was doing my job." Natasha looked down at her hands.

Everyone at the table looked skeptical. Tommy searched for a way to explain what she and Natasha did. Natasha beat her to it.

"I know you aren't convinced. I haven't seen the videos. I don't know what they show, but I can tell you what happened. The man with the pipe was having an acute psychotic episode. Every police officer in the state could've drawn their weapons and screamed at him, and it's unlikely he would've dropped the pipe and put his hands in the air."

Tommy had wondered if the man heard them yelling at him. He seemed on another plane of existence.

"Folks in mental health crisis, substance use crisis, those are the folks Tommy and I have been helping. He was one of ours. We could help him and probably save his life. Tommy and I were on the same page about that, so I stepped in. They could've shot him, but for what? Being scared and having no idea what was going on around him? I had to step in."

"By thoughtlessly throwing yourself into the path of everyone's fire if something went south?" Cody obviously wasn't convinced. Priya put her hand on his arm.

"Your sister was covering my back. I was being neither reckless nor a glory-seeking showoff. It *wasn't* thoughtless. It was a calculated move based on what we've been doing and knowing my partner was right behind me."

Tommy saw the slightly stunned looks at the table. "I told you, she's been yelled at more than once today."

"Sorry. It's been a stressful day and Tommy's right. I've been accused of a lot already. Tommy and I work together, not against each other. I think today was a good example of that. In a really high stakes situation, no physical force was used and an ill man is getting evaluated at the hospital. Maybe he'll get treatment, maybe we'll see him again tomorrow, but it was the best outcome today."

"And what does Natasha Blackstone have to do with the events of today?"

Tommy looked at her mother, whose face was unreadable, then she looked at Natasha who had gone as pale as a suspect ensnared in a lie. If a drop of gravy shifted in its bowl, Tommy was convinced she'd be able to hear it, so quiet was the table.

"She doesn't have anything to do with today." Natasha kept her head high, but her voice was subdued. She looked defeated.

Tommy's stomach churned.

Her mother pressed further. "But you're Natasha Blackstone, correct?" She held up her phone with a picture of Natasha at a swank family gathering years ago, beside a photo of her today in full crisis mode. It had been Tweeted by a gossip rag.

Natasha shook her head and looked at her hands. "Not anymore." She looked up and straight at Tommy. "My name is Natasha Parsons. I'm a social worker who lives by the same principles I did five minutes ago before you found out who my parents are."

Tommy knew Natasha was waiting for her reaction. What the fuck was she supposed to say? The Blackstones were one of the richest families in the country and the whereabouts of their daughter had been the speculation of gossipy tabloids for years.

"Why didn't you tell me?"

"I did, sort of. I don't want people to know. This is going to make everything so much harder." Natasha ran her hands through her hair and pushed back from the table.

"Oh sure, I can see how being richer than some small countries is a real inconvenience." Tommy bit her lip. That was a dick thing to say. She looked around the table, and most everyone looked like they were watching an enthralling theater production, but her mother was casting a disapproving look her way.

"You just proved my point." Natasha sighed, her shoulders slumped. "You're looking at me like I'm a bank account. People don't connect with bank accounts. I can't do my job being seen as a bank account."

Tommy didn't want to continue the conversation in front of her family. She got up and motioned for Natasha to follow. She saw her mother nod her approval. At least she hoped it was approval.

Once they were on the back deck, Natasha made no move to close the distance between them. She sat on one of the patio chairs and looked smaller and less sure of herself than Tommy thought possible. One of the most attractive things about Natasha was her assertiveness and her confidence, and that was stripped away now.

It tugged at Tommy's heart. She went to Natasha and knelt in front of her, putting her hands on Natasha's knees. "I'm sorry for what I said in there. Mama dropping that bombshell caught me off guard. I didn't react very well, but that's not fair to you."

"How do you think I feel?" Natasha leaned back in the chair and looked up at the sky. "I've never lied to you, Tommy. I've never hidden the fact I have money. I told you why I became a social worker and that it disappointed my parents. The way you reacted inside, that's why I changed my last name. I care too much about the work."

Tommy hung her head.

"Do you still trust me?" Natasha lifted Tommy's chin.

Tommy didn't hesitate, she knew what Natasha said was true. "Yes."

"Then buckle up, buttercup, because things are going to be bumpy. Work will probably be harder for a while. I doubt you're the only one who'll react the way you did. I'm going to need your help."

Tommy reached up and gently cradled the back of Natasha's head. She pulled her forward until they were within kissing distance. "I'll help with anything." She kissed her, reveling in the softness of her lips.

Natasha broke the kiss far too soon for Tommy's taste.

"As much as I enjoy having you on your knees promising your service for any of my needs, we agreed no more kissing, and I'm supposed to be here as your partner. We should get back inside."

Tommy grumbled, but Natasha was right. She held Natasha's hand until they slid the patio door open and stepped inside.

As soon as Harry saw them she got up and started to collect dishes from the dining room table. "Oh good, I thought you two were going to leave me with all the dishes."

Tommy joined her. She carried serving dishes into the kitchen. "I wouldn't dream of shirking my duty." She turned and almost ran into Natasha.

"Where should I put these?" She had a stack of plates with silverware balanced on top.

Tommy cleared a spot on the counter. "Harry and I do the dishes. If you need to get home, I can get a ride from Harry or Cody."

Natasha smiled slowly. "I don't have anywhere else I'd rather be, but if you want time with your family so you can talk about the scandalous turn of events, I can head out."

"The only one I want to spend time with is right in front of me. Please don't go."

"Ugh, not again. Come on, guys. I thought dinner might be a cold shower for you two. Is it safe to come in there or am I gonna get pheromones all over my clothes and stuck to my shoes? Those are impossible to get out and then I won't be safe to walk home. Take pity on me and stand on opposite sides of the kitchen or something." Harry shooed them away from each other dramatically.

Tommy swatted her in the arm.

"You know we need to talk about this, right? Not to mention your big news, Natasha. You two need to be careful. You're going to fuck it up if you keep fucking each other."

"Harry, we're…you know what? It's none of your damn business." Tommy wanted to punch her sister in the face for talking to Natasha so crudely.

"Just some sisterly advice. Now, since you two can't be within ten feet of each other, Tommy, you wash, I'll rinse, Natasha, you dry."

After the dishes, the three of them ended up on the back deck. Listening to the crickets, Tommy let her thoughts wander. Maybe it should've felt strange having another person joining her dinner, dishes, back deck routine with Harry, but it didn't. At least not to Tommy. She wondered how it felt to Harry.

Why were emotions so hard to figure out? Maybe it was the stress of the day heightening the obvious attraction between them. Perhaps it was something else, but it felt like Natasha belonged at that table, at least before it had taken a sudden turn. Given that they weren't even supposed to be engaging in the activities they were, it scared her a little to think of Natasha having a natural place at her parents' dinner table. Did Natasha still have a place there, after the big reveal?

"I'm sorry if I offended you inside, Natasha. I forget what delicate little ears my sister has."

"I'm not all that easily offended, Harry. I appreciate you looking out for us."

"I have to ask because it's been bugging me since Mama outed you. The tabloids have been looking for Natasha Blackstone for years and it turns out the *you* formerly known as *she* was sitting at our table this evening. So, did we have a runaway princess dining with us tonight?"

"No one has ever called me a princess before. I'm not sure if I should be flattered. I'll think on that and get back to you if I want to whack you in the nuts the next time I see you."

Harry winked. "Something to look forward to."

Tommy was glad Natasha and Harry were getting along, but she was still annoyed Harry was sticking her nose where it didn't belong. "Why's it any of your business what Natasha and I do in our off hours?"

"It's not, Tommy, except I'm your sister, and I love you. How many times have we stood out here talking about work? I've seen the evolution of your thinking about your 'Natasha calls' since you two started working together and I know how important your career is to you."

"It's not that easy, Harry." Tommy wasn't sure how much to share with Natasha standing next to her. What if she freaked out and bolted?

Natasha snuggled closer and looped her arm around Tommy's bicep, then leaned her head on Tommy's shoulder. Harry couldn't possibly say anything to counter how good Natasha felt against her.

"I never said it was easy. Natasha, you *fit* at the table tonight. If you were anyone else, I'd be planning a bachelor party and writing my best man speech. But there's only one of you in the city. And you both care about the work you do together."

"What if?" Tommy didn't want to finish her thought.

"I don't know. You might have to choose. No offense, Natasha, but, Tommy, are you absolutely sure this is worth the risk to the career goals you've had since you were a kid? What if it affects your move to detective? How do you know it's not a head rush from what happened today, and tomorrow you'll both stick it back in your pants and move on? This is why I don't do emotions."

Tommy felt Natasha laughing against her. At least she thought it was funny.

"I like you, Harry. And I really like that you've got your sister's back. The job's important to me, and as apparently everyone on social media now knows, my career goals are important, but Tommy's important too. I guess the two of us have to figure out how to solve that puzzle."

Natasha relinquished Tommy's arm and was standing again, but she was still touching Tommy. She was facing Harry with her arm around Tommy's waist. Tommy was happy to stand all night and let Natasha put her hands wherever she pleased.

Harry pointed her beer bottle at the two of them. "While you figure it out, do me a favor and no more dry humping against a car in the middle of the street like two horny teenagers."

On the way home, Natasha held Tommy's hand while she drove. "What would happen if the captain found out we were sleeping together, or dating, or whatever?"

Tommy had been thinking about that question all night. "If you were a cop, one of us would have to leave. I don't know if the same rules apply for you since you're a civilian. No way she lets us stay partnered though. Although since I'm Alice Finch's daughter who knows? But even with that, it's probably not great for my future prospects, like Harry said."

"And now we have to contend with Natasha Blackstone too. I'm going to be treated differently now, even though I don't want to be. What do you mean by leave?"

"One of us would have to transfer to a different station in the city."

Natasha looked horrified. "That's ridiculous. I see how hard you work. You earn what you get in this life. Why couldn't we work together?"

Tommy pulled Natasha's hand to her lips. "Don't the privileged always think that? I mean me, not you, being privileged. It's easy to think you earn your way when you already have every advantage."

"I knew what you meant, Tommy. Stop worrying so much just because you know one detail you didn't this morning. If you wouldn't have made a big deal about something yesterday, don't make it a thing tomorrow, okay?"

Tommy nodded. She could do that. Probably. "Okay, well, like I was saying, I think I'd lose my shit now if anyone messed with you. Or if you asked me to cover up a crime for you or take a bribe with you, I'd still say no, I think, but I'd consider it. All objectivity is out the window."

Natasha parked in front of Tommy's house. "I won't tell anyone, but you're incredibly sweet."

"What was Mama saying to you before we left earlier?"

"She told us to take care of each other." Natasha traced Tommy's cheek and down her jawbone to her chin.

"She knows we're partners. That's part of the job." Tommy was distracted by Natasha's hand on her face. Why did they have so much trouble keeping their hands off each other?

"That's what I told her. She said that wasn't what she was talking about."

Tommy sat up, fully focused on what Natasha said. "She knows? About this?" Tommy pointed between them.

Natasha shrugged. "Apparently. You think Harry told her?"

Tommy shook her head. Harry wouldn't have said anything. "She knows, and she's okay with it. That's unexpected."

Natasha laughed. "Tommy, does kissing me make you happy?"

That had to be a trick question. She nodded.

"What about spending time with me outside of work?"

"Of course. If I haven't made that clear, I'm sorry."

"Shh. It's not about that. You make me happy. I make you happy. She's your mother. That's what mothers want for their kids. At least that's what they're supposed to want for their kids."

Tommy saw the sadness Natasha tried to hide. She thought about what Natasha told her about her family. She said a silent thanks for the familial love that had always surrounded her. Tommy hadn't considered that anyone in her family would advocate she buck the police rules and regulations because Natasha made her happy. It seemed a little too…simple.

"So I guess now we have to decide what to do." Natasha sighed and closed her eyes.

Tommy leaned over the center console and kissed her. It was slow and deep. She had no agenda except connection. She wanted Natasha to feel what she was feeling.

When they broke the kiss, Natasha kept her hands on Tommy's face and their foreheads together. "God, I could kiss you all day. I don't know what's better, seeing you all day but getting rid of this, or having more of this, but losing you during the day."

Tommy took a deep breath. She already regretted the words she hadn't yet spoken. "I think we both know which way we have to lean. I want as much of you as I can get, but we've both worked hard on our work partnership and I don't want to piss off the captain. What we've set in motion is fragile. Losing one of us would snuff it out and we'd have to start over. I don't want to go back. You told me we have to like the work a little bit more right now, and I think you're right. I know there will be a time for us."

"I never would've said such a stupid thing." Natasha leaned back in her seat and blew out a breath. "You're right. But I refuse to like it. I don't want to jeopardize your goals, and I actually think you should steer clear of me for a while outside of work. But once this baby bird of ours has strong enough wings and you're on to the next rung of your career ladder, I'm going to kiss you everywhere."

Tommy felt her cheeks heat. "Do you mean everywhere?" She pointed out the window. "Or everywhere?" She pointed up and down her body.

"We better get this work thing sorted out so I can clarify. Now get out of the car before I invite myself inside which will make work tomorrow awkward."

Awkward sounded nice to Tommy, but she did as Natasha asked. She walked to the driver's side and leaned in to kiss Natasha one last time.

"Thanks for having my back today, Tommy."

"That's my job. I told you I'd lose it if anything happened to you. No one wants to see that."

Tommy watched Natasha drive away, climbed the steps, and flopped on the couch once she was inside. She didn't care if she made it to bed tonight. She'd slept on the couch plenty of nights when she came home too exhausted to walk another step.

Harry called before she fell asleep. "You okay?"

"Nope."

"You look at the media reports about her?"

"Nope."

"Anything I can do?"

Tommy sighed. What was there to do? "No. You tried to warn me about getting involved with my partner. My fault for not listening."

"What are you two going to do?"

Tommy didn't want to think about it. "Just partners. Nothing else. For now, anyway."

"I'm sorry. I'm always here to talk."

Tommy threw her phone on the coffee table and pulled a blanket over herself. Work was going to be torture in the morning. Natasha's smile was like a cloudless day after a rainstorm. It wasn't just that Natasha could stop traffic with a hair flip and a smile, there were plenty of beautiful women in the world. Natasha had unrivaled beauty, but she was intelligent, empathetic, courageous, and the slightest bit cocky, a combination Tommy found irresistible. She thought about calling her and asking her to lie. Maybe they could hide the fact that they were more than partners.

She dismissed it immediately. That wasn't who she was and she didn't think it was who Natasha was either. She didn't want it to feel like a dirty secret, and she wasn't willing to flaunt rules designed to maintain the integrity of the force. So she was left with a day of yearning to look forward to. She could've made it easier on herself and tied herself in knots over a barista or a rodeo clown. She thought of Natasha again. Complicated or not, she didn't want anyone else occupying her thoughts as she drifted off to sleep. They'd figure it out together.

CHAPTER TWENTY

Natasha stumbled wobbly legged after Kayla. Somehow Kayla had talked her into another round of hell with the active seniors. Absence hadn't made her heart fonder or muscles stronger. She was stumbling her way to dinner, a burger and milkshake the only thing keeping her upright, when her phone rang. She never sent Tommy, Kayla, or her mother straight to voice mail although she wished she could send her mother other places. It was probably that kind of thinking that had her mother's name flashing on her screen now.

"Damn it. I'll meet you inside." Natasha held up the phone to Kayla.

Kayla jumped away and pulled open the door quickly.

"Hello, Mother."

"I need to know if you're bringing a plus one to the gala. I've already arranged clothing and jewelry." Her mother's tone was curt and businesslike as always.

Natasha looked to the heavens for strength. "I haven't RSVP'd yet."

There was a pause on the end of the line. "That stunt you pulled is costing your sister and brother dearly. You'll show up and fix the damage you've done."

Before answering, Natasha counted to five slowly. When she still felt like screaming, she counted again. "It wasn't a stunt, it was my job. I'm sorry that it's caused issues for Valencia's campaign, but going to the gala will cause issues for me at my job."

"Dear, I think it's about time you put down that hobby and returned to the fold. You know you can have much greater influence on the world working through the family charity anyway." Her mother's voice was cold despite the term of endearment.

"Even if I believed that to be true, my work isn't a hobby, it's a career, and not one I'm about to give up. We're done here." Natasha fantasized about hanging up dramatically, but she'd never had the balls.

"Come to the gala, shake a few hands, give a quote to the media supporting our cause or I personally guarantee that career you care so much about will disappear before your eyes."

There was probably steam coming out of Natasha's ears and she was sure she could breathe fire if asked. "Always nice talking to you, Mother." This time she did hang up.

She stared at the phone a moment before pulling the door to the restaurant open with more force than was necessary and searching for Kayla. Once she found her she flopped into the booth.

Natasha held her frustration at bay until after they'd ordered and the food arrived. She squirted ketchup on her plate but didn't bother with her burger. Her stomach was still in knots.

"It's been a while since you hit level three on the Cricket scale. What did she do this time?" Kayla pointed at Natasha's plate.

When they were kids, they'd developed a one to five scale for how far under Natasha's skin her mother, Cricket, dug. Level three sucked her appetite.

Natasha picked up her burger and took a bite. "No, no levels anymore. I'm a grown-ass woman. I wear a ballistic vest and step in front of guns for a living."

"I really wish you'd step in front of fewer guns for a living. But since you brought it up, what do your parents have to say about the video?"

"My parents don't get a say on that video or anything else." Natasha jammed a fry in her ketchup too hard and splashed some off the side of the plate.

"Oh please. They've had you by the tits since you were born, and if I were wrong you wouldn't have changed your name and tried to hide them as your dirty little secret. It's not right, but I know they have an opinion." Kayla had stopped eating and was giving Natasha her full attention.

Natasha threw down the fry she was about to enjoy, a sour taste in her mouth. "You're right, they have plenty to say, none of which I want to hear. No matter what's happening in my life, they always manage to be the most complicated and annoying. Their list of demands is surprisingly short, but I don't see how I can possibly comply."

Kayla frowned and then her expression quickly changed to shock. "Isn't your sister-in-law running for state senator?"

Natasha nodded.

"And isn't the centerpiece of her campaign a pledge to defund the police?"

"It doesn't seem fair to offer you three guesses to solve the mystery of my parents' current anger at me. How about three words? That's all you get." Natasha picked up a fry again, her appetite back.

Kayla tapped her chin. "That's easy. 'You're a problem.'"

Natasha gave Kayla a thumbs-up, since her mouth was full, and they high-fived. She was playing the part of disinterested, unemotional, rock, but truthfully, her heart was breaking. It was too much to hope anyone in her family would express pride at the work she did, but the derision and anger that had greeted her as a result of the video's moment of fame on social media had caught her like a rogue wave.

"Poor Tommy was so confused when I tried to explain all of this to her. She's devoted her life to service so she can't understand the quest for power and money above all else. If you haven't seen it firsthand, it's hard to describe how much of both my parents have, and how they wield it to obtain more of each."

"So what do they want you to do?" Kayla drummed her fingers on the table, a telltale sign she was in problem-solving mode.

"I have to attend a gala fundraiser for the campaign." Natasha pictured Tommy in black tie finery. If only she could come as her date.

"Is that what the call was about?"

Natasha rolled her eyes and nodded. "My clothes are selected, my seat is arranged, I'm sure the reporters are lined up and my statement has been written. All I have to do is show up and my puppet master will pull the strings."

"What if you don't go?" Kayla looked thoughtful.

Natasha laughed although there wasn't anything funny about the call she'd had with her mother. "I go or my job in the police department's in jeopardy. It's a public relations nightmare to have me working for the police when they're trying to yank funding from the department, no matter how similar our goals are on paper."

Kayla reached across the table and took Natasha's hand. "And what happens if you do go?"

"I don't know. I'm sure it's going to be a circus and my mother has already made it clear I'm expected to talk to the press as often as possible. I don't imagine that would play all that well at the station."

"Or with Tommy." Kayla smirked.

"It's silly, but I looked for Tommy the entire walk over."

She'd been with her all day at work, but she still missed her. Off-the-clock time was different, better on a personal level, but they'd been limiting that kind of time because it was too hard. No dinners or drinks after work, no hanging out at Chet's for some flirty banter. It sucked.

"If we'd seen her, I would've shoved you really hard into her path, so she had no choice but to wrap her big strong arms around you and hold you for a while. Chivalry would have demanded it." Kayla looked at her seriously.

"There's a reason you're my best friend. I'm sure if you had happened to trip on a rock, leap into the air and had landed in Harry's arms, she'd have had no choice but to catch you too."

Kayla fanned herself dramatically. "That certainly is a pleasant thought. But tell me about you and your Officer Dreamy. Enough talk about your family. I don't like seeing you so sad."

"So you want to talk about Tommy, who I spend all day with, but can't be mine? You really know how to cheer a girl up. But I don't really have anything to complain about. We see each other every day and the work is going really well. This is a decision *we* made." Natasha's heart clenched as the words left her mouth.

Kayla laughed. Natasha wanted to throw her menu, napkin, and utensils across the table.

"I'm not laughing at you or how you're feeling. I'm thinking about the conversations we had early on about how much she made you crazy. This is the same woman who left you behind on your first day. Now you're practically in love with her and moping around your house, my house, exercise class, our burger place. You're a moper."

"I'm not in love with her." That would be crazy. Right?

"Fine, you're in 'like her a whole lot' with her."

"That's not a thing." Natasha smiled around her straw as she took a sip of milkshake.

"I just said it is and it's what you are. So what are you going to do about it? Avoiding each other is just going to make you both nuts. Either there's a thing there, or there's not, but you aren't going to find out by playing cop all day and then going home to your separate beds."

Natasha balled up her napkin and took a deep breath. "How many times do I have to tell you, we don't 'play' cop. I wear a ballistic vest for a reason, and the work we do together has a real impact on the people we interact with."

Kayla reached across the table and took her hand. "I know. I'm sorry, sweetie. The video of you jumping in front of all those raised guns is still a little too fresh in my mind. I like to think of you out there playing a very safe video game version of your very dangerous job."

"What's the other thing I've told you a million times?" Natasha squeezed Kayla's hand.

"That Tommy's watching your back. I know. I worry about both of you. Now you've gotten me liking her and I have double the worry."

"When did this become all about you?"

"By all means, let's keep talking about you. I have a gazillion more questions. How are things at the station now that Ms. Blackstone has been unmasked?"

Natasha laughed. "Well, no one has curtsied in days. I'd say things have finally settled down. But if they think I've been lying to them this whole time and my end goal is to support pulling funding, I might as well quit tomorrow."

"You know what would help take the edge off?" Kayla waggled her eyebrows suggestively as they cleared their dishes and headed for the door.

"Not going to happen. There are rules and regulations in place. The consequences are high if we get caught and it puts the integrity of the work we're doing at risk even if we're never found out."

Kayla put her hand on Natasha's chest. "Heart's still beating, so you're alive." She made like she was going to take a peek down Natasha's pants. "Everything okay down there? Tommy I figured for a Boy Scout. You've never been constrained by rules and regulations. What's going on?"

Natasha slapped her away. "Unhand my lady bits. That's invitation only and you're not on the guest list."

"I beg your pardon, ma'am."

Natasha scuffed her shoe after a pebble on the sidewalk. "Kay, if someone like me had responded the night Joseph was arrested, his life probably would've turned out very differently."

"You don't know that." Kayla pulled her to a stop.

"Sure, it's something I can't know for sure, but it couldn't have gone much worse than it did. There are more Josephs in the world. How selfish of me if I don't follow through on the job I signed up for because I can't get Tommy out of my head. I'm not willing to skirt the regulations and torpedo this experiment. My being a social worker freaks out everyone at the station and that was before the Blackstone business. I don't want to be lying to them on top of that."

"Okay, okay. No Tommy, got it. I'll go elsewhere for my juicy gossip fix."

Natasha face-palmed and walked on. "Ugh. Have I told you she's a really good kisser?"

"A few times."

"And that her mother's amazing?"

"More than once."

"And when I'm with her I feel like I belong for maybe the first time in my life?" Natasha put her hand over her mouth.

"That's new." Kayla hurried to catch up. "Tell me more."

"Let's talk about something else." Natasha needed some time to examine that admission from every angle. Maybe it was like a Christmas tree and there was one ugly side you needed to hide against a wall. You couldn't put a declaration like that out in the world if there was an ugly side.

Kayla didn't look like she wanted to move on, but thankfully she allowed the transition. "How's your crisis training coming? Are they more open to your brand of policing since you went viral?"

Natasha's shoulders relaxed now that they weren't talking about Tommy and their no-win situation or her parents and that sticky wicket. "They've been asking a lot of questions and are interested in what Tommy and I do. In some ways I think the Blackstone thing has helped because they all want to know about it but don't want to come right out and ask, so they make up other reasons to talk to me. I've gotten a lot of compliments on my big ass balls."

"Gross. Why is that a good thing?"

Natasha shrugged. It was a good thing though. She'd had more meaningful conversations with other officers in the station in the past month than she had the entirety of the rest of her time at the station. She'd even had a couple of cordial chats with Justin. She had a feeling he wasn't a lost cause even if he was young and a complete idiot.

"My first official training's in two weeks. I still have a lot to put together. I keep reminding myself I don't have to teach everything on the first day. The most important thing is getting everyone on board and willing to come back for more."

"Aren't they mandated sessions?"

"Sure, but what good does that do if everyone tunes me out? I'm going for rock star, sold out, triple encore performance."

"Good that you're moderating your expectations."

"It's always been one of my strengths."

Kayla grinned and nodded. "What's the ultimate goal of all of your hard work and sacrifice?"

"What do you mean?" Natasha pulled open the car door and slid into Kayla's sleek sports car.

"All this change you're creating. It's keeping you away from the possible love of your life."

"Stop or I'm going to dig a nail into this beautiful upholstery." Natasha traced a finger along her seat menacingly.

"You wouldn't." Kayla was smiling, clearly not taking Natasha's threat seriously. "You're transforming this station a little at a time, but changing something from one thing means it turns into something else. What is that something else?"

Natasha thought back to her conversation with the captain. "I think I'm the something else."

"No you're not. You're the change agent. You're Rodin, not *The Thinker*. So what are you sculpting?"

Natasha couldn't answer, but it was an excellent question. She knew in general terms what she wanted, but she wasn't the only one with a say, and she hadn't considered the ultimate end game. Maybe it was time to come up with concrete goals for the officers and the station. And maybe by doing that, she'd see a path forward for her and Tommy. Too many maybes. They felt like quicksand. No foundation survived on quicksand. Tomorrow she'd outline a solid foundation. This change agent was ready for action.

CHAPTER TWENTY-ONE

Tommy's heart was racing. She and Natasha were on their way to a call for someone in crisis. The caller wasn't specific except they were in distress and needed Tommy and Natasha. The caller had been clear about that.

They pulled up in front of an apartment building with boarded windows, an unkempt lawn, and a front door as sad and decrepit as the rest of the block.

"Can't imagine we're going to find anything good in there." Natasha patted Tommy's leg. "In you go, partner. Let me know when it's safe. And please be careful."

Tommy wanted to lean over and kiss her. Just a quick kiss letting her know she'd be right back. That she'd be safe and that she'd miss her. It would be so easy. But she didn't. She nodded and slammed the door shut on the patrol car and the emotions that served no purpose now but to distract her.

She was halfway up the front walk, what was left of it, when the front door swung open and the Zookeeper lurched out. She was usually controlled and calculating, keeping her own confidence. Tommy never knew where she stood or what the Zookeeper was thinking.

This version of the Zookeeper was the exact opposite. She was gesturing wildly, looked happy to see Tommy, and had lost her guarded countenance.

"Tommy, get Natasha. I need her inside."

"Zookeeper, that's not how this works. I can't let her walk in there until I've cleared the house. I need to know it's safe before she goes in."

The Zookeeper bent over laughing. "I like her a hell of a lot more than you, Officer Finch. I like her so much my opinion hasn't even dimmed now that I know she's a Blackstone. I called for her, not you. If I wanted to mess you up, I could've done it anytime. I'm not going to hurt your pretty little head. But I need her inside. Now."

It felt like a vague threat even though it was delivered amidst laughter. The Zookeeper was acting strangely. She'd never known her to dabble in drug use, but this seemed like the behavior she'd seen in those under the influence.

"I need to check the house. I'm as concerned with Natasha's safety as you claim to be."

Anger flashed across the Zookeeper's face and she looked more like the Zookeeper Tommy knew. "You're going to cost someone their life and me some of my flock. I need her help. Ask her if she's willing to go in. There is no danger in there to either of you, I stake my life on it."

"I'm not willing to stake hers." Tommy crossed her arms.

"Tommy, can we go in together? If I stay behind you and you clear as we go?" Natasha put her hand on Tommy's shoulder. "I trust the Zookeeper if she says there's no danger."

Tommy didn't like that Natasha had gotten out of the car before she knew it was safe. *She* didn't trust the Zookeeper, but drug dealers and the police had a naturally fraught relationship. She thought about the difference between her interactions with the Zookeeper and Natasha's the day Natasha got the tip about a suspect they'd been after. If Natasha trusted her, Tommy trusted Natasha.

"Okay, but you stay behind me. And you stay in front where I can see you." She pointed at the Zookeeper. "If anything goes wrong, Natasha, get out if you can, get under cover if you can't. Your job is to get yourself to safety, no matter what's happening with me, understand?"

Natasha nodded, but Tommy had no confidence Natasha would follow her directions if things went sideways inside. This was why officers weren't allowed to partner with people they were in relationships with. What would she do if something happened to Natasha and she couldn't protect her?

The interior of the house was, remarkably, in significantly better shape than the exterior would lead you to believe. Tommy had a hard time figuring out what the place was. There were clear signs of active drug use, but also very little signs of the garbage, grime, and filth she usually encountered in shooting galleries.

"Why did you call us, Zoo?"

Natasha was keeping behind Tommy as she promised.

The Zookeeper waved them forward toward one of the rooms off the small kitchen. "One of my flock. I've been having trouble keeping track of things. I let her down. She's been saying things, Natasha, things that need your professional assistance. Can you help her? Please?"

Natasha started to move around Tommy to the door. Tommy put her arm out and caught Natasha's eye. She shook her head and reached for the knob herself. She put her hand on her weapon as she entered but didn't unholster it.

She hated walking blind into a room, but she needed to know it was safe. If someone needed her, Natasha would go in no matter the danger. It was one of the best and most infuriating qualities about her.

There were two women on an ancient couch, but nothing else in the room. Both women shrunk into themselves at the sight of Tommy. Whether it was because of her uniform and badge, or because she was a stranger, she didn't know.

She approached slowly and spoke softly. She had no desire to terrify these two who did, in fact, look like they needed Natasha immediately. Once she was sure the room was free from weapons and danger, she waved Natasha in.

"You okay if I stand just outside the door? Or would you prefer me to stay inside?"

"I'll be fine in here. I know you'll be there if I need you."

Natasha trailed her fingers along Tommy's shoulder as she passed. It wasn't a sexual gesture and to any of the other women watching it likely looked like a casual touch, immediately forgotten. To Tommy, it felt possessive and intimate given all they'd shared and were holding just below the surface. Her stomach jolted.

Tommy nodded, not trusting her voice, and took up position outside the door. The Zookeeper paced nearby. Tommy could tell something was off with her. Drug use seemed the most obvious answer, but the Zookeeper was famous for swearing off her own product. Ruining lives was fine for turning a profit, apparently, but wasn't allowed to touch her personally.

She knew the Zookeeper had an underground network keeping women and kids safe from those threats on the street worse than her, but to Tommy, that didn't cancel out what she did for a living. She and Parrot Master still sold poison and ran a street gang. So what if they had lines they wouldn't cross and a twisted sense of guiding principles? What about the destruction they left behind? That was usually what Tommy and her fellow officers were left to mop up.

"We don't have to be enemies, Officer Finch." The Zookeeper stopped pacing and stood in front of her.

She was blocking her view of the room and Natasha. Tommy wanted to force her out of the way, but she was an officer of the law, not disorder. She motioned the Zookeeper to move over.

"I think cops and criminals are always enemies. Isn't that the definition of our relationship?" Tommy pointed between them. "How did you end up doing what you do anyway? Weren't you destined for a courtroom?"

"That's what I'm saying. It doesn't have to be that way. You think of me as a criminal but don't look twice at the corporate lawyers covering up unimaginable wrongs for their clients."

Tommy shook her head. "If they break the law, I'll happily arrest them."

"No, you won't. That's not how the system works. But we've drifted afield. I've got a flock to take care of, and I've gotta sort out some of my own shit right now. I need your help. Natasha seems to like you so I figure I can trust you."

"Okay, fair enough. But what happened to your lawyer vocabulary and closing argument persuasion? And since when do you admit any weakness around me?" Tommy glanced in to check on Natasha.

"Are you going to help me or not?" The Zookeeper looked agitated.

"You haven't told me what kind of help you need."

"These drugs, they're muddling my mind. I need to get myself right again, but until I do, my flock is vulnerable. Look what happened with Armadillo. I need your help keeping them safe."

"Armadillo? What? Keeping who safe?" Tommy focused on the Zookeeper fully for a moment. At least the abnormal behavior was explained.

"Why do you think I'm called the Zookeeper? Each of my flock are given animal names to join my zoo. It keeps them protected. Until now. Will you help me?"

Tommy could see the desperation. You couldn't fake that kind of emotion. "Have you considered treatment?"

"Officer, I'll mind my side of the street. Will you help me mind the other?"

Those addicted to substances, especially those on the street, or marginally housed, were often victims of circumstances and trauma difficult to comprehend. Even those with every advantage who fell under addiction's grip were victims of a disease with no mercy.

Substance use had always been one area Tommy had been willing to bend the rules of policing. She'd never been interested in arresting anyone for drug use in isolation if there were other options available. Technically, it was illegal, but the individual was often suffering far more than greater society. Time in jail would serve little purpose but to further entrench the addiction. Perhaps she'd always been interested in "Natasha calls" without realizing it.

"I don't know what I can do, but Natasha and I will assist if we can." Tommy checked on Natasha again. She couldn't keep her eyes off her and was glad the job required her to watch her constantly.

The Zookeeper nodded vigorously. "Good, good. Today was a start. I needed you. It's not just her. I needed you too, and when I called, you both came. I need to know there's someone on the inside I can trust."

Tommy jabbed her finger at the Zookeeper. "I'm not a cop you've got a line on. I won't do you favors. If you think my agreeing to respond when one of your flock is in danger has bought you a dirty cop, I'll call for an ambulance and Natasha, your armadillo, and I will be gone, right now."

"That's not what I'm asking you. But if you'd jumped to that conclusion and been amenable, I wouldn't have turned down the free two for one. There are some people I trust taking over the day-to-day with my zoo, until I can do right by them."

What kind of people did the Zookeeper have available to take over this specialized task? Knowing the Zookeeper, it could be anyone from a neighborhood corner boy to a US senator.

"If they're taking over for you, why do you need us?"

"The members of my flock, and my new caretakers, are vulnerable. The two I've asked to help are doing so despite the risks to themselves. I don't want legal entanglements for either of them, especially my baby giraffe, a kid named Frankie. That's where you come in. Frankie and Kit can take their caretaker role only so far, but eventually there may come a time when they need to call on you and Natasha both."

Tommy held up her hands. "I already told you, you aren't negotiating for a dirty cop here and you seem to know Natasha pretty well. She's above board."

The Zookeeper considered her carefully. "I'm beginning to understand what she sees in you. I'm not asking you to break the law, Officer. I'm asking you to not leave the neediest behind when you put on that badge every day."

"Go find something else to do before I have to decide if I like you." Tommy turned her full attention back to Natasha.

"Be around if you need me. And, Officer, I'm a criminal, and pretty fucked up right now, but I don't think standard police procedure when watching your partner's back involves staring at their ass."

Tommy knew her cheeks were on fire, but the Zookeeper was already heading to other parts of the house. She needed to be more professional. And more careful.

Natasha poked her head out in the middle of Tommy's self-reprimand. She looked questioningly at Tommy, probably due to her flustered appearance, but didn't say anything about it.

"I need to get our Star Recovery team out here as quickly as possible. Can you call them and let them know it's a crisis call with SI? They should also call one of the legal aid groups they work with to consult."

Tommy nodded and pulled out her phone. SI meant the woman Natasha was evaluating had suicidal ideation. It must not be acute enough that Natasha felt they needed to go to the hospital immediately. Tommy was thankful she wasn't the one to make the decision, or to sit with someone's pain and despair.

She dealt with other people's big, overwhelming emotions often on the job, the flash and bang of anger or grief or pain, but sorrow that had crept into a person's marrow was something she felt powerless against. But she wasn't powerless here, because she had Natasha.

Star responded quickly. As was their protocol, two staff members arrived and joined Natasha. Five people in the small room looked like an overcrowded subway car, but Tommy stepped just inside the threshold anyway. Adding a new element to the delicate chemistry could cause unexpected reactions, and she was now responsible for the safety of Natasha, two Star employees, and two community members. Perhaps she wasn't as much of a hood ornament as she thought on these "Natasha calls."

From what Tommy could tell, the addition of the Star staff was a negotiating chip Natasha had brought to the table. One of the two women was there as support only, the other was the Armadillo, whose real name was Taylor. Natasha seemed to think she needed to be evaluated at the hospital, but wasn't interested in forcing her, except as a last resort.

Watching Natasha talk with Taylor highlighted how ill-equipped she'd been to respond to a similar situation on her own and why what Natasha could provide was so vital to the station. Watching Natasha, she'd learned not only what to ask, but how to ask the important questions. But she'd also been taught over and over, that no matter her own feelings, empathy and caring would not be perceived the same way filtered through a uniform and badge.

There had to be more they could do to get Natasha in everyone's ear as they walked their beat. One training in response to an acute event wasn't enough.

Finally, Natasha stepped out of the room and pulled Tommy with her. "We have a plan that everyone's comfortable with. Taylor and her friend are going to ride in the Star van to the hospital. You and I are going to follow and make sure they get there okay."

"Are you worried they don't know the way?"

"I'm worried that if they don't make it for some reason, I let someone who needs to be evaluated go without making sure she got the care she needs. I'm a clinician, and I'm responsible for her well-being until she gets to the hospital."

Tommy put her hands on Natasha's shoulders. "Why is this one different than the others who have driven with Star? Why don't we drive her?"

Natasha shook her head. "You'd have to handcuff her to get her in the back of our car. And it's different because she's suicidal and I'm clinically liable if she doesn't make it and something happens to her. I'm not thrilled about the seating arrangement, but it's better than traumatizing her by forcing her into a situation she doesn't feel okay with. But we're going to put all those fancy cop driving skills to good use or I'm climbing into your lap and taking over."

"I know that was supposed to be a threat." Tommy silently admonished her body for reacting like Natasha had just given her a lap dance. "You should keep working on your verbal deterrents. They need some work. But I promise not to lose the large van with no intention or desire to ditch us."

"I knew I could count on you."

"Why not an ambulance if you're worried about her?"

"She's had more than one traumatic experience being forced to the hospital against her will and strapped to a gurney. Tommy, look, I said we have a plan that will work. Trust me, please."

"I'm sorry. I do. Always."

They got Taylor squared away with the folks from Star and followed them to the hospital. Natasha was uncharacteristically silent on the drive.

"You okay?"

Natasha leaned her head back on the headrest and looked out the window. "Sometimes life isn't fair. We shouldn't be following Taylor to the hospital for a psych evaluation. We, society at large, shouldn't make it so damn hard for the Taylors of the world."

Tommy reached over and put her hand on Natasha's leg. Natasha covered her hand with her own and squeezed. It only lasted a moment before Natasha broke the connection and Tommy pulled her hand back to her side of the car, but that brief connection was enough. It calmed the background noise clamoring for attention, demanding she ignore her values, her job, her hard work and run away with Natasha.

"Tell me about Taylor."

Natasha sighed. "Do you know she's called Armadillo? The Zookeeper's had a few zebras and a lemur or two, but I don't remember an armadillo."

"I don't understand that woman. We should talk about her later."

"No one does. She and Parrot Master are a unique breed. You noticed she's struggling?"

Tommy nodded. "That could have repercussions in the city. She asked for our help."

"The ripple effects are already starting. Taylor is the first example although she didn't blame the Zookeeper. You're familiar with the general setup of the Zookeeper's underground protection network? She keeps vulnerable women and young people safe from sex traffickers and others on the streets? She has an assortment of places she stashes her zoo when she needs to get them out of sight."

"The library across town from our station is one, if the rumor mill is to be believed."

"Exactly. The head librarian over there, Thea, she's good people. Anyway, the Zookeeper helps out in other ways sometimes too. She was helping Taylor get street methadone to try and clean up."

"Why would she do that?"

"I'm sure she has a few reasons. My cynical view is a drug sale is a drug sale. My altruistic view is she wanted to help Taylor and there are plenty of other fish in the sea. Losing one customer wasn't going to put them out of business."

Tommy snorted. "I'm sure you can guess where I stand."

"Being able to see the angelic qualities of a drug dealer? You continuously surprise me, Officer Finch." Natasha grinned.

"Why did Taylor need to get methadone off the street? Why not go to one of the clinics?"

"Ah, that's what brought us out today. Taylor was arrested about eighteen months ago for drug possession, and while she was in jail for a couple days, her kids were placed in foster care. She has an open case with child services because of it. She was using methadone to kick the drug habit since clean urines are part of the deal with child services."

Tommy pulled into a parking spot outside the hospital. Taylor, her friend, and one of the Star workers all headed inside.

"I still don't understand why she was getting methadone from the street and not a clinic."

Natasha unbuckled her seat belt and turned to face Tommy. "Money. Every bit she had left over she was using to pay off court fines. If she didn't keep up her payments, she'd get scooped up and tossed in jail for a couple of days to 'pay down her debt' which just adds more fees and her kids would get placed again."

Tommy shook her head. She didn't always stop and think about some of the asinine systems for folks after they left her custody.

"Let me guess, in her current condition, the Zookeeper didn't keep up with the methadone?"

"Good guess." Natasha looked close to tears. "Taylor said the cravings and withdrawal was worse than heroin. She couldn't take it. Her last urine was dirty and her kids were removed. I doubt that was the only factor, but it played a role. She's understandably distraught. She wanted to get clean. She wanted to be there for her kids. This isn't a good outcome for anyone."

When kids were involved there were no easy answers and usually hundreds of opinions. Tommy had certainly seen situations she'd wished kids had been removed from their parents the day they were born.

"What about the kids? Are they better off?"

Natasha blew out a breath. "I don't know all the details, so maybe. But having kids pulled away from their parents is always traumatic. I know Taylor loves them and reunification is the goal, so hopefully there'll be a happy ending there. Assuming Taylor can really get clean and be there for them."

One of the Star workers came over and knocked on the window. Natasha got out. She popped her head back in and told Tommy she was going inside to talk with the doctor seeing Taylor.

Tommy got out of the car to wait and texted Harry. *Do you feel like you know what you're doing when you get called to a mental health crisis?*

Like a suicidal person or someone hearing voices? Wish I felt more comfortable, Harry wrote back.

Just had a call. Natasha took the lead.

Did it end up the same way it would've if you were in charge?

Tommy could picture her sister's teasing grin.

Not even close. So much better.

I mean this seriously. I think every station should have someone like her. Maybe she could do some rounds.

Tommy couldn't argue, but the thought of not spending her days with Natasha made her stomach churn.

She saw Natasha exit the hospital and head back her way. Natasha caught her eye and smiled the smile that made Tommy catch her breath. If life were a movie, Natasha would smile that smile and everyone would break out in an earworm pop song, she'd have brightly hued backup dancers, and there'd be fountains exploding behind her.

Tommy's mini rom-com moment was interrupted by Natasha's arrival and her radio returning her to the police procedural she actually inhabited. She listened and responded.

"Well, this call is a first. You all good here?" Tommy pointed at the hospital.

"All set. Where to now?" Natasha slid back into the car and buckled up.

"Ramirez called in a backup request and asked for us specifically. I think he's asking for you, but he was polite about it and asked for both of us."

Natasha patted Tommy's knee. "Look at that, my work here is done. I've taught all of you about feelings."

Tommy kept her eyes on the road. "You've taught me a lot about feelings."

"I've been learning a lot too."

Tommy caught Natasha's eye. They both smiled.

"I've also learned to appreciate the beauty I'm surrounded by every day."

Natasha's grin widened.

"I like that park, look at how gorgeous that is." Tommy pointed out the window behind Natasha's head."

Natasha scowled.

Tommy laughed. "Oh stop. You know if you're in my field of vision, there's nothing anyone could wave in front of me that would get me to take my eyes off you."

"Sports car?"

"Nope."

"Monet's *Water Lilies*."

"No."

"Lenny's fancy hot dogs?"

"Maybe I should be asking you about that one. But still no."

"The family jewels?"

Tommy looked at her crotch. "Ah, no."

"Well, those might distract me, but I guess I'd still be looking at you. God, Tommy, I miss you."

Tommy took Natasha's hand. "I miss you too. Let's get through this call and then the one after that. I don't know how, but we'll figure it out, I promise."

They responded to the backup request from Ramirez, a homeless man he'd rounded up more times than he could count, but this time he thought maybe Natasha could help navigate a different outcome. Tommy was shocked Ramirez thought to call them and even more floored when he took a step back and let Natasha work. When that call wrapped up, they signed out for the day and went their separate ways until the morning. For Tommy it was the worst part of the day.

She drove home alone. She couldn't remember ever feeling more confused or lost. What she always knew about being a cop had shifted under her feet. She could nearly recite the study guide for the detective exam, but when she looked at it now, it felt foreign. How was that possible? Even if the change was a positive one, it still left her a little dizzy. And Natasha. It was harder and harder for Tommy to deny her feelings for her. She was struggling spending all day with her but not being able to kiss her good night. Where would this end?

When Tommy got home, Harry was sitting on her front steps. She had a six-pack of beer and a hug.

"Something about your text earlier made me think you could use company."

Tommy nodded and sat down next to Harry. She put her head in her hands. "I'm with her all day, but it's not enough."

Harry nudged the six-pack closer to Tommy with her shoe. "Does she feel the same?"

Tommy thought back to Natasha's teasing about Lenny's and the family jewels. *She said she misses me.* "Yes, I think so."

"Tommy, you said you're building something. What's it going to look like once it's built? Are you and Natasha going to keep doing this together forever? Or are you building something bigger than the two of you?"

Tommy grabbed one of the beers and popped the top. "I don't know. We said we'd see where we were at once this was off the ground, but we didn't talk about when that might be. Why does it matter?"

"Because if it's bigger than the two of you, then you might not be partnered forever."

Tommy's gut lurched. The thought of not seeing Natasha all day was miserable.

"Hey, you're a little green there, J2. I'm not saying you'll never see her. If you're not partnered, you've got the world open to you."

Tommy wasn't sure. What if this career detour was a magical moment destined to dissipate? That detective position that seemed inconceivable right now was the next step for her. What if Natasha didn't like what she saw when inconceivable became routine?

Then there was the Blackstone thing. As much as Tommy didn't want to admit it, Natasha being a Blackstone had thrown her. It still threw her, if she stopped to think about it, even with a couple months to get used to the idea. Natasha told her she'd been summoned to a fundraising gala for her sister-in-law. Tommy had looked it up and saw that tickets were five thousand dollars a head. She'd choked on her orange juice when she read it. Natasha came from a world she couldn't even really picture, outside the movies.

But she kept returning to Natasha's bravery, integrity, her smile. She wasn't living a fake life. She worked because she loved it, not because she had to, and Tommy was the same cop whether she was handing out tickets or heading up the homicide division, and for some reason, Natasha seemed to like her fine how she was. The question remained though, what the hell did they do about it?

Chapter Twenty-two

Natasha waited in Captain Gillette's office. It had been three months since her annual review so the meeting request was unexpected. Maybe the captain wanted to talk about the training she'd been running every Wednesday afternoon. She'd cycled through it enough now that she'd gotten to almost everyone at the station, so maybe that was what this meeting was about. She hadn't been nervous when she sat down, but the captain was five minutes late, which had given Natasha time to think, so now the doubts were creeping in. Why wasn't Tommy here too?

She'd stand behind the work she'd done, but it was always possible the department wanted to use the money elsewhere. Had her parents gotten involved somehow? She hadn't given them an answer about the gala yet, but she wouldn't put it past them to stick their thumb on the scale.

Then there was the issue of the future. That was making Natasha most nervous. She wanted to propose expanding her role, something the captain might not be on board with. Natasha hadn't been shy about arguing for what she wanted before. It was annoying to have butterflies now.

"Sorry I'm late. Captain Marcetti and I were chatting after an administrative meeting and he was quite interested in talking about you and your work for us. I lost track of time."

Captain Marcetti was at Harry's station. Had Harry had anything to do with that?

"I'm happy to wait, ma'am. Gave me plenty of time to overthink my time working here."

"Relax, Parsons. This isn't going to be contentious. In fact, Marcetti was trying to poach you. You've gotten yourself a bit of a reputation."

Natasha laughed. "I usually do."

Captain Gillette smiled. "I knew that when I hired you."

Natasha wondered what she'd heard. "You didn't know everything before you hired me."

"We talked about your family history at your review, Parsons. I don't care if you wipe your ass with hundred-dollar bills as long as you do good work, and I'm not unhappy with the work you're doing. Quite the opposite. I'd like to talk to you about the future of your position and the ride along clinician program."

Natasha took a deep breath. "This doesn't sound good. Shouldn't Tommy be here for this conversation?"

"You and Tommy are close." It wasn't a question.

Natasha wasn't sure how her poker face was holding up. "Something I learned pretty quickly around here is the importance of developing a good relationship with your partner. That's especially true for me since I'm unarmed and really rely on Tommy. It started out a little rocky, but we've made it work."

"You know, I chose to pair you with Tommy because I knew she'd give this assignment her full attention and care no matter her personal feelings about the program. She's so concerned with living up to the Finch name, she's stifling herself."

Natasha's insides knotted. "All she wants is to be a good cop."

Captain Gillette held up her hands. "Oh, don't get me wrong, she's an excellent officer, but you've been good for her. She's grown into herself when there's no playbook to consult or study."

Natasha had the urge to pull out her phone and ask Captain Gillette to repeat herself so she could record it and play it back for Tommy later. Especially the part about Tommy being an excellent officer.

"I think the program has benefitted from both our perspectives on cases and the trust that we've built. As I said, it was bumpy at the outset, but we both held on and saw the potential."

"Indeed you did. The program is why I asked to meet today."

Natasha squirmed in her chair. "Are you dropping the hammer on my position? Do I need to start looking for another job?"

Captain Gillette looked confused. "No. Of course not. I actually wanted to talk to you about how we can expand your role. The ride along clinician program has been a pet interest of mine for years, and there is real momentum to expand programs like ours now. Our city, our country is demanding change in the ways communities of color and vulnerable populations are policed. We have a role to play, so let's be part of the change."

Natasha thought about the current protests and calls to defund the police, about the gala for her sister-in-law's campaign. Would she be hesitating to attend if she were on the outside looking in instead of talking to her boss, Captain Gillette, sitting in the police station where she worked? It didn't really matter. She was sitting in the police station with her boss. There were a lot of ways to effect change.

"What did you have in mind?"

Captain Gillette's face lit up. "None of this is approved, so don't spread it around, but I've gotten enough nods and handshakes I think we can move forward with some plans. I know you get frustrated with the pace of things around here, so don't bang down the police chief's door if this takes a couple of months, okay?"

"I don't know what I may or may not be annoyed with yet, so I make no promises."

Captain Gillette cocked her head and smiled slowly. "I would expect nothing less. I'd like more clinicians, to start. But getting single clinicians into cars only helps that single officer. Your full station training was well received, but I think we can expand that aspect of your job."

Natasha nodded. More clinicians would help, but the captain was right. The officers themselves needed skills to handle what they encountered on their own, over and above what they already had.

"And Marcetti wants to set up his own program, modeled after ours. Do you know Harry Finch?"

"Tommy's sister? I've met her a couple of times."

"Well, according to Marcetti, she's been agitating for a ride along of her own."

"Are you sure he said Harry *Finch*?" Natasha shifted in her chair.

"Apparently, you've impressed the entire Finch family. Rumor has it Alice Finch has endorsed the ride along program as well."

Natasha ran her hand through her hair. "No pressure there."

Captain Gillette chuckled. "Her reputation is intimidating, but she's a very nice woman."

If only Captain Gillette knew.

"So how do I fit in to all of this since you don't want me banging on any doors to hurry things along? I have some ideas for a couple of additional station-wide trainings, if you're interested. I think some of our community partners might be best suited for a few I have in mind, too, if you're amenable to bringing in some outsiders to partner with."

Captain Gillette put her elbows on her desk and steepled her hands. She leaned forward. "I want you in charge of it all."

Natasha sat back. "What do you mean, exactly?"

"All the trainings, the ride along clinicians, the entire program. I want you at the top of the food chain. You and I are on the same page about how this can help the police department and the community. If you're running it, you can make sure everything put in place lines up with our vision."

"Does that mean I'm off the street?" Natasha was struggling to process. This wasn't how she thought this meeting was going to go.

"Probably. At the very least your time will be cut down, but you still might want to do some street training with other clinicians, show them how you do it. You, like me, would probably get intimately acquainted with your desk and chair. Think it over. I know it's a lot. You and Tommy are doing great work, but your skills can be spread around to greater effect. We can expand this and do even more."

Natasha stood up and took the captain's offered hand. "What happens if I say no?"

"I'm going to push for this with you at the helm or not, Natasha. If you say no, you and Tommy can continue doing the excellent work you've been doing and you can report to whoever is hired to do the job you should be doing."

Natasha stood up straight. "Yes, ma'am. I understand."

She left the captain's office, grabbed her work bag, and headed for the door. She pulled out her phone as she approached her car. Tommy or Kayla? She went back and forth before going with her heart and calling Tommy.

It only rang once before Tommy answered. "Hey, how was your meeting with the captain?"

Natasha heard people in the background. She remembered Tommy saying she was going to her parents' for dinner. "I forgot you were at your parents' house. We can talk about it tomorrow."

"Hang on." There was a long pause and then the background noise disappeared. "What's wrong?"

"Nothing. I didn't mean to bother you. The captain caught me off guard with an offer that didn't feel like an offer, but I don't have to decide anything tonight."

There was another long pause. "Nat, what aren't you telling me?"

It was the first time Tommy had used her nickname. She liked the way it sounded. Inexplicably, Natasha felt like she might cry.

"Tommy, it'll all keep until tomorrow. I didn't mean to call and worry you. I'm really fine."

"I know you're lying to me." Tommy's voice was soft. "Come over. Mama and Senior won't mind. It's just me tonight and they don't like an empty table. Don't say no, or I'll come find you."

All that was waiting for her was an empty house and leftovers for dinner. She longed to see Tommy.

"Nat, come over."

Natasha still hesitated but her rational self lost. "Okay. I'll be over soon. Maybe your mother can help sort through what the captain said."

Tommy was waiting for her on the porch. She pulled her into a hug as soon as Natasha was up the first step. "Are you okay? You sounded sad on the phone." Tommy held her out at arm's length and searched her face.

"Tommy, I'm fine. I should be happy. The captain wants to give me more responsibility and grow the program. But it felt overwhelming. I don't know what it means for our partnership and for us." She rested her head against Tommy's shoulder.

Natasha felt better. They'd talk through the captain's offer and figure it out together. No need to freak out.

"I'm a little embarrassed I worried you enough that you thought I needed a rescue." Natasha pushed some dirt around the porch with her shoe.

Tommy tilted her chin up so they were eye-to-eye. "Maybe I wanted the excuse to see you."

Natasha's chest filled with warmth. In another world she'd have already fallen in love with this wonderful woman. *Is that where I'm headed?* Tommy took her hand and she was content to follow wherever she led.

"Come in, dinner's almost ready. Mama will be happy to see you."

Alice was happy to see her. Senior was too. She wasn't used to being welcomed warmly and genuinely into a family home. Once again, she felt tears close to the surface. What was wrong with her tonight?

"Whatever it is, dear, that table has always been a good place to sort through quagmires, minefields, sticky situations, tough decisions, all manner of emotions, and forks in the road." Alice patted Natasha's cheek and pointed into the dining room.

Natasha nodded, not trusting her voice. Alice handed her a serving dish piled with potatoes and shooed her to the table. Natasha took the seat she'd had the last time she ate here. This time Tommy sat next to her. Senior raised an eyebrow but didn't say anything. Natasha wasn't sure of the significance of the seating arrangement.

"Tommy, how's work?"

Senior's question sounded like part of an opening soundtrack on a well-loved, long running television show. It was a familiar precursor to the good stuff to come.

"It's good. I know I've said it before, but I honestly didn't think I would feel so fulfilled by this work. I feel like I'm growing as an officer. I thought I'd need to become a detective to really stretch my wings, but I'm learning a lot right where I'm at. Natasha and I have been thinking of ways to expand her influence to give more officers at the station advanced skills when they're engaged with the community."

Alice and Senior looked pleased. "Promotions will come, Tommy, and breadth of experience and knowledge makes you a good leader. And what about you, Natasha? How's work?"

The question caught her off guard. It felt familial, as if she belonged at this table, being asked about her work. She wanted to belong here, which made her heart ache. She'd never belonged at any family table. Her family certainly didn't care about her work, or much else about her.

"I met with Captain Gillette today. She actually wants to expand the clinician ride along program, and help train other stations as well."

Alice scrutinized her. It made Natasha desperate to squirm, or hide under the table. How many powerful women, that she admired greatly, were going to stare her down today?

Natasha could see Tommy looking at her in her peripheral vision. "What would that mean for us?"

"If the captain gets her way, you lose me as a partner. I'm off the street. She wants me to oversee new clinician hires and plan and coordinate trainings for our station and Harry's, to start with." Natasha looked down at her plate.

"That sucks." Tommy said it quietly and put her fork down. She put her hands in her lap under the table. After a few beats of silence, Tommy reached out and found Natasha's hand.

"Why the long faces, you two?"

Natasha looked up. Alice was looking at them kindly.

"Promotions are always a cause for celebration at this table. I think we should toast this one heartily. Won't it solve the real problem you've been bumping up against?"

Natasha looked from Tommy to Alice to Senior. She wasn't fluent in Finch family undercurrents, dramatic pauses, and raised eyebrows.

Tommy was staring at her mother. Suddenly, her eyes went wide. "Mama, we haven't... We're not... I know my duty."

Senior folded his hands and fixed them both with a pointed look. "Tommy, service is built into this family's DNA. I know the job is important to both of you. But there is no job on this earth that is worth the risk of losing someone who can cut through all the noise, can understand you, and make you happy. Your mother and I aren't advocating throwing the rules out the window, but you can't hide from the world outside the job either."

"Both of you answer me honestly."

Alice leveled them with a stare that Natasha was sure would pull out all her inner truths.

"Natasha, in a moment of crisis out on the street, if Tommy were injured by someone you were evaluating, would you be an effective clinician to that individual or anyone else on that call? What about you, Tommy, if the situation was reversed?"

Natasha wanted to be able to say yes. She thought about the question and played multiple scenarios in her head. She didn't need the time she was buying herself. Her gut reaction was "fuck no" and she was sure with a million simulations the outcome would be the same.

"No, ma'am. If someone hurt Tommy, I'd say all bets are off."

Tommy looked a little queasy. "I don't want to think about that scenario, Mama."

"Exactly. All we're saying is don't hide behind the rules as a way to run from your feelings. And don't think that a literal interpretation of the regulations means you can't still be violating them. The answer appears to be right in front of you, assuming the promotion is something you want, Natasha."

"But, Mama—"

"Don't 'but, Mama' me, Tommy. I'm speaking as your mother, not anyone in your chain of command. You can't help who you fall for." Alice looked at Senior. They shared a smile years in the making.

"You certainly can't. Not advisable to try, either." Senior leaned over and kissed Alice's cheek.

"Does she make you happy, Tommy?"

Tommy looked at Natasha and smiled. She pulled their joined hands up from under the table and rested them on the tabletop in plain view of Alice and Senior. "Yes, Mama. She does."

Natasha tried to hide their joined hands, even if Alice and Senior knew, it still felt disrespectful to flaunt it, but Tommy held firm.

"And what about you, Natasha? Does Tommy make you happy?"

"Extremely happy, ma'am." Natasha hadn't taken her eyes off Tommy.

"Well then, as far as I'm concerned, let's toast to a brand-new day." Alice picked up her fork and returned to dinner.

"Fine with me." Natasha took another serving of green beans and resumed eating. It only felt seventy-two percent okay with her, but Alice Finch was giving it the green light, so who was she to argue? Especially at her dinner table?

"You're on board with this too?" Tommy looked like her head might explode.

"Why are you arguing so strenuously?" Natasha poked Tommy in the ribs.

"I'm not. It's just…" Tommy scrubbed her face. She looked like someone had just told her Santa wasn't real.

"Hey, look at me." Natasha ran her fingers up Tommy's forearm. She spoke quietly, but at the table with only the four of them, she knew Alice and Senior could hear them. "The ride along program, this thing between us, ignoring everything you believe in for some social worker you met at work, none of it has to be figured out tonight. I'm not going anywhere."

Tommy took a deep breath. Natasha could see her body relaxing. This morning, she had no idea how weird the day would be.

"I'm still not sure what's gotten into you two." Tommy was staring with a bewildered look at her parents. "But let's toast. Whether being with you is as easy as your taking the promotion, I don't know, but no one deserves the recognition more."

Alice looked at both of them with what Natasha could only describe as love. Her own mother had never looked at her like that. "You two keep trust in each other. It may take some time and patience, but from my vantage point, what you have is worth the wait."

After dinner, Alice brought out a cherry pie that was the best Natasha had ever tasted. Alice seemed delighted when Natasha told her as much. Being with Tommy, having permission to celebrate the promotion, surrounded by the Finch family, Natasha felt at peace.

"We'll clean up. You two go on out back. Sounds like Natasha has a lot to catch you up on." Alice shooed them out the door.

"I still think you both are nuts. I expect my parents back when we come inside."

They were followed out the door by Alice's and Senior's laughter.

The back deck felt intimate with only the two of them. Natasha hadn't noticed how magnificent the view was when she was last out here with Tommy and Harry. Alice and Senior lived along the river, and the setting sun reflecting off the water was so stunning Natasha wished she were an artist.

"I don't think I've ever seen anything so beautiful," Tommy said.

"I know, this sunset is spectacular." Natasha couldn't look away from the river.

"Sure, the sunset's nice too, but that's not what I'm talking about."

Natasha looked at Tommy this time. She was leaning with her back against the deck rail, hands in her pockets, and one foot crossed over the other. Natasha's breath hitched. She changed her mind. This was what she'd use artistic skills to capture.

"Harry's the one with the roguish reputation, but look at you baiting me."

Tommy looked taken aback.

"You're so damn sexy posing there for me. If I could capture you just like that, I'd take the picture home and hang it in my bedroom. Since I can't have the real thing. A picture on my phone won't do you justice, I'd need a painting."

Tommy's cheeks reddened. Natasha inched closer.

"What if my parents are right?"

"Of course they're right. They're your parents and want what's best for you. Your mom kindly pointed out we have a solution if I take the promotion."

Tommy reached out and traced along the side of Natasha's face. "What if I don't want to wait?"

Natasha straddled her legs and moved close so their bodies were nearly pressed together. "What are you saying, Tommy?"

Tommy rested her forehead against Natasha's and put her hands around her waist. Natasha wanted to melt into her touch and stop talking, but they couldn't do that.

"I'm saying, I barely noticed that sunset because you're all I could see. Things that make me happy or make me laugh are dulled when you're not there to share them, and when I'm at home at night, without you, I fight the urge to call to say good night and that I miss you."

"Tommy." Natasha pulled away a few inches and then stopped. Tommy wasn't holding her in place, and she didn't want to leave.

"Mama's right, if anyone laid a finger on you, I don't know what I'd do." Tommy pulled Natasha closer. "I can't believe she told us to ignore the rules she's drilled into me my whole life."

"That's not what she said. For someone as meticulous as you, you weren't listening all that closely."

"Probably because my parents suddenly lost their minds and the woman sitting next to me was very distracting."

Tommy leaned forward. Natasha wanted the kiss so badly she almost didn't stop Tommy before their lips met.

"Tommy, the next time I kiss you, I don't want to stop." Natasha stroked Tommy's cheek. "But while we're still partnered, and it's not going to be forever, I want to be able to look the captain in the eye and tell her sleeping together is a line we didn't cross. Maybe it's a stupid place to draw the line, but it's the one I'm drawing, especially since we've crossed all the other ones. And no matter what you're feeling now, I think you want that too."

Tommy tilted her head back and cursed under her breath. When she looked back at Natasha she had a lopsided grin on her face. "I want to argue with you, but you're right, as you usually are. So what do we do? Because you can't stay here but I can't make myself let you go."

"You don't have to let me go because I'm not going anywhere." Natasha took a deep breath. Her heart raced. "Tommy, I'm yours. You know that, right?"

Tommy looked surprised, then a wide grin spread across her face. "You tell me something like that right after you tell me I'm not allowed to kiss you? Heartless."

"Little reminder who steers our ship."

Tommy laughed. "As if there are any doubts."

Natasha kissed Tommy's cheek and moved out of her arms. She desperately wanted to stay, but the longer she was close to her, the more likely she was to lose her resolve. She leaned on the railing next to Tommy and stared at the river. Tommy settled next to her. Natasha scooted closer so you couldn't slip a playing card between them.

"I'm going to take the promotion."

"Nat, you didn't seem sure earlier. I know we were toasting and celebrating in there, but don't do it so this will work. We can find another way if it's not what you really want."

"I'm not doing it for us. I'm doing it for me. Well, a little for us too. Your mom was right, we're both compromised when we're together. I love being partnered with you, but we shouldn't be teamed up anymore. If we're not partnered, you and I don't have to feel guilty being together and you're free to finally take that detective exam I know you study for every spare minute you have. Besides, you aren't rid of me yet. The Captain said it's going to take a couple of months to get off the ground. Getting good ideas off the ground in the police department is like turning an aircraft carrier."

Tommy opened her mouth as if to argue, but shut it again. She looked resigned.

"Babe, it's okay. When I took this job, I wanted to see if this program was feasible and change some hearts and minds at the station. Not only is the program feasible, but I'll have the chance to grow its footprint to include another station and train the next crop of clinicians. It's an even better outcome than I could've imagined. We did that."

"No." Tommy shook her head and looked at her feet. "You did that."

"Officer Finch, look at me."

Tommy snapped upright and looked at Natasha. She thrilled at the response.

"Don't you undervalue what you've done. I'm not having it. Understand?"

"I hear you. But what if I do?"

Natasha leaned toward her.

Tommy looked expectant.

Natasha whispered in her ear. "Until you make detective I'll stick you with the clinician I know will make you the craziest. An opera fan maybe. Or someone who's just taken up bonsai and wants to discuss every detailed pruning."

"That would backfire on you, you know. Do you really want me getting off work every day that wound up?"

Natasha raised an eyebrow. "I wouldn't mind helping you unwind."

Tommy blushed. "Okay, so the promotion sounds good for you. Did the captain say what it means for me?"

"No, but tomorrow, first thing, we find out together, okay?"

Tommy nodded but looked conflicted. Natasha reached out and took her hand.

"We're bad at this." Tommy lifted their joined hands.

"Actually, I think we're pretty good."

"Tell that to the captain when she busts our asses."

"I will." Natasha winked. "I'm not going to the gala my parents are throwing either."

Tommy squeezed her hand. "Why not? Didn't they threaten you?"

Natasha sighed. "I care too much about everyone at our station. Can you imagine Lieutenant Smith's face the morning after the gala when I'm quoted supporting defunding the police? Because that's how it's going to be spun, no matter what I actually say."

"I know you explained it to me, but I don't understand why they need you to be there at all. Who cares that you work for the police and are doing the work you're doing? Isn't it in line with what they want?"

Natasha stared out at the river. She felt the weight of deep family wounds descend. "Valencia, my sister-in-law, actually cares about the issues on her platform. My brother probably thinks he does, but his wife has brought him a long way in his thinking. My parents don't believe any of it. They don't have opinions on anything except what will help them the most."

Tommy wrapped her hand around Natasha's waist and pulled her close. "How do you fit in?"

"My parents have crafted a public relations campaign strategy to help get Valencia elected. I'm sure they've paid a lot of money to test a winning strategy. The message needs to be tightly controlled and I'm the out-of-control outlier. They need to rein me back in."

"Your outlier tendencies are some of my favorite things about you. I wish I could do something about your parents. They kind of suck. What about your sister-in-law? Is she going to get screwed if you don't go?"

Natasha paused. She didn't often stop to think about what Valencia must feel like having married into the Blackstone family. She made the choice to join up, after all.

"I don't know, actually. I think I can make sure everyone knows I support her without stepping into a ball gown."

Tommy raised an eyebrow. "Maybe for me sometime? This is probably none of my business, but do you still get money from your Blackstone side? Will your parents cut you off if you piss in their Cheerios?"

"I don't have secrets from you, Tommy. Well, not anymore." She quickly amended when Tommy gave her a look. "I am sorry I didn't tell you about my parents, but look at all the trouble they cause once you know about them. But no, they can't cut me off. Once I turned eighteen I gained control of my trust. They can't touch it."

"You said a bunch of words there, but strung together like that, they really don't mean anything to me."

"That's okay, I'd rather you tell me more about some of those favorite things you mentioned." Natasha turned and smiled at Tommy.

"Something for you to look forward to. A few of them aren't things I should share with my partner. You know what I can't stop thinking about, though, besides you of course? My parents were so enthusiastic in there about us and our being together, no matter what rules we'd be breaking. Why is that? If we get caught, will Mama call in some favors and everything will be fine?"

Natasha leaned her head on Tommy's shoulder. "Hey, no. No way. There are surely officers in the department who would welcome nepotism on that scale, but think about Alice Finch for a moment. Would *she* ever pick up the phone to make those calls?"

Tommy shook her head. "When you put it like that, it does seem ridiculous to even consider."

"No, it's not. My parents made those kinds of calls all the time to clear the way for my brother, for me, I'm ashamed to admit. Preston got in trouble a few times as a teenager, 'youthful indiscretion' my parents called it. One phone call cleared it right up. He doesn't have a record. Your mom is nothing like my parents."

Tommy looked relieved. Then she frowned. "Okay, here's another thing kicking around my brain. Before you, my life as a cop made sense. Then you jumbled it all up. But you put it back together better than it was before, and I liked being that kind of cop. But without you everything changes again. I might not get another clinician partner. Maybe I don't want one, if it's not you. Maybe I'm a detective and you've ruined me because the world doesn't look the same anymore."

"Tommy, that's the point. But let's take this one step at a time, okay? Tomorrow we talk to the captain. It's her call anyway right? But I'm sure she'll listen to what you want."

Tommy took a deep breath. "All right. You know, I didn't need so much hand-holding before you came along."

"I didn't realize hand-holding was such a bad thing." Natasha pulled her hand away from Tommy and jumped out of reach.

Tommy chased after her and caught her around the waist. She spun her into her arms. They were inches away from each other. Natasha could feel Tommy's breath on her cheek. Tommy had one hand on her lower back, the other woven in her hair.

They looked at each other and the world seemed to recede. Natasha was happy to stay here, in Tommy's arms, until the world needed them again in the morning.

Tommy pulled away. "I can't be this close to you without short-circuiting my gentlemanly instincts. If we're going to present ourselves to the captain in the morning with what's left of our clean conscience, I think we should head back in."

Natasha said good night shortly after they went back inside. Before she fell asleep that night, her mind was filled with thoughts of Tommy, the job, and the possible future with both. She rolled over and stared at the empty space next to her in bed. She pictured Tommy there.

Heat shot between her legs. She moved her hand down and covered herself. It wouldn't take much after so much buildup on the deck. She rolled over and removed her hand. Tommy was worth the wait.

CHAPTER TWENTY-THREE

Tommy pushed through the doors to the station feeling the lack of a Broadway chorus and full ensemble. If she had them, and today would be a perfect day for them to come on board, they'd be singing and dancing every up-tempo show tune ever written. Tommy couldn't wait for her shift to start.

Technically, Natasha's promotion was still pending and they remained partners, but in reality their new way of life at the station had already begun. Although Natasha was largely riding a desk and up to her eyeballs in paperwork, logistics, and phone calls, she still rode with Tommy at least once a week. Natasha had sold it to the captain as a way to not lose the momentum in the community, and as a way to introduce new clinicians to their community contacts. Tommy was happy to be close to her all day, and she'd also grown accustomed to their new schedule.

What was making both Tommy and Natasha crazy was the wait. Although it felt like they were partners in name only, neither one of them thought their superiors would see it that way if they were openly crazy for each other. They'd waited this long, but it was starting to feel like the last week before summer vacation.

Today, however, was one of the days Natasha was riding with Tommy, thus the need for backup dancers. Harry had threatened her with bodily harm when she'd mentioned her tap shoes, so Tommy was left to celebrate quietly, sans chorus. But internally, she was center stage hitting a glory note the minute she set foot in the station.

"What took you so long to get here? I almost left without you." Natasha was half sitting on her desk with her legs crossed at the ankles.

She was wearing the pants that drove Tommy crazy. Tommy could tell from the look on Natasha's face that she'd worn them for that purpose.

"I have the car and the keys, smart-ass." Tommy swung the keys from her index finger.

"Trouble has a way of finding me. I'm sure I could've kept myself busy."

Tommy shuddered. She didn't want to think of the trouble Natasha could get into by herself. Not that she couldn't handle herself, but Tommy preferred to be there watching her back. She tried, and failed, to stop watching Nat's ass as they walked to the car.

"I saw you were busy last night. Were your parents satisfied?"

Natasha had, as she said she would, declined her command performance at the family gala. Instead, she'd made an appearance on the local news and stumped for her sister-in-law. She'd also pointed out the merits of their ride along program, which might not have been in the official Blackstone family script.

The clip had aired the night before, and Tommy had been mesmerized watching Natasha. She'd been everything Tommy knew her to be, but somehow extra. The reporter seemed enamored with her as well and hung on her every word. Tommy wondered if this was the power and influence Natasha had tried to explain.

"My parents are never satisfied, but hopefully it will be good enough. It's all they're going to get."

"I'm going to miss this once it's gone for good." Tommy pulled the car away from the station.

Natasha stared out the window looking contemplative. "I don't like thinking of someone else filling this seat in your car."

"Jealous?" Tommy's heart raced at the thought.

"Territorial."

Natasha's look was possessive. Tommy liked it quite a bit.

"Any luck filling that seat?" Tommy felt like she choked on the words as they came out.

Natasha tilted her head slightly. "A few promising leads. I'll know more once we check references. Might be able to fill the spot at Harry's station too. Which reminds me, did you threaten your sister with her old tap shoes this morning?"

"I knew Harry being your point of contact over at her station was going to bite me in the ass."

Tommy was ready to explain further when a call came through the radio. It wasn't a "Natasha call," but they were the closest available to respond. The call was about an infant in distress. Tommy turned on lights and sirens, flipped a U-turn, and sped back in the direction they came.

"When we get there, stay in the car. Please, Natasha. I'm not going to be able to clear the scene if the baby's in trouble." Tommy was running through every scenario she could think of that she might encounter. The caller hadn't been specific.

"Tommy, I might be able to help calm the parents."

She looked at Natasha. Adults were one thing. A baby in distress was something else. Natasha was right, she might be able to help.

"At least wait until we see what we're walking into, okay? And if it's *at all* dangerous, I don't care how helpful you could be. I won't be able to do my job if you're in the line of fire."

"But I'm supposed to watch you in trouble buckled in safely here in the patrol car?"

They didn't get a chance to finish the argument. Tommy pulled to the curb and jumped from the car. As soon as she pulled up, the door opened and three adults rushed at her. She tensed until she saw one was carrying an infant and all were yelling not in anger, but distress.

"Okay, slow down. Something's wrong with the baby?" Tommy focused on the woman holding the infant.

More chaotic shouting followed.

"He's not breathing? He choked on something? Okay, give me the baby." Tommy slowed her breathing.

She took the baby with steady hands. He was tiny in her arms. He followed her with his eyes and she repositioned her grip. That was a good sign.

"I'm going to try to clear his airway." Tommy supported the baby's neck and head and flipped him so his belly rested along her forearm and he faced the ground. She tilted his body so his head was lower than his body and rested her arm on her thigh.

The three adults wailed. One tried to pull the baby from her arms.

"No, I need to get him breathing again. I know you're scared." Tommy took a step back.

"Do what you need to do, Tommy." Natasha stepped between her and the group of terrified adults.

Tommy delivered a series of quick back blows between his shoulder blades with the heel of her hand. When he didn't begin crying or resume breathing, she flipped him to the other arm, facing up.

Fear crept up Tommy's spine. She knew an ambulance was on the way, but right now, this child's life was hers to save.

"Come on, little guy." Tommy placed two fingers in the center of his chest and compressed.

On the second chest thrust, the baby screwed his face in displeasure and screamed. Tommy got a finger quickly in his mouth and swept for any remnants of what had just been dislodged. She couldn't tell what had been stuck, some sticky, gooey food of some sort, but it was out now, thankfully. As soon as she was satisfied his mouth was clear, she stepped forward and returned him to his family.

The moment the baby was out of her arms, she felt the adrenaline sweep through her, threatening to send her into jittery overdrive. She still had work to do, but for a moment, she wasn't able to make her body follow any command.

"It's done now. You saved him. Take a couple of deep breaths." Natasha moved close to her and spoke quietly.

Tommy nodded. She looked at Natasha and got lost in her smile. That was her beacon home from any dark night.

"Thank you. I'm all right now."

The ambulance arrived and Tommy explained the situation to the paramedics. All three adults with the baby filled in the details.

Once the family was squared away with the paramedics and the parents had thanked Tommy for the fiftieth time, she and Natasha left the scene. Tommy still felt shaken, but some calls hit harder than others. And there was another possible outcome she was glad she ⸱⸱⸱ ⸱⸱ ⸱ ⸱⸱⸱ to grapple with.

"God, Tommy, you just saved a baby's life. Most people would take a week off and get fifteen minutes of fame. You're finishing your shift."

Tommy waved her hand dismissively. "*We're* finishing our shift. And don't downplay what you did. I'm not exactly sure what it was, but I know you helped keep the parents calm enough that I could work."

"That felt like the easy part."

"Now you know how I feel when I stand around looking pretty while you do your social worker thing all over the city." Tommy flashed her most charming smile.

"Do you think Captain Gillette and Lieutenant Smith will reassign you to be my personal desk ornament? I'll pose you all day so I have something sexy to look at while I work."

Tommy almost spit out the sip of water she'd taken. "I'm sure you having sexy things to look at during your workday is right at the top of Lieutenant Smith's priority list."

"Maybe if I tell her what a great—"

Natasha was cut off by the dispatcher. Tommy responded and steered them toward their next call. Tommy missed the daily patrol with Natasha. They had chemistry. It was probably why Tommy was crazy about her. As much as she missed Natasha at work, the carrot of finally spending non-work hours with her, not skulking in the shadows, but free to be together, was worth this particular loss. Only a few more weeks and they could forget rules and regulation and focus on dinner dates and bedtime kisses. Natasha was the first thing more important to her than work. It was terrifying and exhilarating.

As their shift neared its end, Tommy's cell rang from an unknown number. She ignored it. Her phone rang again. When she didn't pick up, it rang again. Finally, a text came through.

Answer your damn phone, Officer Finch. Zoo.

She pulled over and accepted the call on the first ring. Natasha looked at her questioningly. Tommy shrugged. No point trying to speculate what the Zookeeper might be after.

"Officer, I need to turn myself in, but I don't want to walk up to the first officer I see. No offense, but I don't trust the reception I'll get with just anyone."

"What are you talking about?" This wasn't good. Zoo wasn't into histrionics, and she sounded far too serious.

"I fucked up and I need to make amends for that. It's time I grew a pair and made the changes I need to make for myself." The Zookeeper sounded sad.

"I thought jail was one of your most lucrative markets. What makes you think you can get clean there?"

"Officer Finch, are we going to talk business, or are you going to help me? I'm in the park near the library. That's your sister's territory, correct?"

Harry was either going to love or hate her. "Yes. I'll have her meet you in front of the library. Why is she arresting you, exactly?"

The Zookeeper explained her situation. Tommy's stomach knotted. Natasha wasn't going to be happy.

Tommy stepped out of the car and called her sister. She filled her in and asked her to meet the Zookeeper. Harry seemed more than happy to arrest one of the most well-known drug dealers in the city. Parrot Master and the Zookeeper had always been Teflon when it came to law enforcement. Probably because the Zookeeper was a lawyer.

Natasha looked at Tommy curiously when she slipped back in the car. "Did you get promoted to James Bond? What's with all the secrecy?"

Tommy sighed and wanted to drop her head to the steering wheel. She started the car and drove back to the station instead. "International espionage would be more fun. I called Harry and asked her to go arrest the Zookeeper."

"You what?"

"She asked me to. That's who called. She was high and needed money to keep withdrawal at bay. She robbed an electronics store. She knows she's on the store's surveillance footage, but I get the feeling she'd be turning herself in even if she wasn't."

"Tommy, jail isn't the place for her to get help."

Natasha looked angry, as Tommy knew she would be.

"She committed a crime, Natasha. She confessed and asked to be arrested. She's the unicorn of criminals. This is straight up burglary, Nat. Not the shades of gray of someone in crisis."

Their argument continued after they returned to the station. It got heated when they reached Natasha's desk. Tommy was aware they had caught the attention of most of the station, but they were too far in to back down now.

"She was high and looking to stave off withdrawal. Do you know what withdrawal looks like? How bad it is? How are those *not* shades of gray?" Natasha leaned against her desk and crossed her arms.

"If you go to holding, everyone down there will come up with a special circumstance that made them do what they did. Why does this get consideration when theirs don't?" Tommy waved back over her shoulder toward the door to the holding cells.

"You know why, Tommy. Addiction and mental illness are diseases. This isn't some idiot who got mad over a spilled drink in a bar. And what about the Zookeeper's flock now? She asked us to help them."

"She also asked to be arrested." Tommy refused to look away.

Lieutenant Smith came over and Tommy realized they could have handled this a little more quietly.

"Explain to me why you two are yelling at each other in the middle of the station?" Lieutenant Smith crossed her arms.

"Professional difference of opinion." Tommy avoided looking at Natasha.

"Are you sure? Sounded personal to me."

"It is personal." Natasha roughly smoothed her pristine shirt.

"Natasha—" Tommy's heart rate kicked up to high intensity cardio level.

"Whether a woman gets sent to jail or has the opportunity for drug treatment *is* personal to me."

Lieutenant Smith appraised both of them for an uncomfortably long time.

"I'm surprised it took you two so long to get here. Walk me through it."

Tommy wasn't sure where they were or if the lieutenant was happy they'd arrived, but she could regurgitate the facts of her call with the Zookeeper. So she did.

"I saw the police report for larceny at Gregorian Electronics. The Zookeeper was named as the suspect by the owner."

Inexplicably, the confirmation of the Zookeeper's story made Tommy sad. It would've been easy to blame the new emotions on Natasha and her forcing Tommy to soften, but that would be shifting ownership where it didn't belong. Tommy had begun caring about the Zookeeper all on her own and it was annoying as hell. What was the Zookeeper thinking? If her addiction had more fully consumed her, she probably wasn't thinking. Tommy thought of the women in her flock. Hopefully, the plan B the Zookeeper had mentioned was in place because their benefactor was about to be unavailable.

"I'm not discounting the seriousness of the Zookeeper's actions or the real impact on Gregorian Electronics." Natasha kicked her desk chair out and offered it to Lieutenant Smith. "But there is a flip side to this coin, even if it's uncomfortable to look at. The Zookeeper is struggling with substance use and would be better served in treatment than jail."

"She committed a crime." Tommy grabbed a chair from another desk.

"Frank punched you in the face, Tommy. He went to the hospital, not jail. Sean broke a window at this station with a pipe. No jail. Taylor's friend told me she trades sex for drugs or money when she can't make ends meet. Again, no jail. So what's different this time?" Natasha was glaring at Tommy and Lieutenant Smith.

"There was no victim in those other cases, Natasha. If someone breaks into a store, the owner has a right to expect the perpetrator is punished."

"Sean was in very real danger of being shot to death. If there was no victim, that would make his death murder. So explain to me again, why it was okay for him to end up in the hospital, or the morgue, rather than jail?"

Natasha's foot was tapping and she was drumming her fingers. Although she was doing a fairly good job of controlling her temper, Tommy could tell how close to the surface her fury was.

"And do you really think Mr. Gregorian's Electronics would want the book thrown at a desperate woman in the throes of addiction? Or would there be room for another solution that satisfied everyone? Are you treating this differently because the person Harry arrested is the

Zookeeper? How much more evidence do we need that criminalizing drug use isn't effective?"

Tommy loved watching fired up Natasha. She loved her passion and commitment. It would be more enjoyable to watch if she wasn't the focus of Natasha's ire.

"She's not a desperate woman. She's not a random substance user. She's the Zookeeper and she turned herself in to both Officer Finches. If she chooses, she can seek a drug diversionary program through the court system." Lieutenant Smith stood. "She didn't turn to a rehab, Parsons, even though she knew it was an option. She committed a burglary and then called a cop because she knew she'd done something wrong."

"You just proved my point." Natasha looked like she was going to say more.

Tommy reached out to get Natasha's attention and tell her to give up the fight. She meant to tap her arm, but ended up grabbing her hand. She cringed when she saw Lieutenant Smith staring at their joined hands. Natasha seemed to see it too. She pulled her hand away quickly.

They were saved explaining the awkwardness of the moment by Captain Gillette summoning them to her office.

"Finch, Parsons, in here, now."

Tommy had an uneasy feeling. Captain Gillette closed the door behind them.

"Don't sit. This shouldn't take long."

Tommy stole a glance at Natasha. She looked angry. Angry and sad. Did she know what was going on?

"You two have one chance to tell me what the hell's going on here." Captain Gillette pointed from Natasha to Tommy.

"I'm not sure what you mean, ma'am." Tommy stood at attention. She saw Natasha give it a good shot next to her.

"Officer Finch, you were out there yelling at your partner. She expected you to allow a criminal to go free because she asked nicely and you were just holding hands in the middle of my station."

Tommy's stomach dropped. "Ma'am, I think you have the wrong idea."

Now she's done it. Tommy tried to catch Natasha's eye, to calm her down, but that train had already thundered through the station.

"All due respect, ma'am, but what you overheard was a *professional* disagreement between partners, not some lovers' quarrel. And I'm pretty sure you've had other partners here have a tiff or two as well. And I wasn't asking Tommy to let a criminal go free because I was asking *nicely*, as you put it. I was providing my opinion as a social worker and questioning the thinking behind an arrest decision. Something you're paying me to do. But if everyone's just going to ignore my advice, then why am I here?"

Captain Gillette looked taken aback.

"As for what's happening here." Natasha pointed between herself and Tommy "We have done and continue to do the job you've charged us with. We've demonstrated the feasibility of a program that I know you care about deeply. Over strenuous objections and skepticism within the station and outside it. And now we're taking it even further, and it's going to be amazing. And Tommy wasn't holding my hand. She was warning me to shut up. Advice I'm finally going to listen to."

Tommy was feeling all kinds of things in all sorts of places watching Natasha go to bat for them, but this was their boss she was dressing down.

"Care to add anything, Officer Finch?" Captain Gillette looked like Natasha had chased any remnants of good mood that might have been hanging around right out the door.

"No, ma'am. I agree with Natasha's description of our work together. I'm proud of what we've accomplished. And I don't think everyone can agree all the time."

The captain nodded. "Glad you enjoyed it. Might be the last time either one of you does anything enjoyable in this department again. What the hell were you two thinking?"

She pulled an envelope from her top desk drawer and emptied the contents onto her desk. Tommy figured the blood probably drained so quickly from her face it was leaking out her shoes. Spread across the desk in eight by ten glory were close-up photos of her and Natasha holding each other, walking hand in hand, and kissing.

"Fucking paparazzi. I'm going to kill them." Natasha looked furious. "Tommy didn't have anything to do with this, ma'am. This is my parents doing and they're coming after me."

"She looks pretty involved from where I'm standing."

Tommy couldn't stop looking at the pictures on the captain's desk. The pictures that would likely torpedo the career she'd been meticulously plotting as long as she could remember.

Captain Gillette gave Tommy a look that felt like it burned through her. "Finch, I expected better from you. I expected your career and the job to mean enough to you to take the rules seriously."

"It does, ma'am. It means almost everything to me." Tommy snuck a look Natasha's way.

Natasha reached out and squeezed her hand. Captain Gillette raised an eyebrow.

"I was going to stop at offering Tommy quick comfort, but I can invite her to sit on my lap if my parents didn't give you enough ammunition to fire me." Natasha lifted her chin, clearly unwilling to back down.

Captain Gillette laughed. Tommy wasn't expecting that. Natasha looked surprised as well.

"God, do you know how much easier my life would be if you'd just followed the rules or done all of this indoors?" Captain Gillette picked up a couple of pictures, waved them in their direction, and then threw them back on the desk.

"Yes, ma'am," Tommy and Natasha said in unison.

"I'm getting a lot of pressure to fire both of you and I was pissed enough to consider it. But you have some powerful allies in the department after the work you've done over the past nearly, what? Eighteen months?"

It almost sounded like the captain was ready to offer them a lifeline, but Tommy wasn't ready to hope. If it was snatched away it would be worse than the initial blow.

"Powerful enough to go toe to toe with the Blackstones?" Natasha looked skeptical.

"Parsons, if you want to keep this job, it might be time you remembered what last name you were born with. There are Blackstones on both sides of this power struggle, and if the name carries as much weight as you seem to think, put it to use."

"What do you want me to do, Captain?"

"I don't know, Natasha. Unfuck this mess you two made. These photos came with some financial incentive to send you both out the door, but like I said, you've made powerful friends of your own. Until the brawl happening way above my pay grade is settled, you can't be partnered and I have to reassign both of you." Captain Gillette looked at the photos again and shook her head before shoving them all back in the envelope.

"Reassign us where?" Tommy resisted the urge to wipe the sweat bead off her brow.

"You're out of the ride along program altogether, Finch. You're with Pete, you report to him. Natasha, I can't send you back to traffic duty and you're already riding a desk, so I made the case that a demotion meant going back on patrol and field training one of our junior officers. Natasha, you're back on patrol five days a week with Justin. You're lucky neither of you is looking for a new job."

"Justin will get her killed." Tommy felt like she might explode. She didn't want to lose Natasha. She couldn't imagine anyone but her watching her back. Natasha's safety was more important than her job, her career plan, those stupid photos, anything.

"Justin is green, but he'll be fine. Anything else?" Captain Gillette was dismissing them.

Tommy wanted to get out of the captain's office as quickly as possible. She felt like she'd let down her family name. Shame ate at her, making her ill. So much for making detective. She should reschedule the exam she'd been studying months for. No point taking it now.

They made it out the door before Natasha grabbed her arm and stopped her.

"Tommy, I'm going to fix this. You shouldn't be punished because of me."

Tommy's heart broke. She didn't want Natasha to think this was her fault. But they couldn't continue the conversation here, either.

"I knew what the risks were. This isn't your fault. Can we talk about this later?"

Tommy didn't expect the look of hurt on Natasha's face. It was fleeting. Natasha was professional and they were still at work, but Tommy saw it. She felt like an ass.

"I'll see you tomorrow, Tommy. Congratulations on your big prize today."

Ouch. Tommy wanted to run after Natasha and…she wasn't sure what she'd ask for when she got to her. A smile, a reset button, a hug, anything to make the uncomfortable feeling in her gut go away. How had the day that she'd been so excited to begin end up being one that would never end?

She packed up and headed out the door. She called Harry as she drove home, and they met at their parents' house for dinner. Before they went inside, Tommy pulled Harry up short and unloaded the last hour. She wasn't ready to share it with the rest of the family.

At the end of her monologue, Harry laughed. "I have zero experience with relationships, but pissed off women are a specialty of mine. Sounds like she's hurt. You rejected her twice. First, professionally by locking up the Zookeeper over her protest, then personally. I bet that stings."

Tommy thought back. "I didn't reject her personally."

"Sure you did. She wanted to tell you things were going to be okay, that she has your back, and you shot her down. You blew her off. On the heels of the Zookeeper thing, I bet that felt like shit." Harry bounded up the stairs. "You coming in? I'm starving and my captain's thrilled with me. I'm looking forward to being the one with good news and you having the lady troubles. Our parents won't know what hit them."

"Should I wait until dessert to tell them my career is fucked?"

Harry either didn't hear or ignored her.

Tommy plodded up the stairs after her. She didn't have lady troubles. She and Natasha had a rough day. If they couldn't withstand this, the relationship was doomed before it began.

She considered Natasha's perspective on the Zookeeper. Was Tommy set on arrest and jail time because of the Zookeeper's profession? She didn't think so, but it was hard to say for sure. That bothered her. Wasn't that what Natasha had been trying to do at the station, change the way they reacted to those with substance use and mental illness? Change their assumptions and biases?

The Zookeeper case still felt solid. It was burglary, regardless of motive. She was confident it was the right decision. The rest, she wasn't sure. Was her career effectively over? Natasha said she was going to fix it. Why hadn't she said she'd do the same for Natasha? They'd played an equal part getting into this mess. She needed to step up to the plate and do her part to get them out of it.

She opened the door to her parents' house, took one step inside, and knew this wasn't where she belonged tonight. She yelled her apologies to the family, turned, and ran down the steps. She had somewhere else to be.

Chapter Twenty-four

Natasha stomped around her kitchen. She tried to slam a cabinet door and then cursed when the force of her anger was tempered by the no slam, gentle close technology. She considered calling Kayla, but there was no reason to subject anyone else to her bad mood. Kayla wouldn't mind, but grumping to her wasn't going to steer her dinghy out of the shit storm it was sailing through.

She replayed the meeting with Captain Gillette. She tried slamming another cabinet after she pulled out a wine glass. No luck. Why had she paid extra for no slam cabinets? She'd have to get an old one just to keep around for moments like this.

She picked up her phone and tapped it on her chin trying to decide if calling Preston and Valencia was stupid. She didn't care if it was. She dialed.

"Tash, hey, you never call. Everything okay?" Preston sounded worried.

Natasha hated the nickname her brother had given her as a kid, but he'd been the only one who seemed to care enough to come up with a term of endearment. Preston got Valencia when Natasha asked, which she knew probably ratcheted up his anxiety.

"Did you two know?" No point making small talk none of them cared about.

There was a long pause.

"Know what, Natasha?" Valencia sounded confused.

Natasha looked at her traitorous cabinets and thought about kicking them to vent some frustration. "The gala, the threat, the photos, the torpedo aimed at my career, fucking over my partner as collateral damage?"

The silence stretched on longer this time.

Finally, Preston sighed. "Tash, we don't know what you're talking about, but it doesn't sound good. Can we help?"

"Sweetheart, you know she hates when you call her that, right?" Valencia's tone was businesslike as always, but the edges were softened tonight.

"Really?"

"Preston, you're an idiot sometimes. You guys really don't know anything about the photos that ended up on my captain's desk this afternoon and nearly got me fired?" It would be easier to interrogate them if she could see their faces. She should've insisted on a video call.

"Natasha, the work you're doing is amazing. Wouldn't it be hypocritical of me if I tried to get you fired for doing the kind of work I'm advocating for during my campaign? I want to defund the police to force them to clean up their houses, but having you and your program in-house is doing exactly that. I can point to it as something being done right and the way forward."

Now Natasha was the one stunned into silence. "According to Mother, I'm a liability to your campaign."

"Preston, this is getting out of hand. You have to talk to your mother."

"Val, I know they're a little intense, but they did extensive focus group interviewing and issues polling. That's why it's important to stick with the message and make sure everyone is on the same page."

"No matter the collateral damage?" Natasha pulled her phone away from her ear and silently screamed at it. Maybe it was good it wasn't a video call after all.

"No, collateral damage isn't okay with me. Your career and the career of your partner is too high a cost to pay. This is why we're losing, Preston, everyone's been told what to say, so there's no heart behind it. Why should voters care if we don't?" Valencia sounded more heated than Natasha had ever heard her.

"Whoa, let's all take a breath here." Preston sounded like their father. He was about to impart some "wisdom." "We need to stick with the campaign roadmap until after the election. Tash, you need to come on board, this is family. Then, after Valencia is elected, there will be plenty of time to debate each of your proposed avenues for police reform."

"Preston, I've had a long day, so do me a favor and slap yourself in the face and consider it sent with love from your sister. I don't have the energy to come over there and do it myself."

"What's the issue?"

Natasha ground her teeth. "You're a rich white guy, you have all the time in the world to sit and debate the merits of anything you want until your wingback shapes your ass in its image. The folks I work with don't have the luxury of time. The streets are often life or death, and if I can be the thing between those two options, I'm going to continue to step in and tip the scales as often as I can. I just want to know that my dear family isn't trying to sabotage me."

Valencia laughed. "I wish you could see the look on your brother's face. Whatever you need, Natasha, we're behind you. Whatever those photos contained, we had nothing to do with them. I want to win this election, but not at your expense."

There were as few banal pleasantries at the end of the call as the beginning. Natasha didn't care, she'd gotten what she needed. She felt better knowing Preston and Valencia hadn't been involved. They were the family she was closest to liking.

Her parents were a different beast entirely. She'd always known they'd do whatever necessary to get what they wanted, but until now, had held out hope that "whatever necessary" didn't include screwing her. Or Tommy.

They'd had no regard for the collateral damage in their quest to bring her back into the fold, and there was no doubt in her mind they were behind the photos. The paparazzi hadn't bothered her for ages, and after the initial outing of her working for the police, they'd moved on pretty quickly. The captain was right, if she was willing to let her, Natasha Blackstone could be a powerful ally. She needed to make things right whatever the cost. She couldn't let Tommy's dreams die by a hostile power grab.

She kicked off her shoes and took a sip of wine. The day really had ended on a shit note, but the middle hadn't been great either. She still felt strongly the Zookeeper was being arrested for the totality of her wrongs against society, not the current moment of law-breaking. She'd never argue the Zookeeper was an upstanding citizen, or even that the city wouldn't be better if she and Parrot Master were put out of business. But drug ecosystems were delicate, and if Parrot Master and the Zookeeper disappeared, someone else would fill the vacancy, for better or worse.

Based on the circumstances and the Zookeeper's current substance use, Natasha didn't think the criminal justice system was the best place for her, but Tommy was right, she'd committed a fairly straightforward crime. If she went looking, she could argue circumstances stacked against a lot of folks to make crime seem like the only option, but that's not how the criminal justice system worked.

Natasha leaned her head against the back of the couch and fought off tears. Damn it, Tommy. How were they going to fix this? When she'd tried to bring it up, Tommy had blown her off. That was what had really stung.

She was starting to lean into a good wallow when there was a knock at the door. She looked at her watch as if the time of day would explain the knock. No one knocked at any hour unannounced, let alone at night. She ignored it.

Her phone buzzed. She checked the text. It was from Tommy. "Knock knock."

Natasha got up and opened the door a crack. Tommy was standing on her front porch.

"I'm not home." Natasha didn't close the door.

"Okay. Well, I brought pizza in case you're hungry when you get back. Do you think you'll mind if I sit on the porch and wait for you?" Tommy held up the pizza box, looking hopeful.

"I probably will mind. It'll go gloopy. Are you planning on leaving, or waiting all night?"

Tommy held up the food again. "I have food and an empty bladder. I'll wait as long as I need for you to get home. I just want to talk."

Natasha opened the door the rest of the way and waved Tommy in. "The neighbors will start to talk. What do you want, Tommy? Feels like you didn't say most of what you needed to earlier."

Tommy hung her head. "I'm sorry, Nat. I'm sorry for the way things ended up earlier. I got a little blindsided with my own side in this and didn't think enough about how fucked up it is that your parents did what they did."

Natasha took the pizza and got plates. She didn't realize she was hungry until she smelled the food and her stomach growled loudly. She saw Tommy smile.

"Don't apologize for the Zookeeper. We knew there was going to be a point where we disagreed professionally. We did, the lieutenant made the call, it's done. I don't have to like the decision, but I don't expect you to side with me just because we have this thing between us. And believe it or not, I respect your position. There's no easy answer."

Tommy smiled and took the plate Natasha handed her. "For what it's worth, you did make me reconsider my bias when it comes to the Zookeeper. I can't guarantee I'm not lumping everything she's done to this city under one burglary charge in my mind, and that's not fair. As you pointed out, I didn't do that with other folks we interacted with."

"Although it's done all the time." Natasha walked to the couch and motioned Tommy to follow her. "People are prejudged and tried based on all kinds of factors, right? Skin color, criminal history, substance use, any combination of those."

Tommy nodded. "There are a lot of ways to be a bad cop. It takes work to be a good one. I'm glad you joined the station for so many reasons, but even if I set the personal aside, you made me a much better cop."

Natasha pushed her pizza aside. "I'll be better at my job every time we have those kinds of arguments too. I browbeat you all for being too rigid in your thinking, but forget to look in the mirror, from time to time."

"What a mistake. You're missing quite a sight." Tommy traced a line along Natasha's cheek.

"I'm not sure I want you to be charming me. I want you lean and mean and spoiling for a fight. Are you ready for what's ahead?"

"I'm not sure. Am I? What are we getting ourselves into? Gladiatorial combat?" Tommy was laughing.

"Now I'm picturing you in an outfit that's very distracting."

"I guess it's payback for torturing me today by wearing the pants you know get me riled up." Tommy reached out but didn't actually touch her.

"It's okay to want me."

Tommy put her food down and leaned back dramatically against the couch. "You make it impossible not to. How you don't have women lined up outside your windows each night reciting poetry and singing you love songs is beyond me."

"Who says I don't? I chased away five right before you got here." Natasha stifled a laugh when Tommy glanced at the windows facing the street. "So where do we go from here, Tommy?"

"I want you. All of you." Tommy reached for her and caressed her face. "But believe it or not, that's not why I came over tonight. Or it is, but not in the hop in bed naked sort of way."

"How disappointing. Was it something my parents did?" Natasha got up and paced.

"No, it's not about that. Wait, yes, it is, sort of. Jesus, why am I so bad at this? I want you without the hammer over our head. I want to kiss you and not feel like someone's watching. I'm not even sure I should've come here tonight, given, you know, but I wanted…you."

Natasha knew exactly what Tommy meant. She leaned down and grabbed a fistful of Tommy's shirt and pulled her to her feet. Once she was standing, Natasha cupped the back of Tommy's head and, still gripping her shirt, pulled her close.

"Don't think for a minute I don't want you too. Every minute." Natasha tilted her head and kissed Tommy.

Tommy's lips were soft, like Natasha remembered. She kept the pace slow at first, but her resolve deserted her quickly. She pulled Tommy closer and deepened the kiss. She was desperate, hungry.

Natasha was vaguely aware of Tommy's hand moving to her ass, the other in her hair. Her hand was still between them, holding Tommy's shirt. She could feel both of their hearts pounding against her hand.

Natasha shivered when Tommy moved her hand from her ass and pressed it against her back, sliding under her shirt against her bare skin. Tommy moved higher. Natasha broke the kiss and wrapped her arms around Tommy tightly. She left her hand under Natasha's shirt and wrapped the other around her shoulders. If Tommy was confused by the abrupt end to their kiss, she didn't let on.

"Had to see if we were still good at that." Natasha rested her head on Tommy's shoulder.

"What's the verdict?" Tommy kissed the top of Natasha's head.

She pulled out of Tommy's arms and shoved her down on the couch. Tommy leaned back into the corner of the couch and Natasha sat in her lap and leaned back in her arms.

"If you don't know how it was, I'm not sure you deserve any more. I don't trust your judgment."

"My thinking is cloudy when you're around. Especially when you're sitting on my lap. You're killing me a little here, Nat."

Natasha shouldn't have kissed her, Tommy had said she wasn't here to remove clothing, but she'd needed the connection.

"You're going to live, Tommy. You better if you want to finish what we just started once we sort out the work thing."

Tommy let her head tumble back dramatically. "We should've asked the captain if we had to keep our hands to ourselves now that we're not partnered and the photos are out of the drawer."

"She certainly looked like she was in the mood to entertain questions about the parameters of our social life. Tomorrow, will you ask her where she recommends you take me on a proper date?" Natasha slid off Tommy's lap and leaned into her.

"What will your parents do if they don't get their way immediately?" Tommy pulled Natasha closer.

"It's probably best if we don't get caught again." Natasha's throat felt dry as the words choked out. "Until I go Captain Couture on them and put everything back the way it's supposed to be."

"Captain Couture is coming back out to play? Am I going to need to start taking blood pressure medication?" Tommy kissed the top of Natasha's head.

Natasha poked her in the ribs. "If you're lucky."

"Hey. Okay, Ms. Couture, what's the plan?"

"Tonight, I'm going to let you pick the movie and I'll pretend to love the musical you select. I want this." Natasha traced her finger over Tommy's nipple. "But tonight I want your strength, your comfort, and your security."

"And what about tomorrow?" Tommy reached for Natasha's hand and entwined their fingers.

"Tomorrow I guess I'll remember what it is to think like a Blackstone and get my parents to back off."

Tommy laughed. "That's the slimmest of plans, but I'm with you to the end."

"Gotta have something to hang your cock on and it's the best I can do tonight. Thank you for coming over."

"I couldn't leave things the way we did at the station. You mean too much to me. It's going to be torture at work tomorrow."

Tommy tensed and pulled Natasha closer to her. She wasn't complaining about the feel of Tommy holding her tight, but something spooked her.

"What's wrong, babe?"

Tommy was quiet long enough Natasha didn't think she was going to answer.

"If anything happens to you...even a hangnail. God, I'll kill him. She could've picked anyone but him."

Natasha turned so her legs were on Tommy's lap. She leaned her bent arm against the back of the couch and rested her head in her hand. "Don't worry so much about Justin. He's not the only one in the car. Do you trust me?"

"Of course. You know I do." Tommy rested her head back against the couch cushions and turned to face Natasha.

"Then trust that I'll be okay. No matter what happens. Justin's like an egg that just got dropped in the pan. He needs his thinking to be scrambled up a little so he can come out the other side palatable. Pete is already on board, and the other officers are seasoned and can absorb the trainings I've already done. It actually makes sense. We don't have to like it."

Natasha settled back in Tommy's arms while Tommy got the movie started. Once the first big musical number started and Tommy began to sing along, Natasha felt at peace, safe in Tommy's arms.

They fell asleep like that, tangled up on the couch, fully clothed, and wanting more. Natasha dreamed that Tommy carried her to bed. She tried to pull dream Tommy down next to her but couldn't make her stay. In the morning she was in her bed, still fully clothed, and alone. Maybe it hadn't been a dream. She looked at the empty half of the bed.

Tommy's half. She tried to shake the thought before deciding she didn't want to banish it. She cursed her parents. Why should she have to hide the woman she loved so they didn't taint what was so pure?

Natasha stopped short. Love was a big word. It filled her head. She said it out loud and it filled the room. She looked in the mirror and tried it out.

"Tommy, I lo—" She caught sight of the clock behind her. "Shit, I'm going to be late."

She rushed to get ready and flew out of the house. As she always did, she tried to leave her personal feelings tucked away safely inside when she turned the front door key.

Today, more than others, she needed focus. Justin the rookie was watching her back now. Given their track record together, he should be about as excited by the prospect as she was about armor-plated, fire-breathing, sedan-sized mosquitos.

At least she had the torture of Kayla and the active seniors to look forward to after work. It had been a hell of a week and it was only Tuesday.

CHAPTER TWENTY-FIVE

Tommy had been partnered with Pete almost a week. He was a great cop, a good partner, and a nice guy to be around. Normally, she'd have no complaints. But she compared him to Natasha constantly and he came up short every time. That coupled with the fact that Natasha hadn't been able to stick it to her parents yet and she was nursing a terrible mood.

"You going to sigh your way through the day again today, too? Or are we finally going to talk this out?"

Pete was smiling so it took some of the sting from his words. Tommy flipped him off anyway.

"Look, I get it. It's hard to upgrade to someone like me. I'm gorgeous, I smell divine. My hair is like the silky strands of unicorn ass hair. We don't need to touch on my singing. There's a lot to love, you'll adjust in time."

Tommy choked on the sip of water she'd taken. She coughed to try to clear her airway and not die in Pete's car.

"It's all right, buddy, you're not the first to get choked up when we talk about my finer features."

"Fuck you." Tommy coughed a few more times to clear the last of the water.

"Rumor in the station is that it would make me a home wrecker, and I have a reputation to uphold."

Tommy lowered the bottle of water before taking another sip. "Jesus, Pete. Let up on me. You tried to kill me once already. I'm thirsty."

Pete turned serious. "I know you're miserable, Tommy. You wanna talk about it?"

"I'm sorry, Pete. You've been great. I actually think we're pretty good partners. It's just…"

"I know. I'm probably the only one you never had to convince. Natasha's amazing. Is it true you two are, I don't know how to put it without you punching me in the nuts, a thing?"

"Why do you think I'm partnered with you?" It didn't feel right being so flippant. "That's the defensive asshole answer. The real one is yes, sort of, and it's complicated."

Pete nodded. "Ah, so there's something real there then."

Tommy's anger was close to the surface these days and Pete's mocking poked a hole in the thin crust holding it in.

"Whoa. I see you boiling over. I was being sincere."

Tommy downshifted her temper. "I hear the rumors at the station about me fucking our hot social worker. She's been with us for all this time, and just like that," Tommy snapped her fingers, "she's reduced to a hot blonde because there might be sex involved?" She pointed at him. "And there wasn't, for your information. We haven't slept together, no matter what bullshit is going around."

Pete held up his hands. "Well, that explains your terrible mood. But I can clear up the rumors right now. It's two idiots from the swing shift who started that bullshit. You don't have to look around wondering who's being a dick behind your back, because Natasha's one of us. Even Justin ripped into one of those assholes. The kid's learning. Everyone is curious what's going on with the two of you, but Natasha's earned respect."

Tommy's blood pressure felt like it was coming back to a normal range. "That makes me feel a lot better, thank you. We were working so hard to figure out how to make the social worker-cop thing functional, and somewhere along the way, she became more important to me than work, or this new program, or any damn rules and regulations."

Pete looked impressed. "I never thought I'd see the day that Alice Finch's buttoned up daughter kissed the rule book's ass."

Tommy's knee bounced and she ran her hand through her hair. "That's the thing, we tried so hard not to run afoul of the rules. The work partnership and what Nat could bring to the station was important to both of us. We weren't willing to risk it. And we didn't, ever, but we got slammed for it anyway."

"Guess you should've said to hell with it and done what you wanted."

"Apparently. Probably would've ended up with you, the ass hair unicorn, a few weeks earlier. There are worse punishments."

Pete started to answer when their radios blared with the code no officer ever wants to hear.

"Officer down."

Tommy and Pete looked at each other. Tommy could see the fear and anguish she was feeling swirling in Pete's eyes.

"Go." Tommy grabbed the handle above the passenger door and braced for the ride.

Pete flipped on the lights and sirens. Tommy's heart was racing. This was a big city with lots of officers. Tommy was worried for all of them. But there was one duo she needed, down to the marrow of her bones, not to be the source of the distress call.

Her phone buzzed. She pulled it out and stared. It was from Natasha. She reread the text.

I'm so sorry. I love you.

No. No, no, no. Natasha could *not* send her that text full of apology and love right after an officer down call. Coupled with the radio call, it felt like there was finality to the text.

Tommy tried taking a deep breath. Her lungs seemed to have shrunk down to the size of the font on her phone display. There was no reason to assume Natasha's text was related to the officer down call.

She tried to catch another breath. Her lungs rebelled again. She felt like she was gasping for air. Deep down, she knew. There was no such thing as a coincidence. Not on this scale. Natasha was in trouble and Pete was driving too damn slow.

"Move your ass, Pete. Nat's in trouble."

"What? How do you know?" Pete glanced over at Tommy. He didn't say anything else after he got a look at her.

Tommy's fear turned to anger. Why wasn't she with Natasha? Why hadn't Justin protected her? Tommy was filled with the kind of rage that couldn't be dampened or bottled up, but didn't have anywhere to go. Justin wasn't in front of her and she had a job to do that required a clear head. She pushed the boiling anger down where it seared her insides and bubbled in her gut.

They pulled to the curb and sprang out. A frantic woman ran at them from the direction of a multifamily house.

"I called. There were gunshots in his apartment. I was the one who asked them to check on him." She was waving frantically and looked distressed.

"Where?" Tommy felt like an arrow stretched tight on the bow. Point her in the direction of the target and let her fly.

"Billy's apartment is on the second floor, right there." She pointed to the red house behind her.

Tommy ran for it. Pete was right behind her.

"Don't sprint in there and make the situation worse. We should be waiting for backup." His breathing was heavier than it should be from the short run. He was scared too.

"This isn't my first day on the job, Pete. I won't do anything to put her in danger. You're my backup." Tommy pulled the door open slowly and slipped inside the building.

She and Pete climbed the stairs carefully. They were old and creaky. There was no way to approach silently. Tommy heard more sirens. The cavalry was arriving.

There was only one door on the second floor. Natasha had to be in there. Tommy said a prayer she was unharmed. She cursed the old, squeaky floorboards as they groaned and creaked under their weight as she and Pete flanked the door.

She was about to announce herself and make entry when Natasha called out.

"Whoever is about to come through the door, hold your position, please. Billy and I need a little more time to talk."

Tommy tried to answer, but all that came out of her mouth was a choked, gasping, exhalation of relief. She cleared her throat and tried again.

"We got an officer down call, is everyone okay in there?"

"Nothing life threatening, and I'd like to keep it that way. A few more minutes, please."

Tommy could hear the stress in Natasha's voice. She wanted to sweep Natasha to safety, but that wasn't what Natasha needed from her.

"We're ready the minute you need us, Nat."

There was a moment's pause. Tommy felt like she could hear everyone's heart beating. Then Natasha's voice filled her with enough hope to keep her on this side of the door.

"Thank you, Tommy."

Tommy strained to hear the conversation happening inside the apartment. It was easier to hear the man Natasha was talking to, presumably Billy. He was speaking loudly. His tone and words clearly indicated his agitation.

"I shot two cops. I'm not getting out of here alive."

Two cops. Natasha had been shot. Tommy reached for the door handle. Pete grabbed her hand. He shook his head.

"He shot her." Tommy felt like she was coming apart.

"She asked for more time. She wouldn't do that if she or Justin were in real trouble. Trust her."

Tommy stepped back and swallowed hard. She did trust Natasha. She focused on the conversation again.

"Walk out of here together…gun stays here…keep you safe."

"Why would they let me walk out of here after what I did? Maybe I'll use him as a shield. Maybe I shouldn't leave at all."

Tommy didn't like the turn Billy was taking.

"Leave him…talk to me…partner outside…trust me."

Tommy leaned closer to the door. She couldn't hear Natasha.

Billy roared. "I want to pull the trigger and become the monster I feel like I am. I don't recognize myself. But you, you're kind like her. Why do you have to be kind?"

"Told you…here for you…want to help."

Tommy heard scuffling in the apartment. Then Natasha shouted, "No!"

There was a single gunshot.

Tommy and Pete hit the door together. It crashed open, splintering off its hinges. As she crashed through the door, Tommy took in the scene in a quick glance. Billy was on his knees in front of Natasha, head in hands, sobbing. Justin was slumped against the fireplace.

Natasha kneeled on the floor next to Billy, holding a handgun, looking shell-shocked.

Pete targeted Billy and took him to the ground. He got him to his stomach and cuffed him. He didn't resist so the arrest was quick and clean.

As soon as Tommy saw Pete had Billy under control, she moved to Natasha. She looked for signs of blood and trauma. Her hands were covered in blood, but nothing else was obvious. Maybe it wasn't hers.

"Nat, can I have the gun?" She reached for the weapon Natasha was still clutching and eased it out of her hands.

Tommy wanted to take Natasha in her arms and carry her away. She wanted to tell her she loved her. She wanted to be anywhere but where they were. But they were both at work and the job wasn't done. Natasha locked eyes with her. Tommy knew Natasha understood.

"Justin's been shot, we need to get him downstairs."

"What about you? You've been shot too?"

Tommy radioed for the paramedics to come up. She could hear the squeaky stairs as more help thundered into the building.

She nodded. "But I'm okay, my vest took the hit. We need to take care of him." Natasha gave Tommy a little shove. Pete gave Natasha a serious nod as he led Billy from the room and out of the building.

"He was supposed to clear the scene. What the hell happened?" Tommy moved to Justin's side.

Justin's hands were covered in blood and it had soaked his shirt and leaked onto the floor.

"Tommy, the kid got shot, don't you think that's enough punishment?" Natasha followed close behind.

"I can hear you, you know." Justin tried to sit up straighter and winced.

"Sit still. We'll get the paramedics up here to take a look at you." She patted him on the shoulder. "You're all right, okay? You're going to be okay."

"I screwed up. Natasha, I'm sorry. Tommy, I was so scared." He looked up at them with tears in his eyes.

Tommy heard Natasha step back to give her a moment with Justin.

"Of course you were scared. Anyone who says they're not scared is lying. But you can't let fear rule you and force you to make bad decisions. If you want to be a good cop, you have to learn that."

Justin nodded. "I do want to be a good cop. Like you. I think she could teach me a lot too. That guy shot both of us, then she got up again to talk to him. He held a gun to her face the whole time and she never flinched. She kept him talking, looking for a way out of here. Then she saved his life when he looked like he might try to shoot himself. She wrestled the gun from him, Tommy."

"Jesus." Tommy felt a little shaky and leaned against the doorway.

Justin looked at Tommy and grinned. "My grandpa always told me, if you find someone you love enough to make your knees wobble, you better tell them before it's too late."

Tommy rolled her eyes. "What do you know, you're about twelve."

The paramedics rolled in and started working on Justin. Tommy backed away. Justin called after her. "Sure, but my granddad was married for sixty-five years."

Natasha was waiting for her just outside the apartment door. She looked exhausted and haunted and so alone standing on the dark landing. Tommy pulled her into a tight embrace. Natasha whimpered.

Tommy sprang back and held her at arm's length. "You're hurt. What's wrong? You said you were okay."

Natasha tried to shake it off again, but this time Tommy saw the hitch in her breathing and the tears ready to fall. She looked her over more closely. Fury surged when she saw the bullet hole in Natasha's vest.

"You said you were okay, but you're hurt. Do you need a stretcher? How could I not see you were hurt?"

"Tommy, look at me." Natasha grabbed both sides of Tommy's face and held her close. "I'm going to be fine. The vest did its job. Okay? I'm sore, but I'm okay."

They worked their way slowly down the stairs. Tommy didn't mind going an inch an hour if that's what Natasha needed, but it looked like Natasha couldn't get out fast enough.

They made it outside and yielded to the paramedics hauling Justin down. Now that the immediate danger was passed, some of the show of force had gone back on patrol, but there were still a fair number of officers around.

"Let's get you checked out."

Natasha gave her a look.

"You're going to have to get cleared to return to work anyway. One officer down, another taking a round to the vest? You aren't going to avoid getting checked. Trust me, it's better than getting your checkup by Priya at family dinner, although there probably isn't any way to avoid that."

"Tommy, I told you, I'm okay." Natasha put her arm on Tommy's shoulder.

Tommy saw her face contort in pain when she did.

"I thought I might lose you today." Tommy put her arm around Natasha's waist and steered her toward one of the ambulances on scene. "I've never been so scared in my life. You make my knees wobble."

Natasha gave Tommy a funny look.

Tommy shook her head and grinned. "It's something Justin said. The important thing is, I love you."

"I love you too, Tommy. You're all I could think about when I was in there, and I had to text you when I made the officer down call. I didn't want to die because I had too much to live for, but if I did, I had to let you know how I felt."

Tommy reluctantly let Natasha go when they approached the ambulance. Tommy hovered nearby while she was examined. The paramedics didn't think her ribs were broken and left it up to her whether to go for X-rays. Tommy would be more comfortable if she was admitted to the hospital overnight for observation, but everyone had looked at her like she'd lost her mind when she'd suggested it. She worried she might wake up from a dream and Natasha might be gone.

While someone took Natasha's statement, she inched closer. Halfway through, they were next to each other. Tommy sensed Natasha wanted the closeness as much as she did. She reached out and slipped her hand into Natasha's. Some of the turmoil and anxiety she'd been feeling settled. She had tangible proof Natasha was safe.

Toward the end of Natasha's statement, Lieutenant Smith came by to check in. Natasha tried to pull her hand away when Lieutenant Smith arrived, but Tommy held tight. She'd felt the fear of losing Natasha, and the pictures didn't seem that important anymore. Her last name, the differences in where they came from—none of it mattered as long as Natasha was safe in her arms.

"Good work today. From what Justin said, we should be giving you keys to the city. Finch, see that she makes it home safely."

Lieutenant Smith nodded to both of them and walked away without another word.

"I'd love to crack her open and see what makes her tick." Natasha rested her head on Tommy's shoulder. "Maybe she's some kind of steampunk golem."

"Ready to roll?" Tommy had asked Harry to come pick them up and was relieved to see her pull up.

"Let's get out of here. I'm ready to not be a cop's sidekick anymore."

"And I'm ready to not be a social worker's sidekick."

Harry didn't say anything when Tommy climbed into the back seat next to Natasha and sat in the middle with her arm around her.

"I love you." Natasha squeezed Tommy's hand.

"We need to talk about your timing. You dropped that on me in the middle of a crisis. What if that was the last thing…" Tommy dropped her head against the back of the seat.

"If that was it for me, I wanted you to know how I felt."

"I told my parents I wouldn't be at family dinner tonight. I thought you'd want to go home."

Natasha cocked her head and looked thoughtful. "No, if you don't think your parents would mind one extra, I'd like to go." She took a shaky breath. "Today was awful, and I never want to be in that position again. I think your kind of family distraction is just what I need. I want to be somewhere the fear can't follow."

Tommy kissed Natasha's cheek. "They'd love to have you. So would I."

As Harry drove them to family dinner at her parents' house, Tommy wondered what the future held. One panic-inducing, heroic day hadn't changed their standing with the captain, nor removed the

Blackstone-shaped obstacle to their being together. But Tommy had no desire to put the "I love yous" back in the bottle or to unwobble her knees.

She'd gotten a flash of what life looked and felt like without Natasha, and the weight of her crushed heart, heavy in her chest in those few moments of terror, would haunt her forever. Tonight, though, was about healing and family and love. The rest of the world would have to wait until the morning to creep back in. Tonight, Natasha was safe. Tommy would guarantee it.

CHAPTER TWENTY-SIX

"Hero in the house."

Natasha was sure she was bright red at Harry's announcement of their arrival. She jabbed Harry in the ribs. "Quiet."

Alice ran into the room and directly to Natasha. She pulled her into a tight hug. It was the kind of motherly affection Natasha hadn't known or realized she missed. She felt the first tear roll down her cheek. Now wasn't a good time to lose it.

"Mama, easy on her ribs."

"Tomasina Finch, I know more about ballistic vest impacts than any of my children ever will. I also know the power of a mother's hug. Shut up."

That did it. Natasha lost the small measure of control she'd still held over the emotions from her encounter with Billy. She knew the tears were falling on Alice's shoulder. She could certainly feel them, but Natasha couldn't bring herself to raise her head and break the connection. For her part, Alice hadn't let go either.

"All of you shoo. Natasha and I have some things to catch up on."

Tommy started to protest but stopped short. Natasha wondered what look Alice had deployed to stop Tommy cold.

Alice finally let Natasha out of her arms far enough to take a look at her. She wiped away Natasha's tears. "Oh, my dear, you've had quite a day."

Natasha followed Alice to the couch and sat down where directed. "How do you know? About my day, I mean."

"I'm only mildly ashamed to admit I asked my kids' captains to get in touch if something happens to one of them. Call it a perk of my rank when I retired."

Sometimes Natasha forgot Alice was a cop too. When she was in mother mode it was hard to picture her arresting anyone. "Don't tell Tommy that. Part of her worries her success is only because of her last name."

Alice shook her head. "That child has never understood how remarkable she is. There's nothing I could say to anyone that isn't apparent to everyone who knows her."

Natasha smiled and nodded. Tommy was remarkable. "I still don't understand. Tommy wasn't involved today. Not really. Not until the end when she kicked down the door." Natasha wiped angrily at the tears that were dotting her lap anew. Enough was enough.

"Sweetie, Captain Gillette didn't call me about Tommy. She called me about you."

Natasha was sure she heard incorrectly. What she thought she heard didn't make any sense.

"I see that look. I didn't misspeak. I care about you. The fear that shot through me when I heard what happened today, Lord. Natasha, from the first time you sat at my table, it felt like a puzzle piece snapping into place. Whether or not you and Tommy work out, you'll have a place here."

Natasha tried to speak, but a sob escaped instead. She took a breath and made another attempt. "Today, I thought…for a moment I wasn't sure if…I was so scared. I'm still so scared. I close my eyes and see him holding that gun in my face."

Alice pulled Natasha close and held her while she cried. "I was in a situation similar to yours once. My partner and I were ambushed responding to a domestic violence call. There is no more terrifying or lonelier place than looking down the barrel of a gun."

Natasha shuddered. "What did you do?"

"Same thing you did. I used my training and my brain to get myself out of it. From the sound of it, you did a hell of a lot better than I did and most anyone in a uniform would've done."

"I kept thinking my friend Kayla was going to be furious with me. She was worried I was going to get shot on the job and I promised

I wouldn't. And that I might die before I had a chance to get Tommy's career back on track and give my parents what they have coming to them."

"Have you found a solution to that issue?"

Natasha looked at her hands folded in her lap. "There's a woman at the accounting firm my family has used for generations who has always been nice to me. I asked her for a favor."

"Tommy said you might have to become Natasha Blackstone again. It doesn't change who you are, you know."

Natasha looked up at Alice and ran her hands through her hair. "Yes, it does. I asked for a favor using a last name that no one says no to. Now I have proof that my parents paid to have me followed and made sizable donations to the police department the same day the photos were delivered. I also know they wouldn't be on a whole lot of Christmas card lists if some of their banking activity was made public."

Alice looked surprised. "That was quite a favor."

"Exactly. I'm rich with a powerful name. I have influence and leverage, and if I don't, I can buy it. What about the folks Tommy and I work with? Who's exerting influence and power on their behalf?"

Alice patted her thigh. "You are, my dear. Everything you did with your power and influence was to get back to your job helping people. How can I help get you over the finish line? I have a bit of power and influence myself and I'm not afraid to toss it around for a good cause."

Natasha laughed. She wasn't sure what it felt like to love a mother, but she did know she loved Alice Finch.

"I need to get in front of a reporter. The rest will work itself out."

"Would a press conference related to today's excitement do the trick?" Alice took her hand. "If it will add more stress having to talk about it more, say no."

Natasha squeezed Alice's hand. "No, a press conference would be perfect, but I can't call one of those on my own and not make it look like I'm going after my parents. I'd prefer to let everyone save face for the sake of my sister-in-law's campaign."

"I'll make a phone call and see if I can give the ball a nudge and get it rolling."

Natasha brushed a speck of non-existent dust off the knee of her pants. "If this happens, is it possible you could be there? At the press conference, I mean."

"Standing next to you if you want me there." Alice gave her hand one more squeeze.

Natasha swiped at her face, trying to rid herself of the final tears. She wasn't usually such a crier. But she wasn't usually showered with maternal caring. Or sore from being shot.

"What do you say we join the rest of the family? I'm willing to bet Harry is sitting on Tommy in *there* to keep her from bursting in *here*."

Natasha nodded and stood. Talking to Alice and being allowed to cry soothed some of the pain and fear Billy had left behind and her anxiety about facing off with her parents. She was thankful for that. But now she needed Tommy.

When they got to the dining room, Alice hadn't been far from the truth. Harry had Tommy corralled in a dining chair. Tommy looked like she was assessing her odds if she broke the perimeter.

As soon as Tommy saw Natasha, she shoved past Harry and was by her side. She slipped her arm around Natasha's waist and held her close. Natasha recognized the protective gesture for what it was, and definitely didn't mind Tommy keeping her close tonight.

Tommy looked her over, worry written all over her face. Then she looked at her mother when she noticed Natasha had been crying.

Natasha kissed Tommy's cheek. "It's okay, babe. I'm fine."

Tommy refocused on Natasha. She loved the look Tommy saved only for her. Soft, devoted, protective, passionate.

"Priya wants to see you. You're really one of the family once the doc hauls you in for a once-over." Tommy dropped her arm from Natasha's waist and took her hand.

"Natasha, I thought I was safe with you. Didn't expect to add you to my list of family dinner checkups." Priya motioned Natasha to a chair.

"Priya, I'm fine. You don't have to do this."

"Don't argue," Tommy, Harry, and Cody all said.

Natasha sat. She explained the bullet impact and the lingering effects. Priya's appraisal wasn't cursory. She clearly took her role as family dinner physician seriously. Dinner didn't begin until Natasha was released from her appointment with instructions to seek immediate medical care if her pain worsened or she had trouble breathing.

After dinner, she and Tommy skipped the back deck and called it a night. Tommy called a ride share. They sat on the porch and waited for the car.

"My family loves you."

Natasha snuggled closer to Tommy and took her hand. "I've never had a mother who cared enough to let me cry when I need to. I'm really glad your mom can. You've gotten a feel for what my family's like. I didn't know a family like yours was real outside of television. Even the most functional ones I grew up around, like Kayla's, are nothing like the Finches. I love your family too."

Tommy looked up at the stars. "Do you think your leverage is enough to get your parents off our backs? If it's not going to work, I don't want tonight to end. That way we don't ever have to face tomorrow."

"Trust me, Tommy. Billy didn't shoot my ego. It's still fully inflated. I'm going to beat my parents in a blowout and then run up the score for fun because I can."

The car pulled up and they both stood.

"I can have Harry give me a ride back." Tommy stared at the car as though wishing it would go away.

Natasha laughed. "Are you out of your mind? I want you to take me home."

Tommy nodded a little too long. "Okay. I'll make sure you get home okay."

Natasha pulled Tommy close and whispered in her ear. "I don't think you understand. I want you to take me home. I'm not interested in spending the night alone."

Tommy's eyes got wide. She took Natasha's hand and led her to the car without another word.

The ride felt interminable. Tommy never so much as glanced Natasha's way.

Instead of speculate about what Tommy was thinking and ruin what might be about to happen, Natasha whispered in Tommy's ear again. "I've wanted you long enough. I'm tired of waiting. I'm not about to die without having tasted you."

The pulse on Tommy's neck beat more noticeably and she made a tiny whimpery noise.

The driver pulled to the curb in front of Tommy's house, and she practically dragged Natasha from the car. They chased each other up the steps. Tommy unlocked the front door but hesitated before she opened it.

"Are you sure? You didn't want to cross this line until things were settled at work. And what about your ribs?"

Natasha traced Tommy's eyebrow and cheek with the back of her fingers. "I love so much about you, and your tender, caring heart is at the top of the list. But right now, I don't need that. I need you to get your ass inside, show me the way to your bedroom, and then help us both out of our clothes. Make me forget everyone and everything but you."

Tommy threw open the door, pulled Natasha in, and kicked it shut. "I can do that."

Natasha spun them around and backed Tommy against the door. "I knew you were the woman for the job," she said right before she kissed her.

"The only woman." Tommy grabbed Natasha's ass and lifted her.

Natasha wrapped her legs around Tommy's waist. She'd never been literally swept off her feet before. It was hot as hell.

With Tommy holding her, she focused on kissing and how good Tommy's body felt. She needed to get Tommy out of her shirt.

Tommy walked them through the living room and down a hallway. Natasha was too busy working the buttons on Tommy's uniform shirt to care where Tommy was taking her. She didn't even break concentration when Tommy nudged open a door and slipped inside a cooler, darker room.

Natasha tangled her hands in Tommy's hair and pulled her closer. Their kissing became more erratic and wild. Natasha's desire was ramping up fast. Tommy squeezed tighter on her ass, forcing her closer against Tommy's stomach. The friction sent a jolt of arousal through her that would be competitive on a top ten climax list.

Natasha broke their kiss. "Bed, now, please."

The first time she and Tommy had sex she wasn't going to orgasm dry humping two feet from Tommy's bed.

Tommy grinned.

"What are you smiling about, babe? You haven't done anything yet."

Tommy dropped Natasha carefully on her back on the bed. "I guess I should get to work then."

Natasha rose up on her elbows. Tommy made a move to follow her to the bed, but Natasha lifted her high heel and rested it in the center of Tommy's chest to stop her.

"I want to watch you take that uniform off."

Tommy shivered, then pulled her shirt from her pants and started unbuttoning the buttons Natasha hadn't gotten to. Natasha lowered her foot, scooted up the bed so she was leaning against the headboard, and watched. She traced her finger across her chest, then a circle around her nipple. Pleasure shot directly to her clit. Tommy hadn't touched her yet and she already felt lost in her.

Tommy was watching her intently. Her hands were shaking as she worked her shirt off her shoulders. Natasha circled the other nipple. Tommy stopped removing her shirt. Natasha stilled her hand.

Tommy groaned. She threw her head back dramatically before refocusing. Her shirt hit the floor and Natasha covered her own breast and let out a satisfied sigh. Tommy yanked at her undershirt and pulled it over her head, and Natasha covered both breasts and squeezed.

She could see Tommy's arousal building. It was matching her own. The look on Tommy's face when she touched herself was more erotic than her own touch. God, she was going to explode when it was Tommy's hands on her body.

"These too? Or can I touch you now?" Tommy had one hand on her fly.

"Off, please." Natasha traced her finger lazily down her stomach. She wished Tommy still had her duty belt on so she could watch her take that off too. Another day, perhaps.

Tommy unzipped and dropped her pants. She kicked out of her shoes, socks, and trousers. She stood there in her sports bra and boxers, waiting. Even if Natasha weren't enjoying teasing Tommy, the sight of her would be enough to draw her hand to her own sex. Tommy's body deserved odes and marble statues.

Natasha slid her hand down her stomach to the apex of her thighs. She hesitated, making sure she had Tommy's full attention. Tommy leaned forward, waiting for permission to join her. Instead, Natasha covered her sex with her hand. Even over her pants she could tell how wet she was.

She stroked slowly, taking one more minute to imagine Tommy touching her. She moaned and heard Tommy shuffling at the edge of the bed.

"Nat, I'm really enjoying the show, but I don't want to embarrass myself by coming where I'm standing."

"Then calm yourself down and undress me." Natasha removed her hand to give Tommy a breather.

"Sure, that should totally do the trick." Tommy crawled across the bed and between Natasha's legs. She settled on top and kissed her.

Natasha slowly ground against Tommy's stomach, ramping herself up to dangerous levels. Tommy felt too good.

"My clothes, Tommy. Stop being so careful. The doc gave me a clean bill of health."

Tommy turned the tables on Natasha and took her time undressing her. She trailed her tongue down Natasha's neck before slowly unbuttoning her shirt. She followed the path of the incremental opening, teasing, but never actually touching, Natasha's nipples. Natasha was ready to rip her shirt off and send buttons and bra clasps flying around the room, but Tommy was keeping her attention focused on the path of her mouth.

Once Natasha was finally naked, Tommy dipped between her legs and teased her open. She licked the full length of her clit. Natasha nearly bucked off the bed. She rolled Tommy so she was on top, straddling Tommy's lap.

"Enough teasing." Natasha bit down on the side of Tommy's neck.

Tommy pulled her closer. It felt like her hands were everywhere. Natasha's skin was on fire with her touch.

"Put that mouth to use, Officer Finch." Natasha pinched her own nipples.

Tommy laughed. She pushed up against the headboard and dipped her head. She kissed a line from Natasha's neck to her breast.

She circled once before sucking it into her mouth. Natasha rose up farther on her knees to give Tommy better access. Tommy moved her hand to the other breast.

Natasha's clit was throbbing and she was wet with need. Tommy's attention was stoking her desire, but in their current position there was no relief.

"What do you need, baby?" Tommy dragged her teeth along Natasha's nipple as she released it.

"I need more of you. Get your hand where I can use it." Natasha dropped her head to Tommy's shoulder. She was feeling so much of *everything.* How was this amazing woman hers?

"I like this assertive, bossy side of my partner." Tommy moved her hand between Natasha's legs.

"You've always loved this side of her." Natasha lowered herself onto two of Tommy's fingers. "But you never got to fuck her before."

"Have I told you I love you?" Tommy circled Natasha's clit with her thumb while Natasha found a rhythm on her hand.

"I never get tired of hearing it." Natasha kissed her. It was sloppy and frantic.

She raised up and steadied herself on Tommy's shoulders before she relaxed against her, letting her fill her more deeply. Natasha moved her hips against Tommy's hand, riding slow and steady.

Tommy took her breast into her mouth again and sucked hard on her nipple. Natasha loved this position. She could set the pace and depth and she got stimulation on three pleasure points. Plus, she could enjoy the sight of Tommy at her chest. And when she came, she knew Tommy would be watching.

She pumped her hips faster. Tommy raised her knees behind her, forcing Natasha deeper onto her hand. Natasha moaned and leaned forward to brace herself against the headboard. Her hair fell down and surrounded them, bouncing with every jerk of her hips. Tommy dragged her mouth from Natasha's breasts up her chest to her neck. She bit down and released her.

Natasha was so close. Tommy thrust faster, harder, and threw her over the edge.

She cried out Tommy's name and rode her hand through the peak of her orgasm. She didn't want the feeling to end. She rolled her hips lazily through the aftershocks, still wanting Tommy inside her. She leaned down and kissed her. Not the frantic kisses of earlier but soft, possessive kisses. Natasha wanted Tommy to feel what she felt, what Tommy made her feel. She didn't have words to explain so she kept kissing her while they were still intimately connected.

Finally, she rose off Tommy and fell back on the bed, dragging Tommy with her.

Tommy was careful when she landed not to crush Natasha beneath her. Natasha didn't care, she wanted to feel the full weight of her between her legs. She hooked her heels around the backs of Tommy's legs and kissed her again. There was passion again in this kiss. Natasha was having a hard time getting enough.

When they broke the kiss, Natasha forced Tommy onto her back. She rolled on top of her.

"You've ruined me. You're the only one allowed near my body from this day forward."

Tommy frowned. "I better be."

"Jealousy is oddly sexy on you. Don't overplay it though. You have nothing to be jealous of, hot stuff. Let's see if I can convince you." Natasha took the time to remove Tommy's sports bra. "Jesus, Tommy. Maybe I'm the one who should be worried. Do other women know about this body?"

Tommy was all defined muscle and strong body but still wrapped in a distinctly female package. She had soft curves and breasts big enough to wrap your mouth around. And that was just what Natasha did.

As soon as Natasha had Tommy's nipple in her mouth Tommy arched off the bed. Natasha focused attention on first one breast, then the other. Tommy was so responsive, Natasha could have spent hours winding her up, but she was impatient. She wanted Tommy to come. She wanted her to come for her.

Natasha kissed her way down Tommy's washboard stomach and removed her boxer briefs. Tommy was as wet as she was. She ran her finger along Tommy's clit to her opening and teased there for a moment before slipping inside.

Tommy groaned and twisted her hands in the sheets. Natasha pulled out and Tommy whimpered. She wasn't trying to speed up

Natasha's attention even though she was clearly ready. Tommy had relinquished control and allowed herself to be vulnerable.

Natasha had no desire to play with her further. She replaced her hand with her tongue. She dipped inside before teasing along her clit. Tommy clung more tightly to the bed as Natasha swirled her tongue over Tommy's clit.

Finally, she sucked Tommy fully into her mouth and Tommy cried out. She bucked her hips against Natasha's sucking and she could tell she wasn't going to last long. She moved her hand up Tommy's thigh until she reached her opening again. She slid first one, then two fingers inside. Tommy pumped against her, gasping. Natasha could feel the walls of her sex contract as her orgasm built.

She sucked hard on Tommy's clit as Tommy thrust down on her. Tommy cried out and came in her mouth. Natasha swirled her tongue along Tommy's clit and kept her fingers inside. Finally, Tommy was spent. Natasha crawled up her body and sprawled on top of her.

Natasha rested her chin on her crossed hands, right over Tommy's heart. Tommy put her hands behind her head so she was propped up enough to look at Natasha.

"I love you, Tommy. Thank you for today."

"You don't have to thank me for what we just did. And if you want to thank me, you should wait because I hope we're at intermission, not final curtain."

Natasha leaned forward and kissed her. "I wasn't thanking you for sex. Thank you for being outside the door today when I was scared and needed backup. I knew when I called for help, you'd find me."

"If you're in trouble, I'll always find you." Tommy cupped Natasha's face. "I don't think I've ever been that terrified. I can't imagine a world without you."

Natasha leaned into Tommy's touch. "The other part of the thank you is for not letting your fear overwhelm your trust in me. Thank you for listening to me when I asked for more time."

"It was the hardest thing I've ever had to do. And when I heard him say he'd shot two cops…" She sighed and moved one hand to stroke Natasha's hair. "I wanted to rush in. I can't stomach the thought of something happening to you."

Natasha rested her head on Tommy's chest, and she held her while they lay together in comfortable silence. Tommy's breathing was steady, and Natasha wondered if she fell asleep.

She shifted so she had better access to Tommy's entire body. With feather-light touches, she moved across her nipples, down her stomach, and finally to her sex. She cupped her, but Tommy covered Natasha's hand and slowly removed it. This time Tommy was the one to flip them.

She looked down at Natasha with a wicked grin. "You shouldn't start something if you don't intend to finish it."

"Oh, I have every intention of finishing what I started." Natasha repositioned so her legs were spread wider apart. "Right now, Officer Finch, I believe your mouth has somewhere to be."

Tommy sucked her in and Natasha threw her head back. She closed her eyes and focused on Tommy. No matter what had come before or what faced them in the morning, right now, in this moment with Tommy, she was right where she needed to be.

Chapter Twenty-seven

Captain Gillette intercepted them shortly after they entered the station. She motioned for them to follow her. Tommy looked at Natasha who shrugged. Tommy's stomach knotted. Last time they got called to the captain's office she'd blindsided them with the photos. Now what?

"Relax." Natasha put her hand on Tommy's shoulder and gave it a squeeze. "The press conference is in thirty minutes. Don't sweat through your uniform before then."

"Do you two have a moment? I know we've got the thing soon." Captain Gillette closed the door as she asked.

Natasha nodded and crossed her legs casually. If she was nervous or annoyed she wasn't betraying those emotions.

"I know the last time we spoke things were…" Captain Gillette looked like she was searching for the right words.

"The last time we spoke, you broke up our partnership, stuck me with an inexperienced rookie, and he got us both shot. Was that what you were looking for?"

Tommy coughed to cover the "holy shit" that was threatening to escape.

Natasha and Captain Gillette evaluated each other. Tommy held her breath but the standoff went on so long she gave up.

Captain Gillette broke first and laughed. Filleting and grilling both of their asses over a hot open flame seemed more likely than laughter.

"Your old boss, Dinah, told me you'd disregard the hierarchical structure and would give me an earful when you thought I deserved it. Thank God she was right."

"So you're willing to admit you were wrong about pulling me out of Tommy's car?"

"Absolutely not, you two were breaking the rules. I can pull out the photo evidence, but I'd prefer if that stayed locked up out of sight. The rules are there for a reason. But let's focus on the future. If things work out like you say they will, Parsons, we need to figure out what to do with both of you."

Natasha moved to the edge of her seat and leaned an elbow on Captain Gillette's desk. "Hold on, we were bending the rules at most. We're both professionals and Tommy isn't a rule breaker. If you need evidence she wasn't compromised, look no further than the incident Justin and I were involved in."

"I don't follow." Captain Gillette stood and sat on the edge of her desk.

Tommy was interested in where this was going too.

"Tommy responded, knew I was in trouble, but still waited *outside* the door when I asked her for more time. Once she and Pete entered the apartment, the suspect was arrested without the use of excessive force. No threats were made, no shots were fired, by them at least."

"What's your point?"

"I didn't break down the door like an out-of-control girlfriend." Tommy smiled her thanks to Natasha.

Captain Gillette looked thoughtful. "You're right. You acted like I would expect my officers to act in that situation. Point taken. You still can't work together."

"Fine, but don't sideline us either." Tommy sat forward in her chair until she was perched on the edge.

"Relax, Finch. I'm not going to sideline you. I didn't have much choice in getting you two away from each other. You forced my hand there."

"I'm sorry, Captain." Tommy put her hands flat on her knees and looked Captain Gillette in the eyes.

"So am I." Natasha looked like she considered mimicking Tommy's rigid posture but decided against it. "So where do we go from here?"

Captain Gillette leaned forward like she was about to let them in on a secret. "Natasha, if you can clear up the Blackstone complication the chief and mayor are thrilled with the work you two have done and the community response to Natasha's viral moments. They're ready to authorize funding for a larger expansion of our program than I asked for. Natasha, do you have any ideas?"

"Yes, ma'am. One or two."

"Finch, there's a detective position with your name on it if you want it. You'd have to pass the exam, but I assume that's only a formality given the care you take in everything you do."

Tommy leaned back heavily in her chair. Eighteen months ago, she'd have jumped at the chance for detective. Now the prospect made her sad. She looked at Natasha and knew why.

"With all due respect, ma'am. I think I'd like to stay in the ride along program for a little while longer. I know that might mean my shot at detective is gone, but that's okay. I really believe in this program."

Tommy felt like a weight was lifted. She knew what she wanted from the job and now the captain did too. What to expect and what was expected from her was on the horizon line again.

"Detective positions will come up again. You'll be an asset to whoever you get paired with. Final order of business is your personal life."

Tommy and Natasha started to state their case and protest simultaneously.

Captain Gillette held up her hands to stop them. "Believe it or not, I'm on your side. I would prefer not having to talk about it at all, but there's a way to keep everything in line with the rules on paper and in the court of public opinion."

Tommy wanted to shake Captain Gillette to get her to speed up already.

"You know Marcetti's interested in piggybacking on our ride along program. He wants to use our expertise to get his officers on board."

Tommy nodded. "Moving me to Harry's station seems like a bad idea, ma'am."

"Who says *you* have to go? Right, Captain?" Natasha sat back heavily in her chair.

"Exactly. You can oversee both programs but be based at Marcetti's station. I know it's a change, and getting uprooted to a station where you don't know anyone is daunting."

Natasha shook her head. She looked at Tommy and smiled. "It's fine with me. It's a perfect solution actually. Harry's had nothing but good things to say about Captain Marcetti and her co-workers."

Captain Gillette stood. She shook hands with both of them. "Marcetti and I will work out the paperwork. I'm sorry there's not a better solution. Even when we expand, the ride along program is going to be so small, you two would end up working closely together."

"Nothing to apologize for. Thank you for taking the time to give a damn and not shuffling me off to career purgatory." Tommy hesitated then turned and followed Natasha to the door.

She couldn't ask what she always wanted to know when some special accommodation seemed to come her way. Natasha would've been ballsy enough to ask, but she wasn't.

"Tommy, you didn't get special treatment because of your mother. I know you're wondering. You're a good cop. That's why I give a damn."

"Yes, ma'am. Thank you, ma'am." Tommy pulled the door shut behind her.

"You ready to slay some dragons? You should be up there with me. This program is ours." Natasha looked like she'd had too many energy drinks.

"Is there a button or a nob on you somewhere to turn down this energy level and get you back in the human range?" Tommy pulled Natasha's ear playfully.

"You explored my body pretty thoroughly last night, I think you would've seen it." Natasha leaned in and whispered in Tommy's ear before walking away.

Tommy didn't move for a few seconds. How could Natasha do that to her? Stop her in her tracks, derail her thoughts so easily with a look or a flirty comment? Must be love.

She hurried after Natasha once her legs seemed willing to obey brain signals again. They had a press conference to get to.

Tommy took a seat in the front row. Harry sat next to her. She was happy to see her sister, even though she didn't have to be there.

Natasha and their mother were sitting behind the podium talking quietly. Captain Gillette and the chief of police were also there.

Harry elbowed her and pointed behind them. Tommy turned. She hadn't realized how many people had filed in after she'd taken her seat. There were a few fellow officers and one or two individuals she couldn't identify, but the majority were members of the press. She'd been to a few of these before and never had they been so widely attended by the local media.

The press conference started with the police chief and Captain Gillette talking about the ride along program and Natasha's contribution. After that they shifted to the incident with Billy and her heroism. Natasha looked uncomfortable. Tommy saw her mother whisper something to her.

Captain Gillette concluded her remarks and asked Natasha to step to the podium for questions. Tommy could tell she was nervous although most people probably couldn't.

"Hello, thanks for being here. First, I'd like to acknowledge my police partner, Tommy Finch. None of the work I've done over the past eighteen months would've been possible without her. I'm happy to take questions now."

Tommy held her breath. Now was the moment. The wall of sound from behind her hit fast and hard. Every reporter seemed to have twelve questions they asked at once. As long as one of them asked the right question.

"Ms. Blackstone, there's a rumor you're leaving the police department and returning full time to supporting your family enterprises, especially that of your sister-in-law's campaign. Can you comment on that, please?"

Bingo. Tommy wanted to fist pump, but that was inappropriate.

"I've not heard that rumor, but I can assure you, I'm not leaving my job here. Valencia Blackstone is intelligent, thoughtful, and a woman of integrity. I look forward to voting for her in the upcoming election, but I don't think she needs me knocking on doors to help her get elected. I'll be right here, continuing to work in this remarkable program the police chief and my captain have put in place. I'm also happy to report that the Blackstone empire is in full support of what we're doing and have promised sizable contributions to help make our program a success. Giving officers additional tools to respond with empathy and skill to citizens who are in a mental health crisis makes the streets safer for everyone. Also, please make sure you spell my last name correctly in any story you may write about this. It's spelled P-a-r-s-o-n-s."

Tommy smiled. Of course Natasha had heard that rumor, she was the one who leaked it, but the press conference had served its purpose. Publicly, she'd supported her sister-in-law, and privately, she'd undoubtedly pissed off her parents, but they couldn't go back on that kind of public promise, whether they'd agreed to it or not. Tommy knew that would be the harder of the two steps in this reckoning.

After the press conference, Natasha followed Tommy to her car and slipped into the passenger seat. Tommy dropped into the driver's seat and looked over.

"Were you attached to the idea of going home alone?"

"I'd never hitch my wagons to an idea as wild as that." Tommy started the car and headed toward her house.

"Do you mind if I make the phone call to my mother while we drive? Then we can lock all the bad mojo in the car for the night and not bring it inside. I don't want it lurking in a corner when I'm naked."

"Weird and creepy. Get that phone call done quick." Tommy wasn't getting out of the car until Natasha was off the phone.

She listened to some of the details of the call, but she knew what Natasha was going to say. The money trails Natasha had uncovered showed her parents dealing with unscrupulous individuals in ways that stretched the bounds of legality. Even some of the perfectly legal transactions would be damaging given some of the political images her parents had cultivated recently.

What struck Tommy most was the way Natasha sounded when she spoke with her parents. She was flat and stifled. She lost her sparkle, her vivaciousness. She willed the call to be over quickly so her Natasha returned.

"I'll go straight to the press if you threaten her again. This is your only warning."

Natasha's anger caught Tommy's attention. Tommy held out her hand and Natasha took it. It was silent while Natasha listened to her mother's response.

"That's where you're wrong, Mother. I've got nothing to lose. I'm not a Blackstone. I'm Natasha Parsons. I'm a social worker employed by the police department, and if the money I promised on your behalf doesn't show up, you'll understand what it's like to squirm under a microscope. I don't think public opinion will judge you kindly."

Natasha hung up and tossed her phone in her bag at her feet.

"Went well, then?" Tommy pulled into her driveway and cut the engine.

"They won't bother us anymore. I'm not worth the embarrassment I could cause them."

"Could they still hurt you? You said they couldn't cut off your money, but are you sure?" Tommy opened Natasha's door for her and then unlocked the side door to the house.

"They might be able to get at some of it, but like I told you before, most of it's in trusts and all that boring stuff. And I have more than I need as it is. Do you really want to keep talking about my parents?" Natasha grabbed Tommy by the belt and spun her around.

Tommy's heart rate kicked up. She shook her head.

"I'm so happy to hear it. What I'm desperate to know is which room you want to come in?"

Natasha's wicked grin was sexy as hell and her hands on Tommy's body were ramping her up fast. She pulled Natasha's shirt up and over her head and tossed it. She knew she wouldn't be able to wait and go slow.

"Can I choose more than one?"

CHAPTER TWENTY-EIGHT

Tommy waited inside the door of the large classroom at the police academy. Two stations' worth of officers were intent on talking to Natasha so Tommy had plenty of time for her thoughts to wander. They didn't stray far from the woman at the center of everyone's attention. They never did.

Natasha had just finished the first mental health training for officers at their station, as well as Harry's. It was more in-depth than anything they'd gotten at the academy or through continuing education and had elements of assessment, de-escalation, and stabilization until help arrived. Natasha was going to repeat it until all the officers at both stations had received the training.

"Do I want to offer a penny for your thoughts, or am I going to be spammed by porn starring my sister?"

"Don't sneak up on someone with a gun, Harry. What's wrong with you?" Tommy jabbed her in the ribs.

"You were staring at me the entire walk over here. Maybe I should ask what's wrong with you, except the answer is clearly over there." Harry pointed to Natasha across the room. "Being adored by her new fans."

Tommy knew she should be embarrassed by what she knew must be a goofy grin on her face, but she wasn't. Loving Natasha had opened up an emotional spectrum she hadn't been aware humans could feel.

"Love looks good on you, Tommy."

Tommy didn't have a chance to answer before Natasha appeared by her side and took her breath away, like she always did. She beamed at both Tommy and Harry.

"Tell me the truth, Harry. What did you think?"

"I don't have to try and sugarcoat, it was great. I expected more grumbling and pushback from my station mates, but there hasn't been any that I've heard. I think it helps that you've had a gun in your face and you've been shot. You're one of us now."

"Oh, that's all it took?"

Natasha's tone was light, but Tommy saw her hand tremble.

"Come on, Harry, seriously?" Tommy gave her a backhanded slap on the shoulder.

"I don't like it either, Tommy. Nat, I'm just saying I think it took away some distance between what you do and what they do, in their eyes. And your station is lined up behind you."

Tommy wanted to punch Harry in the teeth to get her to shut up.

"Boys, at ease. Tommy, I appreciate your protectiveness, but I don't think Harry deserves your biggest growl."

"She can stow it as a down payment for the next time she does deserve it." Tommy blew Harry a kiss.

All three of them laughed.

"I'll see you two at family dinner. Great job today, Natasha." Harry bounded off.

"Ready to get out of here?" Natasha touched Tommy's shoulder lightly and let her fingers linger.

Tommy looked around. There was no one in the room. She wanted to pull Natasha close and kiss her or take her hand and lead her to the car. But they were at work, and on the clock they were colleagues only, even if the day was done and they were alone walking to the car.

"What are you thinking, babe? And don't tell me nothing because I'll know you'd be lying. You suddenly have the same look you get when you're hoping I'm about to strip you down to nothing."

"That's not exactly what I was thinking."

Natasha gave her a pointed look.

"Okay, a little bit was that. It started that way, but then I was thinking how I slept alone without any problem my whole life, and in a couple of weeks you've made it impossible for me to sleep when you're not next to me."

"Sometimes, Tommy, you say the sweetest things. I'll invite myself over later in the evening. I packed my toothbrush, clean underwear, and maple syrup."

Tommy stared at Natasha over the roof of the car. "Maple syrup? I have maple syrup at my house."

Natasha pointed at her looking offended. "No, what you have is sugary goo that calls itself maple syrup. I brought my travel size pure maple syrup. I'm going to be in the mood for pancakes in the morning. I'm planning on working up an appetite."

Tommy laughed and slid into the car. "Just when I think I can't love you any more, you tell me you have travel sized maple syrup. Tell me why we're not going straight to my place now?"

"So impatient. I told you pancakes aren't until the morning. It's dinnertime now. Take me to Lenny's. I want to watch the sunset across the river with you."

"You want me to take you on a date?" Tommy's heart raced, like she had first date nerves. This time they could walk by the water, hold hands, kiss, without the guilt and without holding back from each other. She felt like she was reading the first page of a good book having already read the ending.

Natasha's smile was more beautiful than any sunset. Dinner at Lenny's was easy to say yes to, but Tommy knew if Natasha asked for the moon she'd find a way to give it to her.

Natasha dropped a bag of food on Tommy's lap and sat next to her on the bench facing the water. She decided she wasn't close enough so she switched spots with the food bag.

Tommy reached around her and peeked in the bag. "Did you get anything for me?"

"There are seven hot dogs and potato salad in there, Tommy. I don't think you're going to starve." Natasha took a bite and made appreciative noises.

"You said you were hungry." Tommy kissed her cheek and pulled out food for herself.

"It's strange not seeing you every day." Natasha slid off Tommy's lap so they could both eat more comfortably, but kept her legs crossed over Tommy.

Natasha cupped Tommy's face. She was so beautiful it made Natasha's heart ache.

"Back when we first met, did you think, in your wildest imagination, we'd end up here?"

"It was the only way it could ever end. Total destiny."

Natasha threw a napkin at Tommy. "Liar. You threw a temper tantrum at the thought of having to spend time with me."

Tommy covered her face with one hand and peeked through her fingers. "I did, didn't I? And then you kept putting me in my place, over and over again. It was annoying and a bit of a turn-on."

They sat and ate in silence. Plenty of other people were out enjoying the walking path and the beautiful night, but it felt as if the evening was made for them.

After speaking with her parents and getting them to back off Natasha felt like she could finally take a deep breath after trying not to disturb the current for months. Captains Gillette and Marcetti were on board with the work she loved, and the new station wasn't bad. It was a new batch of officers, but they were more open to her presence than when she'd first started at Tommy's station.

Now the job she'd grown to love was expanding and she was the one in charge of nurturing it and she and Tommy could just be together. No more skulking around or worrying about crossing lines.

"I've been thinking about something the Zookeeper told me about making changes where you see a need." Natasha finished her third hot dog. "That's why I agreed to join the ride along program in the first place. I thought I knew what I wanted to get out of it, the impact I thought I'd have. But I wasn't really prepared for how the community embraced us, how the captain supported us, how the station got behind us."

"That was through a lot of hard work. Mostly yours. It didn't just happen, Nat. Look how hard you had to work to get me to buy in and your parents to butt out. But the change that's going to ripple through the community? It's remarkable." Tommy wiped her hands on a napkin and tossed it on the trash pile.

"Is it enough?"

"You're not done yet. This program isn't out of diapers, so who's to say what it can do? But policing is in need of some soul searching. The ride along program can help, but there are issues that are greater than this program can solve by itself. I'm saying that as someone who bleeds blue."

Natasha shook her head. She wasn't satisfied with that.

"The Zookeeper gave me a similar pep talk when she asked me to keep an eye on her flock. Since the Zookeeper's going to be locked up a while and we're call number one to her new Zookeepers, we might as well listen to her advice too." Tommy stroked Natasha's legs. "We tackle the problems we can impact first. Let's build our program. Then we have more influence with our two stations and in the community. Then maybe we go after bigger issues. To be honest, I don't think there's anything you can't do if you work at it."

"There's plenty I can't do. Pole vaulting for one. Walk past a free sample table at the grocery store. Remember what kind of toothpaste I like when I run out."

Tommy leaned her head back on the bench and smiled at the sky, then she sat up and pulled Natasha into a deep kiss. Natasha's stomach fluttered and her heart raced. Tommy could always rev her up with a passionate kiss, but she was also good at conveying emotion, and right now, Natasha felt incredibly, wildly, loved.

When they finally broke the kiss, Tommy pulled Natasha around so she was leaning back in Tommy's arm.

"Do you see that?" Tommy pointed across the water at the setting sun. "That's how loving you feels."

"Like a setting sun about to turn to darkness?"

"No, loving you is like that sun. It's a burst of energy, fire, and light. It can pierce darkness and create life. Usually, it's hidden away, only for us, but sometimes when things are just so, it bursts out and reflects off everything around us. It's a cacophony of color and beauty and everyone who sees it has to stop and stare."

Natasha felt a tear roll down her cheek. "I'm never going to look at sunsets the same way again."

"Good." Tommy pulled Natasha to her feet and kissed her as the sun slipped below the horizon. "From now on, think of them as my promise to you. My promise to never stop loving you. Because we're something where no change is necessary."

Epilogue

Tommy pushed open the door to her parents' house and held it open for Natasha. They shivered against the cold and deposited their boots in the pile by the front door. The house was decorated for Christmas. Tommy loved her parents' house at any time of the year, but especially at Christmas.

Natasha had told her she'd always dreaded the holidays because of her relationship with her family, and she'd spent more than one holiday completely alone. This year she used Tommy as an excuse not to go to her family gala and stayed home to celebrate with Tommy and her family. The entire Finch family had been thrilled when Tommy told them, especially Alice.

"Tommy, Natasha, did you bring presents?" Tommy's nieces and nephew skidded to a stop in front of them.

Cody scolded them.

"Sorry, Merry Christmas. Did you bring presents?"

Natasha leaned down and kissed each of their heads. "Merry Christmas, my favorite rascals. What kind of Christmas would it be without presents? Of course we brought you gifts. Aunt Tommy loves you so much she had a little trouble knowing when to stop buying them this year."

Tommy smiled when Natasha winked at her. It was a complete lie. Tommy was a terrible shopper and would gladly have just handed out gift cards. Natasha had brought home a mound of presents for everyone in the family and left Tommy speechless. She was going to be the most popular gifter this year. Or she would be, if everyone didn't immediately assume Natasha did the shopping. Which they would.

"There you two are. You'd think now that you live together it wouldn't take you so long to get here." Her mom pulled Natasha into her arms and then did the same to Tommy.

Tommy wasn't going to tell her mom that getting ready takes longer when you lather and rub the way they had in the shower.

Her mom pulled Natasha away almost immediately and Tommy was left to unload the car. Harry followed her out and helped with the perfectly wrapped boxes.

"There's no way you're responsible for these. You wrapped my gift last year in a grocery bag and duct tape. It had strawberry juice stains and a piece of lettuce stuck to it." Harry handed Tommy a pile of gifts.

"Who cares what it's wrapped in? You rip off the paper in thirty seconds anyway. But yes, she's much better at wrapping than I am."

"Living together still the best thing that's ever happened to you?" Harry opened the door and dropped the boxes inside. She didn't take off her boots.

Tommy put her boxes down and pulled the door closed behind her. She shoved her hands in her pockets against the cold and sat on the porch swing. Harry sat next to her.

"*She's* the best thing that's happened to me. We've lived together a couple of months, and I thought maybe I'd find something annoying or intolerable, but I haven't. I'm not saying I won't, but it's good. Really good. I think I want this to be a forever thing."

"No shit, man. Everyone can tell that. You two make me think about changing my ways. I'm really happy for you. When are you going to get around to asking?"

"Kayla seems plenty interested if you're serious about giving a relationship a go." Tommy turned the box in her pocket over and over.

"Nah, I don't think she's looking for anything different than I am." Harry drummed her finger on the arm of the swing.

"Never know unless you ask."

They headed inside when Natasha stuck her head out and waved them in. Dinner was almost ready. Tommy felt butterflies readying for supersonic flight.

She had trouble concentrating at dinner. The conversation flew by but didn't hold her attention. Her mind was elsewhere.

"Are you okay?" Natasha leaned in and whispered in her ear.

Tommy didn't make eye contact. Natasha would see through her. "I'm fine."

Finally, the dinner dishes were cleared and they returned to the table. There were still a few minutes before dessert. Senior called it the "settling time."

Now or never. Tommy took a deep breath. "I know we don't usually do presents until after dinner, but I was hoping you would allow me one exception."

Harry sat up straighter. All eyes were on Tommy.

"As you know, change has been a big theme in our lives since we met. A change in the way we felt about each other, changes in the way policing is done at both of our stations, changes in both of our jobs, a change in our living arrangement."

Tommy saw Natasha's eyes get wide. She seemed to sense this was going somewhere big. Tommy forged ahead. She needed to get through what she wanted to say before she lost it.

"Natasha, you're the best thing that has happened to me. Loving you is easy because we fit together, we respect each other, and care for each other, and protect each other. So I'd like to ask you to make one more change."

Tommy pulled the small velvet box she'd had in her pocket since they left the house, opened it, and dropped down to one knee. "Will you marry me?"

Her mom gasped. Priya squealed. Senior chuckled. Tommy only cared about Natasha's reaction.

Natasha put her hands to her face and nodded. "Yes." She dropped to her knees to Tommy's level. "Of course. Yes. Absolutely, yes."

Tommy slipped the ring on Natasha's finger and kissed her. She thought her heart might explode. Natasha was going to be her wife. She'd marry her right now if she could.

"Get up, we can't see what's happening. We want to see the ring."

Before they could get up, her mom came around and joined them kneeling on the floor. She wrapped both of them in a crushing hug. "Natasha, you were already part of this family, but welcome to the family. I'm so glad to have another daughter."

Her mom pulled them back to their feet, and one by one, every member of the family offered their congratulations. Natasha had been warmly welcomed before, but it seemed as if she'd crossed an invisible barrier into full membership with the ring on her finger.

Later in the evening, after all the presents were opened and they were on their way out the door, her mom and Senior gave them one last hug. "Thank you for sharing that moment with us."

Natasha slipped her hand in Tommy's as they walked to the car. Tommy liked the feel of the cold metal and diamond against her skin. She opened the door for Natasha, but instead of getting into the passenger seat she slipped into Tommy's arms.

"Tomasina Finch, I love you. I'm looking forward to being your wife."

"Natasha Parsons, I love you too. I like how that ring looks on your finger."

Natasha looked thoughtful. "I think I might try out Natasha Finch."

Tommy's stomach flipped again. "Really? I never would've pegged you as wanting to give up your name."

"We'll see, but names are about family. You and yours are the first family I've felt part of my whole life. Why wouldn't I want to be a Finch?" She pulled Tommy closer and kissed her. Their breath fogged around them with every exhale.

Natasha stepped back and held up her hand. She looked at the ring on her finger and smiled the wide smile that made Tommy's knees wobble.

"Thank you, Tommy, for giving me one hell of a sunset moment. Now let's get home and see how hot our sun can burn."

About the Author

Jesse Thoma wishes that Swiss Army Knife was an official job title because she would use it.

Jesse grew up in Northern California but headed east for college. She never looked back, although her baseball allegiance is still loyally with the San Francisco Giants. She has lived in New England long enough to leave extra time in the morning to scrape snow off the car and use the letter "r" inappropriately.

Jesse is blissfully married and is happiest when she is spending time with her family or working on her next novel.

Courage is Jesse's sixth novel. *Seneca Falls* was a finalist for a Lambda Literary Award in romance. *Data Capture* was a finalist for a Golden Crown Literary Society "Goldie" Award.

Books Available from Bold Strokes Books

A Fae Tale by Genevieve McCluer. Dovana comes to terms with her changing feelings for her lifelong best friend and fae, Roze. (978-1-63555-918-7)

Accidental Desperados by Lee Lynch. Life is clobbering Berry, Jaudon, and their long romance. The arrival of directionless baby dyke MJ doesn't help. Can they find their passion again—and keep it? (978-1-63555-482-3)

Always Believe by Aimée. Greyson Waldsen is pursuing ordination as an Anglican priest. Angela Arlingham doesn't believe in God. Do they follow their vocation or their hearts? (978-1-63555-912-5)

Best of the Wrong Reasons by Sander Santiago. For Fin Ness and Orion Starr, it takes a funeral to remind them that love is worth living for. (978-1-63555-867-8)

Courage by Jesse J. Thoma. No matter how often Natasha Parsons and Tommy Finch clash on the job, an undeniable attraction simmers just beneath the surface. Can they find the courage to change so love has room to grow? (978-1-63555-802-9)

I Am Chris by R Kent. There's one saving grace to losing everything and moving away. Nobody knows her as Chrissy Taylor. Now Chris can live who he truly is. (978-1-63555-904-0)

The Princess and the Odium by Sam Ledel. Jastyn and Princess Aurelia return to Venostes and join their families in a battle against the dark force to take back their homeland for a chance at a better tomorrow. (978-1-63555-894-4)

The Queen Has a Cold by Jane Kolven. What happens when the heir to the throne isn't a prince or a princess? (978-1-63555-878-4)

The Secret Poet by Georgia Beers. Agreeing to help her brother woo Zoe Blake seemed like a good idea to Morgan Thompson at first...until she realizes she's actually wooing Zoe for herself... (978-1-63555-858-6)

You Again by Aurora Rey. For high school sweethearts Kate Cormier and Sutton Guidry, the second chance might be the only one that matters. (978-1-63555-791-6)

Coming to Life on South High by Lee Patton. Twenty-one-year-old gay virgin Gabe Rafferty's first adult decade unfolds as an unpredictable journey into sex, love, and livelihood. (978-1-63555-906-4)

Fleur d'Lies by MJ Williamz. For rookie cop DJ Sander, being true to what you believe is the only way to live...and one way to die. (978-1-63555-854-8)

Love's Falling Star by B.D. Grayson. For country music megastar Lochlan Paige, can love conquer her fear of losing the one thing she's worked so hard to protect? (978-1-63555-873-9)

Love's Truth by C.A. Popovich. Can Lynette and Barb make love work when unhealed wounds of betrayed trust and a secret could change everything? (978-1-63555-755-8)

Next Exit Home by Dena Blake. Home may be where the heart is, but for Harper Sims and Addison Foster, is the journey back worth the pain? (978-1-63555-727-5)

Not Broken by Lyn Hemphill. Falling in love is hard enough—even more so for Rose who's carrying her ex's baby. (978-1-63555-869-2)

The Noble and the Nightingale by Barbara Ann Wright. Two women on opposite sides of empires at war risk all for a chance at love. (978-1-63555-812-8)

What a Tangled Web by Melissa Brayden. Clementine Monroe has the chance to buy the café she's managed for years, but Madison LeGrange swoops in and buys it first. Now Clementine is forced to work for the enemy and ignore her former crush. (978-1-63555-749-7)

A Far Better Thing by JD Wilburn. When needs of her family and wants of her heart clash, Cass Halliburton is faced with the ultimate sacrifice. (978-1-63555-834-0)

Body Language by Renee Roman. When Mika offers to provide Jen erotic tutoring, will sex drive them into a deeper relationship or tear them apart? (978-1-63555-800-5)

Carrie and Hope by Joy Argento. For Carrie and Hope loss brings them together but secrets and fear may tear them apart. (978-1-63555-827-2)

Death's Prelude by David S. Pederson. In this prequel to the Detective Heath Barrington Mystery series, Heath discovers that first love changes you forever and drives you to become the person you're destined to be. (978-1-63555-786-2)

Ice Queen by Gun Brooke. School counselor Aislin Kennedy wants to help standoffish CEO Susanna Durr and her troubled teenage daughter become closer—even if it means risking her own heart in the process. (978-1-63555-721-3)

Masquerade by Anne Shade. In 1925 Harlem, New York, a notorious gangster sets her sights on seducing Celine, and new lovers Dinah and Celine are forced to risk their hearts, and lives, for love. (978-1-63555-831-9)

Royal Family by Jenny Frame. Loss has defined both Clay's and Katya's lives, but guarding their hearts may prove to be the biggest heartbreak of all. (978-1-63555-745-9)

Share the Moon by Toni Logan. Three best friends, an inherited vineyard and a resident ghost come together for fun, romance and a touch of magic. (978-1-63555-844-9)

Spirit of the Law by Carsen Taite. Attorney Owen Lassiter will do almost anything to put a murderer behind bars, but can she get past her reluctance to rely on unconventional help from the alluring Summer Byrne and keep from falling in love in the process? (978-1-63555-766-4)

The Devil Incarnate by Ali Vali. Cain Casey has so much to live for, but enemies who lurk in the shadows threaten to unravel it all. (978-1-63555-534-9)

His Brother's Viscount by Stephanie Lake. Hector Somerville wants to rekindle his illicit love affair with Viscount Wentworth, but he must overcome one problem: Wentworth still loves Hector's brother. (978-1-63555-805-0)

Journey to Cash by Ashley Bartlett. Cash Braddock thought everything was great, but it looks like her history is about to become her right now. Which is a real bummer. (978-1-63555-464-9)

Liberty Bay by Karis Walsh. Wren Lindley's life is mired in tradition and untouched by trends until social media star Gina Strickland introduces an irresistible electricity into her off-the-grid world. (978-1-63555-816-6)

Scent by Kris Bryant. Nico Marshall has been burned by women in the past wanting her for her money. This time, she's determined to win Sophia Sweet over with her charm. (978-1-63555-780-0)

Shadows of Steel by Suzie Clarke. As their worlds collide and their choices come back to haunt them, Rachel and Claire must figure out how to stay together and most of all, stay alive. (978-1-63555-810-4)

The Clinch by Nicole Disney. Eden Bauer overcame a difficult past to become a world champion mixed martial artist, but now rising star and dreamy bad girl Brooklyn Shaw is a threat both to Eden's title and her heart. (978-1-63555-820-3)

The Last First Kiss by Julie Cannon. Kelly Newsome is so ready for a tropical island vacation, but she never expects to meet the woman who could give her her last first kiss. (978-1-63555-768-8)

The Mandolin Lunch by Missouri Vaun. Despite their immediate attraction, everything about Garet Allen says short-term, and Tess Hill refuses to consider anything less than forever. (978-1-63555-566-0)

Thor: Daughter of Asgard by Genevieve McCluer. When Hannah Olsen finds out she's the reincarnation of Thor, she's thrown into a world of magic and intrigue, unexpected attraction, and a mystery she's got to unravel. (978-1-63555-814-2)

Veterinary Technician by Nancy Wheelton. When a stable of horses is threatened Val and Ronnie must work together against the odds to save them, and maybe even themselves along the way. (978-1-63555-839-5)

16 Steps to Forever by Georgia Beers. Can Brooke Sullivan and Macy Carr find themselves by finding each other? (978-1-63555-762-6)

All I Want for Christmas by Georgia Beers, Maggie Cummings, Fiona Riley. The Christmas season sparks passion and love in these stories by award winning authors Georgia Beers, Maggie Cummings, and Fiona Riley. (978-1-63555-764-0)

From the Woods by Charlotte Greene. When Fiona goes backpacking in a protected wilderness, the last thing she expects is to be fighting for her life. (978-1-63555-793-0)

Heart of the Storm by Nicole Stiling. For Juliet Mitchell and Sienna Bennett a forbidden attraction definitely isn't worth upending the life they've worked so hard for. Is it? (978-1-63555-789-3)

If You Dare by Sandy Lowe. For Lauren West and Emma Prescott, following their passions is easy. Following their hearts, though? That's almost impossible. (978-1-63555-654-4)

Love Changes Everything by Jaime Maddox. For Samantha Brooks and Kirby Fielding, no matter how careful their plans, love will change everything. (978-1-63555-835-7)

Not This Time by MA Binfield. Flung back into each other's lives, can former bandmates Sophia and Madison have a second chance at romance? (978-1-63555-798-5)

The Dubious Gift of Dragon Blood by J. Marshall Freeman. One day Crispin is a lonely high school student—the next he is fighting a war in a land ruled by dragons, his otherworldly boyfriend at his side. (978-1-63555-725-1)

The Found Jar by Jaycie Morrison. Fear keeps Emily Harris trapped in her emotionally vacant life; can she find the courage to let Beck Reynolds guide her toward love? (978-1-63555-825-8)